Successful Love

Delmore Schwartz

Successful Love
and Other Stories

Persea Books

New York

The stories in this volume, except "The Statues," were first collected in *Successful Love and Other Stories* (Corinth Books, 1961). "The Statues" was first collected in *The World Is A Wedding* (New Directions, 1948). "Tales from the Vienna Woods," "The Gift," and "The Statues" originally appeared in *Partisan Review*; "Successful Love" appeared in *Avon Book of Modern Writing Number 2*; "The Fabulous Twenty Dollar Bill" appeared in *Kenyon Review*; "An American Fairy Tale" appeared in *Commentary*; "The Track Meet" appeared in *The New Yorker*.

Persea Books, Inc.
60 Madison Avenue
New York, N.Y. 10010

Library of Congress Cataloging-in-Publication Data

Schwartz, Delmore, 1913–1966.
    Successful love and other stories / Delmore Schwartz.
        p.   cm.
    ISBN 0-89255-094-5 : $9.95
    I. Title.
    PS3537.C79S78   1990
    813'.52—dc20   90-41869

Printed in the U.S.A.

To Sidney Hook
and to Robert Penn Warren

Contents

Successful Love

Successful Love

Susan Calhoun thought that Daddy was an old dear, the darlingest dear, although he did make sour remarks sometimes. But it was Mummy who was really keen. She was one in a million, she really was, she understood what it was to be a girl in 1950. Daddums was very sweet too, the soul of kindness, and Mummy would convince him that they would not be in the least mistaken or ill-advised to let their quite attractive daughter go to art school in New York and live in New York City instead of going to college. She was just seventeen, but seventeen was not the bib-and-diaper stage some parents thought it was. She was older than seventeen in the ways of a woman and the world which was more important than anything else for a woman to be if she was a girl. Something was definitely wrong with career girls and career women.

Daddy liked to read books a lot, and he was very clever, very sophisticated, like *New Yorker* cartoons, which made you smile, not laugh, but he certainly did not want her to be a bookworm even if he did want her to go to college. She had overheard by accident what he had said when Mummy first talked to him about her going to art school and living in New York City: Daddums had said that he would have been less surprised if Mother had proposed that Susan become a deep-sea diver or a flagpole sitter, for he had been under the impression that she probably thought Van Gogh was a foreign car, like the Rolls Royce. She did too know who Van Gogh was, he had cut his ear off because of a beautiful girl, and the lives of the painters were truly fascinating as Miss Fisher said in the art history course at Miss Beaumont's last year. Mother had paused before telling Daddy that Susan probably wanted to have an affair. How had Mother guessed? She was certainly clever and keen, but since the affair was in the future, how had she guessed? Mother's remark left Daddy speechless then, which was the way he always was just before he became dreadfully sarcastic. "Sometimes you make me feel just as I feel when I read the Sunday edition of *The New York Times*," Daddy said then, "contemplating a world I never made, nor desired, nor like, nor trust, and about which no one has ever consulted me." Mother said then, trying her hardest to be diplomatic, "Roger, do be patient with me, I've given Susan a good deal of thought. She is a natural lovable and loving child and she is going to have an affair, no matter what we do. All that we can do is to keep her from becoming so serious that the affair ends in a premature marriage, as it will tend to because the child is the soul of respectability: she would certainly get married too soon if she were not free of the sense of respectability which living at home made unavoidable." And when Daddy wanted to know precisely why a young lady of seventeen could not have an affair at college as well as at art school in New York City and particularly since it seemed to be quite customary among many college girls, Mother explained to him that girls at college lived in a community almost as much as they did at home, and Susan's sense of the opinion of other girls might lead to the same disastrous result, since she clearly was an innocent old-fashioned girl.

Susan did not think she was quite as innocent as Mummy thought she was, she did not think she was at all old-fashioned, quite the contrary: and she was absolutely positively certain that she would not rush into marriage. She was going to see life first, and be a woman of the world. But what Mother probably meant was that she was not shrewd, as Mother truly was, nor clever, like Daddums, but she did not want to be: if you thought too much about things, you never had any fun.

Janet Ross's father was just like Mother, he understood what it was like to be a girl in 1950; he took Janet for a drive during Xmas week when she was home from her first term at Fairfield and told her that it would be all right for her to have an affair now, if she knew how to handle it, but did she? Janet's mother was just the opposite. She was a horror from way back, a real pain. She told Janet that she ought not to have an affair even if a lot of the other girls did have affairs, or *just* because they did. If one really felt like that, one ought to get married, and *until* one felt like that, one ought not to get married and spoil something which should be inherently beautiful and meaningful. Honestly! How could anyone think and talk like that in 1950! Janet did not tell her mother that she had already had a perfectly glorious affair, and a very beautiful one too, and the man was beautiful too and also meaningful. But her mother found out and wrote her a perfectly awful letter about how she had been seen registering in a New York hotel with a man and what would people think of her and her brothers and sisters: honestly: as if anyone gave a hoot. No man who had not lost his marbles expected his bride to be a virgin in 1950, not after the way he had been playing around before getting ready to march up the aisle with a member of the fair sex.

And Marion Campbell's father had been like Janet's mother, except worse, when Marion brought her young man for a visit to their summer place on the Cape. Nothing had been going on, absolutely nothing, except a little heavy necking, but Papa had been quite impossible: he had shouted at Marion right in front of her young man that she seemed to think her father's house was a third-rate hotel. It was monstrous: and Janet's father was an art critic, too, and still did not know that he was behaving as if we were still in the middle ages. Marion and the young man had been secretly engaged too; it was broken off in the fall, but no one knew that then: *misere!*

2

Nancy Calhoun had given a good deal of patient thought to her daughter Susan who was seventeen and very pretty and entirely an infant. Nancy wanted to be a more intelligent mother than other wealthy doting parents. Now was the time to be intelligent, now that Susan wanted to go to live in New York City, wanted to live either in her own apartment or in an apartment with other girls whom she knew slightly. She also wanted to go to art school or *some* kind of school: it was clearly a pretext, but Susan must not perceive that her pretense was transparent.

Susan was an only child. She had always been more of a baby than most children, and perhaps she had been babied too much, but it was too late now to brood about that. She had been terrified by her parents' absence as a child, terrified however brief their departure, however great her attachment to the servants. So Susan's desire to live in New York City could mean only one thing, that her beautiful darling lamb of a daughter wanted to have an affair. She had said last summer, surprising her mother with an attitude wholly unlike the child, that necking did get very boring very soon. But Nancy had not expected the next stage so very soon.

In 1950 the right kind of affair would not hurt Susan and might help her very much: provided she learned to take care of herself and did not take the affair too seriously. Which would probably occur if she stayed at home and had an affair with one of the boys who comprised the local talent and whom Nancy had been at pains to scrutinize sharply.

The dear child had a date with herself, a date which she would not keep if caught in the toils and throes of a premature marriage (which was likely enough), and premature motherhood, her own misfortune. Motherhood was even more likely, for Susan would turn to motherhood too soon when astonished and disappointed that the bliss of the honeymoon did not persist forever and ever.

It would be best for her to have a few affairs. Then she would be able to keep her date with herself, then when she knew what men were like, having seen enough of them, when she knew what she wanted in a man because she had been close enough to know how it was a round-the-clock weeklong yearlong lifelong problem, not a matter of good manners and a glib tongue, persiflage and flirtation, or even deftness in the bedroom.

Roger would have to be persuaded. The best persuasion would be to present Susan's departure as a trial which might be quickly ended if it proved unwise. The dear man assented, in the end, to all his wife's desires and decisions; they were natural phenomena to him like summer, the animals in the zoo, the behavior of the stock market and the necessity of suburban commuting. Like all strangers, like all tourists, he expected the behavior only a native or a veteran needed. And like all fathers and husbands, he insisted upon the masquerade of deference to his paternal position without any prior or regular attentiveness . . . it was really tiresome. But Roger was entitled to his foibles and follies like everyone else. Dear Roger! Had there ever been a man so intelligent, clever, and well-educated, yet so unworldly, so foolish, so much the noble savage in the wickedness of civilization?

Intent and intense as Susan had been about living in New York City, it was not at all probable that she had already chosen her young man. It was far more likely that she had chosen the great city to provide the young man, a plenitude of young men. It was best that it should be so. There would be so much chance and so little necessity in Susan's choice of a husband that the simple lamb could hardly help but benefit by being swamped in variety. It was just barely possible that the dear child had already yielded to one of the young men who had been taking her to dances during the past year. And this was precisely the key to the child: that it might be true, she had surrendered, and there was no sign or difference whatever. It showed what she was really like; her dear darling daughter was simple and naive, innocent and old-fashioned, eminently respectable, profoundly conventional. Her respectability was her weakness, the worst part of her innocence. Her innocence was partly impatience: she was impetuous too as only the innocent are. If anything would protect Susan from her own impetuous innocence, it was the freedom and the anonymity of New York: would protect her by giving her, to be blunt about it, sexual satisfaction on a regular basis! She could not have this arrangement with complete impunity in a suburb or at a school in a small town.

3

Roger Calhoun thought that his wife was probably right about Susan. Whether or not she was, he was certainly wrong: since as a young man he had known nothing of the young lady of the era of his youth, he certainly knew nothing whatever now about what it was like to be a young lady in 1950. Nancy's point of view impinged upon him as coldblooded and calculating, but perhaps it was merely her tone, or merely his paternal sentimentality. Still and all, it was always all too easy to be too coldblooded, calculating, and rational about questions of the heart. But was it a question of the heart, regarded in Nancy's light?

It was hardly a year since, while having a quiet drink at the club with Ben Stanton, that Ralph Cox had come over and asked both of them just exactly what one did when one's daughter began to sleep with innumerable young men? Ben who had two sons and three daughters answered immediately that one did nothing: what could one do? Ralph Cox went off shaking his head, silent. Ben had spoken to them of his nephew Arthur who was nothing if not a typical young man. He *worked* at being typical. Now as it happened Arthur had recently been on a week-end house party with his sister and in the midst of it, carelessly, he had entered the wrong bedroom to find his sister in *flagrante delicto* (flagrantly delighted! said Ben caustically) with a young man who was a good friend of Arthur's. "Oh, I beg your pardon!" Arthur had said, mortified, and turned and shut the bedroom door carefully and quietly. Questioned by his uncle, Arthur had said in an offhand way that no gentleman would act otherwise. When Ben remained dissatisfied, his nephew added that he himself had successfully pursued the sisters of his friends: protest would be preposterous and no one ever felt moved to protest: this was not the nineteenth century. One chap had been furious because his sister had been left on the hook by her young man who was too tired and too drunk. The brother requested the tired young man to join his sister in her bedroom, which showed clearly the conception of family duty and honor which prevailed. "We can't halt the course of history," Ben had concluded, which was precisely his resigned comment when Roosevelt had been elected for the third and the fourth time. His tone was a little grandiloquent, but Roger recognized that the cause was the same: he was equally disturbed by the New Deal and the dalliance of his daughters. He had also remarked to Roger that when they had known youth, early in the twentieth century, there had been nice girls and bad girls: now the double standard had been succeeded by open house. A young lady was afraid to hurt the young man's feeling's by refusing to jump into bed with him: she had only one justifiable and acceptable reason for refusing, the fact that she was jumping into bed with some other young man.

Nancy was probably right about Susan. Nancy was not at all unconventional and she would not advocate unconventional behavior on Susan's part. She was profoundly practical and her proposal had a practical purpose: his middle-aged feelings must be mistaken: it was much like the strangeness which had shocked him most of all the previous summer when, reading in his study, he had heard Susan at midnight with her beau on the porch swing, the two of them first licking ice cream cones, then beginning to spoon with no prelude of flirtation as if the spooning were part of a mechanical routine.

"Golly, you have a beautiful pair of knockers!" the young man declared very soon, his utterance inspired by the concreteness of immediate experience. A beautiful pair of knockers was a delightful phrase, in a way; Roger would have been delighted by it in a novel, as he knew very well. When a second beau during the same week told his daughter that she had quite a milk fund, he argued with himself that it was merely a question of speech. Among the young men of his own generation, purity of speech had been directly connected with morbidity of feeling. He had misgivings about Susan's being generous and intimate with more than one man, but it was ridiculous to expect her to be fixed upon her true love at fifteen. Doubtless the child thought of herself as trying to be fair and impartial!

At the beginning of that summer Roger Calhoun had been unable to imagine what the young people found to converse about, assuming that conversation ever occured. "Hi!" said the young man when he arrived. "Hi!" said Susan. When the young man departed, he said: "So long," and Susan chirped: "See you!" Who would have believed that the two had been intimate all evening, concerned with beautiful knockers and prolonged kisses?

After Roger had listened for the first time to his daughter and her beau on the porch swing, he had apologized to her for listening. Susan answered him that she did not mind in the least, which at once reassured and astonished him. He had continued to listen, uneasy about eavesdropping. But his daughter's disavowal supported the curiosity which astonishment awakened and perplexity intensified in him. "You *send* me," one of Susan's four beaux avowed on a brilliant breathless summer night. "And you, kind sir, send me," Susan responded sweetly. "Honestly, I get a big kick out of you." Sometimes there was a mock clash of egos: taunting and teasing preceded the comparative silence of petting: "You are a complete cluck," Susan declared. "So are you," her witty knight countered. "No, I am not," Susan said with heat. "Then neither am I," the young man replied in a tone of greater heat which suggested a conviction of his own brilliance of wit and repartee.

During the course of the summer, the conversation had grown more extended and complex. The young man arrived with jokes as with bouquets or boxes of candy. "Wait until you hear this one," the young man said, impatient and triumphant. "Don't keep me suspended," the beautiful Susan answered. "Man goes into hotel," the beau began, "clerk asks: 'Want a room with running water?' 'No, I never sleep with Indians!' says the man." Susan and her young man were then mastered by convulsions of mirth. The theme of the hotel was popular. "Beautiful lady," said the young man, "arrives at a hotel. Says to desk clerk: 'I would like a room and a bath.' 'You can have a room,' says the clerk, 'but, lady, you will have to bathe yourself!' " Susan was overwhelmed, and the patient perplexed father felt that he must entertain the possibility of the wrongness of his point of view. He had soon remarked that Susan was most amused when a young lady was a leading character in the story: it was then that she was most likely to declare that the story was not only delirious, but devastating. "You just murder me!" she said on the eve of Labor Day in the course of entertaining the most comical of her young men.

Roger Calhoun concluded that his feelings were foolish. He was what he had been, a romantic snob. His youth had been paralyzed by tormented shyness. He had shuddered, adoring the blessed damozel, long since outmoded: if he let himself go his middle-aged mind would give way to the expectation that Susan's suitors would arrive on horseback, knights in mail and clanking armor, armed with ardent and courtly poems in the best chivalric modes. He had been sixteen when he first regretted that knighthood was in flower no more; and now, long past fifty, his daughter's angelic countenance, angelic and cherubic because she was simple and naïve, revived the mores of his adolescent reveries in which the blessed damozel had looked down from an azure distance, infinite and unattainable, at the purity and seriousness, the devotion and dedication of a very shy young man.

4

The idea of going to art school in New York City was quite definitely enchanting to Susan Calhoun. She knew almost nothing about painting, but she did like to look at paintings, it was most enjoyable. But she was certainly intrigued with the prospect of knowing painters, to judge by what she had heard about an artist's life. Artists were interesting people, very clever and amusing, and had interesting parties, and they knew that making love was one of the most important things in life, but they were not stupid and stuffy about it. It must be quite enthralling to sit in a life class when a girl model posed in the nude: how did a girl feel when for the first time she posed in the beautiful altogether ,in front of so many men who were looking straight at her? She was sure that she herself would be quite embarrassed merely when she was just a student in a life class and a girl stood nude in front of the class. She would probably be almost as embarrassed as the first time that she opened the bathroom door in Gloria's house and saw Gloria's father urinating, although he did not seem to mind but smiled at her in a very strange way: if *she* had been in the bathroom and *he* had opened the door, she would have died right then and there, instead of smiling in that peculiar way.

Some people were very strange. Gloria's cousin Phoebe had shocked her whole family and everyone at school when she offered to pose in the nude in the art class one day when the model did not arrive. Gloria said that Phoebe said that you get used to it almost immediately, right after the first five minutes, because you see that you might just as well be an old wornout sofa to everyone staring at you. Phoebe did get used to the nude so quickly that she lost interest and decided to become a nurse, shocking her family still more, but soon after Phoebe had her first affair with a middle-aged man of thirty-eight, old enough to be her grandfather, and forgot all about modeling and nursing. Phoebe told Gloria that sex was not all it was cracked up to be. It was quite enjoyable but nothing terrific or stupendous. But Phoebe changed her mind very rapidly when she had her second affair, this time with a man who practically had one shoulder in the grave, but he was very experienced, Phoebe told Gloria, her whole belly shook with delicious quivers and shivers, and she hardly knew just what she was doing. Gloria said that Phoebe said that the best thing in a way was that after making love like that you did not think of sex for the next few days at least and you felt good at the same time, very good about everything, and patient, and full of energy.

Phoebe was obsessed with sex and when Susan heard about Phoebe's experiences, she felt obsessed with sex too, so it was definitely something if Phoebe did not think of sex at all for several days because she usually thought of nothing else. Some girls at school said that Phoebe was a nympho, and it was incredible that any girl not a nympho should let a man as old and decrepit as that put his hands on her, to say nothing of Phoebe's great enthusiasm about him. She said to Gloria quite seriously that he played her like a piano, she was not joking at all: that was how Phoebe had met him: piano lessons. He was a pianist and Phoebe claimed that only a man of that age had the experience to teach you while the men of your own age are just jackrabbits, it's all over practically before you've begun to respond. Personally Susan herself would rather stay ignorant. She would probably vomit if a man more than thirty made love to her, the very idea disgusted her. But Phoebe said that young

men knew as little as girls did, and you never found out anything from other girls at all the bull sessions at school: you did
find out something about pleasing a man, but not about pleasing yourself: which was basically what a man wanted, believe
it or not, and which gave all concerned the wonderful unbelieva-
ble feeling you never got from necking. Phoebe insisted that
necking was nothing: it just made you nervous.

Susan just adored necking sometimes, no matter what Phoebe
said. She sometimes had too much of it, but usually she liked
it so much that she had had some pretty close escapes and
nothing really important happened not because she stopped but
because the boy stopped. That boy from the South had stopped
and said that it would be dishonorable not to stop and he had
been so polite, he had said May I? before he even touched her
each time, and the Lord knows he had taken so long to ask
permission that she thought she would blow up, she was so
excited by his kisses.

Susan was intensely piercingly bored with this having to
stop: it was an awful nuisance. There were eight million human
beings in New York City and it was hardly possible that she
would not find at least one real and attractive man there willing
to take her on. She would give herself exactly three months: if
none of the painters at art school took an interest in her, she
would go out and pick up the first truckdriver that whistled at
her, and she would not tell him the facts to begin with because
truckdrivers might be honorable like Southerners too.

5

Susan was installed in a New York apartment and at art school
when the winter term began. The apartment was inhabited by
Rita and Consuelo, two girls who were studying art and arche-
ology at Columbia. They were five years older than Susan, which
was the reason that Mother had chosen their apartment. They

were highbrows, but nevertheless had an enormous number of dates.

Susan had never before existed in a state of such continual delight. The climax came after only a week at art school when Anthony Boyd who looked like a Greek god except with pitch-black hair asked her for lunch. She had been afraid that she might get impatient and get involved with her second choice since she had looked at Anthony Boyd directly in the face all the time in class but he never batted an eyelash at her while her second choice kept staring at her as if she were his dream of dreams, a cover girl or a Hollywood starlet.

"Why did you ask me to lunch, Mr. Boyd?" Susan asked in her most aloof tone when they were seated in the lunchroom to which he had taken her.

"Call me Tony," the young man said in a commanding tone, a tone which thrilled Susan.

"Tony," said Susan with a little effort, "tell me the reason that you selected me with all the beautiful girls and models right in front of your naked eyes."

"Do I have to have a reason?" said Tony. Since the chick had to be flattered, he had better not tell her that he had noticed her only because she had gaped at him, starry-eyed, all week long. "It's just natural: you're a girl, I'm a man, we have to eat or we'll starve, so we go to lunch and get acquainted."

He spoke in a gruff husky voice which was so cute and so attractive that Susan forgot the compliment which she had sought.

"I am glad that you did, anyway," said Susan, "whatever your reason may have been." She glowed, looking at his handsome face, and thinking he must have a strong physique, judging by his beautiful-looking, powerful-looking shoulders.

"Look, I told you," said Tony, "I had no reason. I'm not one of those guys who have to analyze everything all the time.

I just keep doing what comes naturally and it certainly pays off. All that brainwork is a big waste of time. Guys who analyze the reasons for everything can't do anything else."

"I never liked reading much either," said Susan, feeling that Tony and she had much in common and felt the same way about life.

"I bet you didn't," said Tony with conviction. "It's the wallflowers who belong on the wallpaper who get the over-developed brains: they're all fatheads with all their fancy talk."

Susan cherished this assertion as a compliment of a kind, for it meant she was not a wallflower, although so far, tech-nically, she might just as well have been.

"How about having dinner dutch tonight?" Tony said at the entrance to the art school. Susan was afraid that she might seem too eager, but she was too delighted with Tony to refuse and too impatient to play the coquette: anyone would know that Tony did not fall for that sort of thing.

Susan soon saw Tony almost all the time, at lunch and at dinner too. He was not only very handsome and strong, but he had an absolute confidence in himself which Susan soon per-ceived was resented by other students. They thought he was too cocky, they thought he was conceited, arrogant, and cheeky, but Susan adored these traits and thought that some of the others must just be jealous because Tony was a real man and very confident and very handsome and the most gifted student. He talked with a Tenth Avenue accent and he had lived in a New York slum until drafted by the army. But the tough accent made him just like George Raft, Humphrey Bogart, James Cagney, John Garfield, Spencer Tracy, all the wonderful stars who played tough guy cabdrivers, mechanics, gunmen, and gangsters in the pictures. She had long worshiped them from afar; now she knew one of them in person, in the flesh.

Tony told Susan during the first week at dinner how he had come to be a painter. He always liked drawing, even as a kid in school, but until he was drafted it hadn't occurred to him that he might become a painter himself. At the army post in Kansas some other G. I. had won first prize and five thousand bucks in a big art show competition. The guy had been a serious painter until drafted, and had nothing else to do with the dough, what else was there to do with five thousand bucks, deep in the heart of Kansas, so he bought five thousand simoleons worth of war bonds. Which the commanding officer heard about, and when the C.O. heard that this well-heeled probably famous bozo was fighting the Axis mainly by peeling potatoes and acting as chauffeur for the Captain's laundry, he thought it was a disgrace to the army, and soon had him transferred to the war correspondents corps, where he diddled away for the duration drawing sketches of the scenes of war. The magic of being a painter astonished Tony: he had never seen anything like it.

"That's for me, I said to myself when I heard about it," he told Susan who did not really understand what he was saying, apart from his superb confidence and ambition. "As soon as I was let out of the army, I took advantage of the G.I. bill of rights, and jumped at the chance of getting to be a painter too. If that guy had the commanding officer kowtowing to him, I was going to be a painter too and get in on all the kowtowing. Besides, I really get a big kick out of painting, anyway. But if you're a painter, you're a holy cow, you are nothing less than the cat's pajamas, you are *it*: you can go anywhere and do anything, no one cares where you come from or how much dough you don't have or if your family did not get a chance to be seasick on the *Mayflower*: you're an artist, so you're it: everyone thinks you're wonderful, and you can act like a dipso on a three-day binge, or a hipster all charged up: everyone says that it's just the artist's temperament. You need talent too, and the funny thing is that you get so interested sometimes in what you're doing, you don't make the most of the artist's temperament and hardly ever feel like going on a tear, like most guys felt most of the time in the service."

Susan felt let down by Tony's conclusion. But what he said about the artist's temperament awakened her hope that as an artist he would not be impeded by a girl's lack of experience, which was not her fault.

6

Soon enough they were going to Central Park after dinner and Susan was not surprised that Tony was wonderful at necking. He was sure of himself, he did not hurry but took his time, but he was not too slow. She felt like inviting him to the apartment because the park was not much good for real heavy necking, someone might pass or a policeman might interrupt them, but she did not ask him for fear that he would think she was bold and forward.

Then one night when they were petting in the park there was a sudden heavy downpour and Tony said they had better get out of the rain before they got drowned and how about going back to his rooming house just until the rain stopped. Susan felt like suggesting the apartment again, but hesitated once more, since Rita and Consuelo might be at home that night, and when Tony took her hesitation as an unwillingness to trust herself indoors with him, she assented fervently and joyously, assuring him that she trusted him and saying she was only sorry that she was wearing her best blouse and skirt which would probably be ruined. They started in where they had left off in the park and Susan took off her blouse which made Tony very excited, but after that he did not go much farther than on any other night, he just stopped at that point and Susan tried to think of what she could possibly do without making Tony think she was a prostitute or a call girl or a pushover, and finally she said that she had better take off her skirt, it was her best most expensive one, it would be ruined, which was enough to make Tony go right ahead before she had the skirt off. She hardly knew what was happening except that it was absolutely marvelous, it was thrilling all over, it was just over too soon, it was not at all painful, not even like having a tooth extracted like that girl at school had said: but it did not last long enough.

Susan lolled in bliss as Tony stood up abruptly and said sternly that she should have told him she was a virgin, it was wrong to start a girl off, only a bastard did that, he just thought all society dames stopped being virgins when they were sweet sixteen at the very latest. "Oh I don't mind, Tony dearest," Susan said, deliciously drowsy, full of pleasure's afterglow.

Susan's reassurance left Tony unrelieved. He said he hated to be a heel, but he was in love with her, she was such a sweet kid, and since he was in love with her, maybe it made a difference. Suddenly he handed her blouse and her skirt to her, although she remained stretched out resting, feeling wonderful.

Tony's mention of love made Susan think of marriage, and she sat up straight and told Tony that although she loved him with all her heart she did not want to get married until she was at least twenty-five years of age: she hoped that he was not shocked, but she wanted to be a true woman of the world before settling down to marriage and babies. As she spoke, Tony moved toward the bed, as she continued he sat down upon the bed and squeezed her hand hard. Susan put her arm about his broad strong shoulders and said that he ought not to feel like a heel, she had been sick of being ch—— (she paused, for the word had shocked Tony, although he himself had just said bastard), but no girl with sense waited until marriage in 1950 before making love and going the limit. She stopped. Tony was shocked again.

"Tony, dearest," said Susan, reasoning sweetly, "if I had told you I was ch—— a virgin, you would have stopped making love to me because you are an honorable gentleman."

Tony was flattered and surprised to learn that he was a gentleman. He had long known that society dames were dizzy, but not dizzy enough to dismiss the loss of their sweet treasure so lightly, demanding no big build-up, pledges of forever, and the rest of the bushwah before you were in. But she' was a sweet kid, and if he had not knocked her up, it was probably all right. No matter what she said, no one but a bastard would break in a girl, but he had not known about it and maybe it made no difference to her just as she said.

Susan moved nearer Tony as his thoughts passed across his face slowly like Fifth Avenue buses lumbering forward. She wanted to begin again, but she did not want Tony to think that she was insatiable. Suddenly Tony stood up. He said that they better not get excited all over again until they took the proper precautions. Susan, disappointed, was nevertheless pleased. Tony was thoughtful and wanted to protect her. As they left, just to be sure, she asked if she would see him tomorrow night, smiling, and soon delighted when Tony said that she was certainly a sexy kid and she sure was going to see him tomorrow night.

7

Susan was soon troubled by the inconvenience and discomfort of making love in a rooming house. She did not like to have to get dressed and go home at midnight when she felt divinely sleepy and also cuddly. When Tony let her stay all night for the first time, it was so much fun to wake up with him as if they were an old married couple. She had to have an apartment of her own and she would tell her parents that she did not like Rita and Consuelo, which was certainly true enough. They were contemptuous of Tony because of his Tenth Avenue accent and Tony detested them, condemning them as snobs. Tony might have stayed with her all night in her room at the apartment, but Susan did not want those two to know how intimate she was with Tony: it was her own private romance which they were utterly incapable of understanding.

Her mother agreed to let her get an apartment without the slightest murmur or comment. Susan found a cute little apartment in Greenwich Village near Washington Square Park. The middle-aged couple who sublet it to her were going to Europe. They were disturbed when she took it practically five minutes after coming through the door and Susan was afraid they might have guessed the reason she wanted an apartment of her own. She was so scared that she left without the key, the husband had to come after her with it, and she acted guilty then, she wondered why. She was not doing anything which she herself regarded as wrong, so, it was hard to understand being ashamed and feeling guilty: how stupid!

She went home for the weekend and on Sunday morning Mother called the couple who were subletting the apartment. While Father was reading the Sunday *New York Times* with a sour look upon his face and Susan was assembling her records, Mother spoke to them at the phone in the foyer and her voice was very clear. Susan saw that Daddums was listening too although he did not lift his head from the paper.

"I am very glad that my daughter has taken your apartment," said Nancy Calhoun. "I am sure that my daughter will take good care of your belongings and your books, Professor Dark. But I am a little concerned about the neighborhood. Susan is only seventeen: will she be quite safe?"

Sometimes Mother made the dumbest most humiliating remarks to total strangers. She was very worldly but sometimes you would never know it. Whatever the man said in answer, Mother just kept it up: he was a professor of philosophy, whatever that was, but the Lord knows what he must have thought.

"Oh, I like Greenwich Village very much," Mother said to him. "I would like to live there myself. I feel that it is high time for the cellophane wrappings to be taken off my daughter. But I want to be sure they are removed gently."

Honestly, how dumb could a worldly and clever woman get?

Father had heard every word, and if she knew Father, he must be making some sour sarcastic remark to himself about Mother making her child seem like a pack of Chesterfields. Father was not supposed to know everything about his daughter's private life and Susan had gone to all lengths the night before to make him feel that she adored going to art school: she told him that she knew a student who had been in the army and was probably as gifted a painter as Van Gogh.

Susan took lots more of her things to New York City and with the help of the family chaffeur she moved to the apartment which would be her very own. She was in so much of a hurry, she was so impatient to get moved that she helped the chauffeur to carry in things, hurting his feelings. Hatboxes and shoetrees fell from her hands as she mounted the stoop, and when it was all in the apartment, Susan looked about the living room and saw that it was an awful mess: shoes, laundry, a bath mat and *Harper's Bazaar* scattered upon the living room floor and upon the studio couch against the wall. She felt bushed: she was eager to see Tony, but so exhausted by her haste that she hardly felt strong enough to rejoice with him in her own apartment.

"I'm just plain bushed," she said to Tony when she called him.

"Take a hot shower," said Tony. "Relaxes you: there's nothing like it. I'll be right down."

When he appeared, Susan, obedient, had taken a hot and cold shower and was wholly refreshed, dressed in her dressing gown, and had fashioned a turban about her head.

"You look like a harem dame!" said Tony, greeting her, kissing her nose and glancing about.

"A nice dump!" he declared, "Good enough" and went in to inspect the bedroom. He sprawled upon the large low double bed, testing the mattress by bouncing up and down upon it.

He closed his eyes in the mimicry of slumber and snoring which signified profound pleasure. Opening his eyes as Susan, charmed, gaped at him, standing between the folding doors, he thrust his arms toward her. She leaped toward the bed and fell into his embrace playfully, gladly, awkwardly, and eagerly.

As she turned aside upon the bed to take off her robe, that the consecration of the house might be consummated fully, Tony sat up, tense.

"Hey, who's that guy?" he said.

"Oh, that's Daddy," said Susan. She had set her father's photograph upon the small bureau which faced the bed.

"He looks like a nice guy," said Tony as he arose and examined Susan's father. Roger Calhoun's studio photograph was one in which self-consciousness showed itself as a solemn gloom of expression.

"He is very sweet," said Susan, drawing her white slip over her head and kicking off her shoes.

"Wait a minute," said Tony. "You know I'm not old-fashioned, but it makes me feel a little peculiar to have your old man staring straight at me when I'm making love to his daughter."

"Oh you silly!" said Susan, unclipping her bra, too absorbed in the movement of the immediate present toward the immediacies of the immediate future to heed Tony's troubled tone. "All that Daddums wants is for me to be happy."

"Sure, that's what they all say," said Tony. "What you can't stop you might as well back."

"Tony, dearest, are you scared that my father will come looking for you with a shotgun?"

"Nah," said Tony, continuing to stare at the photograph and ignoring Susan who was now entirely stripped. "It just gives me a funny feeling."

"But Tony, dearest," said Susan, "when the light is out, you can't see him: you're superstitious!

"You faced death like a brave hero when you were in the

army, Mr. Anthony Boyd," she added in the tone of recitation, as Tony turned the photograph face down, "but my sweet harmless father's *picture* gets you in a tizzy."

"Yup," said Tony, "I'm peculiar that way. Everyone is peculiar in some way, and no one is perfect, certainly not me, so let's just skip the discussion and keep the picture down: maybe I'll get used to it after a while."

"As you wish, my lord and master," said Susan, gracious and playful.

"You're a real honey," said Tony, jumping back into bed, turning out the light, reaching for Susan.

"Now," said Susan sometime later moving to one side, "now let us talk."

She told Tony how a girl she knew said to her boy friend, who wanted to go to sleep after making love, that one must hold a conversation. She tried but was unable to express the sentiment in its first vernacular and unexpurgated form.

"Sure, let's talk," said Tony, feeling heavy and sleepy. "What should we talk about?"

"You decide," said Susan.

"Did I ever tell you that you are a pretty cute trick?" said Tony coyly, teasing her.

"Is that all I am, just a cute trick?" said Susan sadly. Her feelings had been quickly hurt.

"You're the most beautiful girl in the whole world," said Tony, immediately. "You're the most beautiful girl who ever lived anywhere!"

"Oh Tony," said Susan, kissing him for the nobility of his just hyperbole, "Oh Tony, you're so sweet, I would like to eat you, but if I ate you I would not have you tomorrow."

"You can't eat your cake and have it too!" said Tony in a judicious tone, thinking of himself as a chocolate.cake.

"Oh Tony," said Susan, "what would you do if I suddenly died tonight?" The idea of eating Tony had suggested the morbid thought of his death and then of her own death to her.

Tony sat upright in bed, startled by the serious turn the conversation had taken unexpectedly.

"I would beat it the hell out of here in no time at all," Tony answered.

"Oh Tony, how can you be so cruel and unfeeling?" said Susan. "How can you?" She would have burst into tears right then if she had not felt so wonderful.

"What a girl!" said Tony, as if he were speaking of Susan to a third person, "She asks me an absolutely hypothetical question and I give her an absolutely hypothetical answer and then she gets sore! What do you expect me to do, stick around until the cops grab me for questioning and decide that I poisoned you or something, and have to go to the chair, and fry like an egg?"

"No, Tony dearest," said Susan, hardly mollified by his answer, but willing to discuss the question in the lucid light of reason. "I would not want you to kill yourself, merely because I was dead, nor would I expect you to live as a bachelor all alone for the remainder of your days. But if I died, I think that it would only be right for you to go to my parents and tell them that you once loved me very much and hoped to marry me after you became a famous painter and had a lot of money."

Under ordinary circumstances, the allusion to marriage might have made Tony careful, but he was now wholly possessed by images of pursuit in which he made breathless escapes from the police over apartment house roofs: he hardly heard Susan's allusion to marriage.

"That's a good idea," said Tony, remaining bemused. "That's what I will do if you die: I will go to the funeral, hold your mother's hand, and tell your mother and father how much I loved you."

"Would you really?" asked Susan. "Would you really, Tony, dearest one?"

"Sure I would," said Tony, "now that I know that that's what you want me to do."

"If you died," said Susan, reasoned and restored, but still fascinated by the drama of death, "I would kill myself!" she said, violently sitting up. She had not anticipated the conclusion of her sentence when she began it. "My God, woman," said Tony, "don't do that. I don't care what you do after I am dead! What difference does it make to me when I am nothing but a cold corpse."

"I will kill myself!" she insisted with passion. "I don't want to live without you and I don't want to be a sad-looking widow in black. Not only that, Mr. Anthony Boyd, I should think that it would make some slight difference to you to know that I am not going to live after you're dead and in the grave six feet under—"

Susan paused. Tony had fallen asleep while she spoke. He was snoring in his strong and manly way. Susan kissed his forehead gently and fell asleep curled up near him like a kitten.

8

Roger Calhoun's first visit to his daughter's first apartment quickly resulted in a new experience of astonishment. It was truly new, for he had grown accustomed to paternal shocks and surprises, like the inhabitants who live in the shadow of an active volcano. He had winced for weeks after hearing his wife speak of his daughter's cellophane wrappings. But the past now possessed a primitive and illusory character, Susan had come home for the week-end with a sore throat and Nancy had persuaded her to remain until she was well, sending him for Susan's sketchbooks, telling him that the child might be afraid she would fall behind in her art classes.

Having unlocked the double lock which his wife had installed to guard Susan against rape, the patient father followed the urge of natural curiosity and walked through the entire apartment, going from the large living room through the small kitchen to the bedroom in back. At the threshold of the bedroom, he stopped short: his own photograph, solemn and posed, stood on the dresser, facing the long low double bed. A new emotion succeeded curiosity. Surely Nancy was wrong about Susan's desire for an apartment. It was one thing for a young lady of seventeen to have an affair. But was it possible for a simple and natural child like Susan to engage in an affair in this very double bed with her father's image staring directly down at her? If Susan were a special and complicated creature, perhaps. But she was an old-fashioned girl, simple and natural, conventional and respectable, and a little self-conscious too.

Upon the desk where Susan's sketchbooks were, Roger Calhoun saw a book entitled *Successful Love.* It appeared to be a serious handbook on love and marriage, written by a father and a son and dedicated to the wife of the father and mother of the. son. He hesitated a little about borrowing it; but it was not a secret book, it was public domain.

The journey from Pennsylvania Station to the Long Island suburb where he lived took an hour and twenty minutes, and during this time Roger Calhoum rode in a tunnel of absorption, removed from all images, incidents, and passages of the trip, reading of *Successful Love.*

The authors undertook to advise both the unmarried and married on the requirements, which, fulfilled, would make marriage successful. Susan had marked certain passages *N.B.* and her father was pleased that she had been taught the sign *note well,* at Miss Beaumont's school. She had also circled other passages. Many circles occurred in the chapter which dealt with judging the other sex with exactitude: the authors warned against judging anyone when dressed in his Sunday best, at a party or at a dance. Such occasions were at best misleading, often wholly deceptive: appearance was not a reality. It was best to judge those to whom one was attracted not in the evening, but in the morning, after the dance or in the classroom, when they were not dressed up nor intent upon making a pleasing impression. Susan had circled *in the morning,* making her father wonder if she had seen the inescapable implication of the discussion, that perhaps the best time to judge another human being was in the morning, before breakfast, which in turn suggested a night in bed with the person in question?

It was quite logical that the next chapter should be devoted to petting and necking: the choice of a partner raised the question of the propriety of petting. To this intimate and difficult theme the authors addressed a tact, subtlety and delicacy which seemed to Roger Calhoun unexampled. Petting and necking were inseparable from the mastery of auto-eroticism, solo or manual. Petting might lead to auto-eroticism in excess, but privation might also lead to an imprudent excess. Nothing whatever was wrong with auto-eroticism in itself; it was not injurious in a physical sense nor depraved from a moral standpoint: the authors were so determined to make this clear that they stated their view in italics and numbered sentences, like rules or commandments. They continued by declaring that if there were no physical or moral reasons to refrain from auto-eroticism, there were grave psychological risks in such practices. The amorous habits and patterns by means of which auto-eroticism was performed might hinder or prevent the supreme joys of marital love.

The train paused at a station: cars at a crossing waited before white gates. The word, auto-eroticism, had been used at least fifteen times and Roger Calhoun thought it might be linked in the authors' minds with the word, automobile, the vehicle which clearly was the theater of much petting and necking. Returning to the book, Roger Calhoun saw that the dangers of petting and necking had been summarized in an italicized sentence: "In petting there is no Mason-Dixon line."

This sentence struck the father as a stupendous piece of wit. Overwhelmed by it, it set off vivid echoes and versions in his mind, and as the train triphammered eastward into the falling evening, he reflected with pleasure that in petting there is a Bull Run, in petting there is a Gettysburg, an encounter which is ruinous and indecisive, and may very will lead to a Gettysburg Address. There is a Marne, a Verdun, a Château-Thierry; there is just as surely an Austerlitz and a Verdun. If many a Caesar of love must have said that he had just crossed the Rubicon, many an Empress must have mourned a Pyrrhic victory, or perceived that in petting an empire had been overthrown, a Rome had begun to fall. There must be a phase comparable to the fall of France, Pearl Harbor, Stalingrad, and Hiroshima, as there must be an Alsace Lorraine, a D-Day, a V-E Day, a V-J Day.

Neither war nor love were joking matters, as Roger Calhoun soon saw in the chapter devoted to the causes of marital conflict, failure, and divorce. One of the chief causes of these disasters or catastrophes was the tendency to expect perfection in other human beings, although no human being was perfect, neither the authors nor the readers. The expectation was natural, but since one person cannot be everything, it was also vicious and destructive, because the most gifted human being, the greatest genius, suffered from extraordinary defects and limitations. Thus Johann Sebastian Bach, one of the truly great musicians, was the prey of an ungovernable temper which broke out daily or weekly in street brawls and scenes of physical violence in the sanctity of a church. Babe Ruth of the New York Yankees had been the greatest slugger of all times: he had hit more home runs than any other baseball player; but he had also struck out more times than any other athlete, and what is more, he had struck out far more often than he had hit a homer.

Roger Calhoun, pausing, glanced at his wrist watch: how much farther in the brave new world of 1950 would he go before getting to the sanctuary and ancient castle of his own home? Fifteen minutes of sheet-lightning revelation remained: he had not felt as he now felt since he had last taken gas, in 1927, when an impacted wisdom tooth had been extracted from his jaw.

Successful Love next analyzed the chief cause of marital conflict, failure and divorce: it was not alcoholism, cruelty, pathological inclinations, infidelity, nor any of the other reasons frequently cited in court. The true cause was at once simple and complicated: it was lack of respect for the other person, husband or wife. Success was desirable, money might help, kindness assuage, children console: but there was no real substitute for true respect. Yet if too little respect was catastrophic, the presence of too much respect might also be disastrous. Too much respect showed itself chiefly as squeamishness in making love. Once the marriage had been consumated, all squeamishness deserved the utmost condemnation: modesty of any kind was a mockery of the beauty of marriage, the meaning of unity, the oneness of husband and wife.

As the suburban train shuffled and slowed to the station, Roger Calhoun took a last glance at the book on love, and his gaze was caught by a sentence which Susan had circled four times: "Although it is not ordinarily thought of as such, the mind is the first of the erogenous zones."

Rising from his seat, dazed, he dismounted slowly from the train, waving vaguely to his wife who awaited him in the old coupe.

"How are you, dear?" said Nancy Calhoun, kissing her husband lightly. "You look a little haggard."

He motioned incoherently to the book in his hand.

"Susan's book," he said, bending to the car door and taking the wheel. "*Successful Love*. By a father and son. Dedicated to their wife. No, I mean his mother?"

His wife took the book from him and placed it in her lap.

"You look as if it had left you stunned," said Nancy Calhoun, gentle and curious.

"Did you know," said Roger Calhoun in a hoarse voice, shifting gears, "that although it is not ordinarily thought of as such, the mind is the first of the erogenous zones?"

"Dear Roger," said his wife," I see nothing wrong with that

remark. Did you think the book was not a good book for Susan?"

"When in Rome, do as the Romans do," said Roger Calhoun, disregarding his wife's question, preoccupied with his own emotion, "but don't stay too long, or else you will no longer feel at home at home."

9

Out of the unpredictable and literal blue, in the mist of the veritable, mild, and serene summer of their happiness and joy, Tony was recalled by the army. He and Susan had been so preoccupied with each other that they hardly knew there was a war in Korea. Tony was recalled partly because of his age, and his draft board's problems, partly as a result of the special training he had acquired and partly by accident. Although Susan was grief-stricken and Tony was annoyed at first, Tony soon told his dearest sweetheart that one must be a man about these matters, one must place one's duty to one's country first, one must not feel oneself exempt from a man's duty to his country as a loyal American citizen just because one was a painter. His avowals were not smug and platitudinous because they were enunciated in a Tenth Avenue accent.

"You are a hero," said Susan, bursting into tears of sorrow and pride.

When the time to say farewell neared, Susan armed herself with all the vows and sentiments customary on such occasions. Tony found her heartfelt avowals a little trying, resembling a funeral he had once attended. All that she said took it for granted that he was practically dying or dead or was probably going to get killed or at least crippled for life. It was ridiculous except that girls were like that and cried about spilt milk before it was spilled. Not for a split second did Tony suppose that he would be killed in Korea: his whole being suffused him with a sense of his own actuality and hence immortality.

On the night before Tony's departure, the great question of fidelity arose. Susan swore that she would be faithful to her dearest heart and she expected him to be faithful to her, however intense the temptation.

Susan had thought a lot about fidelity. She wanted to tell Tony her thoughts. She did not think that it would be difficult for them to be faithful to each other since they truly loved each other. She had arrived at this conviction while rereading *Successful Love* (returned by her father without her being aware it had been borrowed).

The sentence which had much impressed Roger Calhoun— "although it is ordinarily not thought of as such, the mind is the first of the erogenous zones"—had perplexed Susan and Tony as well. Suspecting a pornographic or recondite meaning, they had consulted the dictionary and sought out the meaning of erogenous.

"The mind is very sexy," said Susan when she arrived at an understanding of the sentence.

"It sure is," said Tony, wondering why such thoughts were not stated in plain English.

Now, in this tragic hour of farewell and departure, Susan, compelled by her emotions to a hitherto unexercised ingenuity of mind, had concluded with a new version of the sentence about how sexy the mind was.

"Since the mind is the first most sexy zone," said Susan, sweetly serious, "and in view of the fact that we are very much in love with one another, our minds are so full of thoughts of each other that we cannot possibly be attracted to anyone else in a sexy way."

Fidelity had never preoccupied Tony, which made it difficult for him to follow Susan. She had to make herself clear in vivid physical detail. When at last he understood, he was very pleased. He grinned at Susan, charmed; grinned so widely that Susan had to ask him what he was grinning about.

"Although I never thought of it as such," said Tony, "the

heart is the first of the sexy zones. And you're a pretty cute chick to figure all this out by yourself."

"You helped me, dearest," said Susan modestly, very pleased, "and anyway if I were not so much in love with you, I would not have been able to figure it out: love is an inspiration!"

"Well I am just as much in love with you," said Tony, "and I did not figure it out, you did!"

Susan was not interested in the question of credit very much, she was far more interested in thinking about the truth that love assured fidelity. And now the mind had been discussed with so much pleasure that the disregarded body asserted itself. Silently, in a hush inspired by love at once sacred and profane, sharpened and intensified by the drama of departure and separation, they went to the bedroom, disrobed as under a spell, hypnotized or drugged, stretched out upon the bed, reaching and surrendering to each other as if for the duration of eternity, making love with the most intense tenderness, sensual sweetness and jubilant joy.

Tony's departure immediately made Susan lonesome and blue, and she felt worse all the time. The apartment made her think of Tony all the time, with pain, fear, longing, and desire. Little as she liked Rita and Consuelo, with them she would at least not be alone all the time. She returned to their menage, and visited her own dear little apartment only to look for letters from Tony. She took his first letters into the bedroom of their love and lay down upon the bed, reading it again and again, unashamed of the hot and bitter tears which rolled down her face, thinking of how strong, handsome and brave Tony was. Susan's letters to Tony were full of declarations of love which concluded with the mind as the guardian of fidelity. Tony's letters disregarded all personal sentiments except for love and kisses at the end. He described army life and his own feats in a boastful unself-conscious way. But at last, when Susan's declarations of eternal love had reached a new summit of dedication, Tony answered in a way which would give the kid something to hang onto after he left the continental United States.

"Beautiful chick," he wrote to her, "if you really mean what you said in your last, then as soon as we get this feud in Korea cleaned up, I'll be back in no time at all, and we'll have to do something about it."

This was the closest he had ever come to a proposal of marriage. He was going by train to San Francisco the next day, and soon after to Japan and Korea. It was not likely that he would come back very soon across the Pacific Ocean.

10

Requested by his wife to look at the apartment which his daughter had ceased to occupy, because the dear child might not have tidied up properly, Roger Calhoun made his second visit to what he regarded, at times, as his daughter's love nest. Going north in a taxi from Wall Street, he questioned the dignity of his mission. There was no point, however, in being pompous or disingenuous about it when his curiosity about youth in 1950 continually mounted.

The living room and the kitchen were ridden by the ruins of a party: bottles of ginger ale, Pepsi-Cola, and root beer, boxes of Cheese-its, Fig Newtons, and Ritz crackers, containers of ice cream, jars of jam, and jars of pickles, dirty dishes and crushed paper napkins were all over. The children must have had a veritable bacchanalia, he thought, which had to be compared to the cocktail parties of his own generation, at which some were unable to converse before gulping four martinis and from which Roger Calhoun withdrew overcome by *taedium vitae* and a contempt for this world to a gymnasium or a Turkish bath.

He went to the bedroom, conscious that he wanted to find

something, unable to think of what it was. He saw it instantly, glancing at the dresser where his studio photograph presided as before, solemn and posed, staring down upon his daughter's bed of sin. The presence of his face sustained a mild modest pleasure, a delightful suspicion of his own misgivings. Perhaps he ought to doubt his doubts about the morality and conduct of youth if he took pleasure in the innocence which permitted his photograph in the intimacy of his daughter's bedroom.

The bedroom was in a state of disorder more extreme than the kitchen and living room. The framed photograph was the only form of order: the disheveled bed resembled the dirty snowdrifts in a city street four days after the worst blizzard of winter. Kicking one of his daughter's dispersed shoes by accident, his own heel trod upon what appeared to be a discarded letter. He picked it up, brushing the dust from it with a coat sleeve. It was Tony's last communication before departing for Korea.

It was not precisely a proposal of marriage, but surely it expressed genuine affection and sympathy, assuming that he was capable of recognizing those sentiments in a generation so distant from himself and the life he had lived. He felt grateful to the young man, certain that he had been kind to Susan. Yet, without knowing why, he felt acute relief that there appeared to be no need to meet the young man.

He left, Nancy would have to send the servants to clean the place. She had been right again, as she so often was. It would be difficult to get a taxi unless he walked to Fifth Avenue.

Gazing at the brittle glitter and nervous exhilaration of the great avenue in the sparkling, hurried hour after work and before dinner, he thought of the restoration of coffee, went to the first drugstore, seated himself on a backless stool at the end of the soda fountain counter, and saw his daughter Susan at a distance, seated so that she could not see him. She was with a very spruce-looking young man. It was very awkward. He must go before she saw him. Susan was succeeding in at once munching her sandwich, drinking her malted milk, and talking with much intensity to the young man.

Pausing to pay his check and feeling furtive, his back was turned to his daughter as the cashier changed his ten-dollar bill, and in the interval he heard what his daughter was saying to her new young man.

"In petting," she said sternly and slowly, as one mastering something to be memorized, "there is no Mason-Dixon line. You must not forget or think that I am holding out on you and being mean."

"Maybe so," said the young man in a tone clipped and intimidated, "but you have to make up your mind sooner or later."

"Although it is not ordinarily thought of as such," said Susan, "the mind is the first of the erogenous zones. If you just give me a chance, I will explain what that means to you—"

Roger Calhoun left as if he were making an escape from a penitentiary and from a period of history. He did not want to know how long it would be before the spruce young man succeeded Susan's true love in the first of the erogenous zones. It might be true that most human beings are much simpler than one commonly supposes them to be; one is oneself far simpler than one often supposes. But it was also true that the simple were extremely complicated. He felt entirely lost in the terror and jungle of innocence.

Tales from the Vienna Woods

To James Hamilton, John Hepburn and The White Horse Tavern

My father told me and he told me true
That marriage is the mystery of joy:
But other mysteries my father knew
He kept from me because I was a boy—

"If only I had the strength of my conviction, or the conviction of my strength," said Tobias Simon to himself, entering the restaurant bar where he had been only once before. It was called *The Vienna Woods*, and in back, behind the dining room, dance floor, and bar, there was a dimly lighted cave-like room known as the Grotto. The walls were decorated by nymphs, nude and in pursuit of each other.

When he had first been there, the slow warm revery which bloomed in him as he nursed his second drink had been broken by the loud and jubilant voice of a drunken girl departing.

"I have more fun than real people," she said boastfully, tossing her head in an effort at bravado and gaiety. For she had been taunted by some of the men at the bar and she had tried to answer them by accusing them of not being able to speak English. But her intention was so clearly to insult them with a random accusation that they merely laughed at her, for they were not foreigners, which was the meaning of the insult, and they were speaking English to her, so that clearly she was too drunk to know how to conceive of an effective insult.

Tobias thought of the drunken girl as he walked through the restaurant and into the Grotto, hoping a little that she would be there again, for he had often thought since that night of what she had said and wondered if it were really true that she had more fun than real people, or people who drank less than she did.

"I've been everywhere and I've seen everything," said Gabriel the bartender. He was big and almost fat and he had a broad heavy face. His remark, an opening gambit, had been directed at Tobias, a young man who looked at once seedy and boyish.

"Are you twenty-one?" Gabriel called out to the gray-haired middle-aged ladies who had just ordered Martinis at ten o'clock in the evening. The ladies who looked like schoolteachers were delighted so much by this gallant query that they blushed.

"Where are you from?" Tobias asked Gabriel. Gabriel looked sharply at Tobias to make sure that the question was a friendly one. He saw that it was.

"I was born in Boston *Mass*," Gabriel said. "When I was sixteen, my father threw me out of the house for running after women. I went to Australia, China, Japan, England, and France. I was in World War One, and then I came back here. I've had more women than you have hair on your head!"

Tobias, impressed, brushed back his thick mop of hair with the flat of his hand.

A customer at a table called to Gabriel, asking for two Tom Collinses.

"Go get them yourself!" said Gabriel as he began to prepare them. He poured the gin into a jigger with a false aplomb, spilling it over each time.

"You ought to get bigger bottles so that you will have enough to spill," said a customer at a table near the bar.

"You're right," said Gabriel. "That's a good idea. I'll tell the Greek. He'll jump at the idea." He looked at the wetness and decided to ignore it.

"This bar has not been wiped since Noah built the Ark," he remarked in general. Then he served the two drinks he had just made and returned to Tobias.

"Here I am," he continued as if he had not stopped, "forty-five years of age, turned down by the army, too old. But let me tell you something, to this day I wear silk underwear and I have a hundred suits."

"What are you trying to prove?" asked Tobias, but in a gentle tone.

"What do you want me to prove?" Gabriel thought that his silks and his suits were radiant, self-evident things like diamonds.

"They killed this place when I went away," he continued. It was a slow and empty Monday evening. "I had a great personal following here. The women used to come here in droves. And you see the way it is now. But I will build it up again."

Two well-dressed women who looked like unhappy wives came in and sat at a table near the juke box and in the lurid light of the juke box, they looked bored and disappointed forever.

"Now I am going to have two quick ones," said Gabriel to Tobias, "and then I am going over there and impress those dames."

A tall plump girl came in and sat down on a bar stool. She wore a tight red dress which declared her plumpness and her roundness. It was clear that she was drunk and it was soon clear that she was angry. The customer at the table near the bar called out and asked her if he could buy her a drink.

"I don't want anyone to buy me a drink," she said without turning to look at the generous customer, speaking to Gabriel who had just returned to the bar. "A fellow bought me a drink, he bought me two drinks, and then he says let's go sit in the park. I meet this ensign at the checkroom in the Ritz where

I work and he says, Let me buy you a drink and take you to dinner, so we go to have dinner, and we have another drink, and then he says, Let's go sit in the park: imagine that! Two drinks and he wants to sit in the park. Not me, brother, I said to him, I don't like that. You picked the wrong customer this time. We were just on the corner near the cabstand, so I said to him, Sorry, wrong number, and I stepped right into the taxi and drove off, leaving him there with his thoughts."

"All he wanted was to be friendly," said Tobias, unable to think of anything else to say.

"Friendly!" said the girl. "He wanted to be *too* friendly. I could see the look in his face."

"What do you want these guys to be, nuns?" said Gabriel. "They're fighting for their country and they're lonesome. Be reasonable, Emma, or at least be polite. If you don't want to play house, then don't let the guy buy you dinner."

"Listen," said Emma, rocking slightly, "the cab driver said I was a deadhead when I told him. But I was hurt once and I don't intend to he hurt again. Nice people get kicked in the face."

"Not all the time," said Tobias. "Maybe the ensign did not want to kick you in the face. He just wanted to have some fun and he just thought you wanted to have some fun."

"Sure, Emma," said Gabriel, "he meant no harm. It is done all the time. Everyone goes to sit in the dark. Why should you be different? How was he to know that you were different?"

"I hate men," said Emma as if she were answering all the questions once and for all and making an exact statement of justice and originality.

"How about a girl?" said Paddles the trumpeter who had just come from the dance floor. "I know some pretty girls. Or do you hate girls too?"

"I don't like girls either," said Emma. "I just like myself."

"What are you after, anyway?" asked Gabriel in a tone of condemnation.

"I want some dollars and then I want some more dollars," said Emma, meaning $: *in hoc signo vince.*

"Baby," said Paddles, who was thin and balding, "if I had what you have, I'd have all the dollars I wanted."

"No one can have it," said Emma. "How about buying me a drink?" she said to Tobias.

"Buy your own drinks," said Gabriel, surrendering to his irritation. But Tobias nodded to Gabriel who proceeded to mix a highball for Emma.

"What are you holding on to your money for, anyway?" said Gabriel as he gave her the highball.

"To get my teeth fixed," said Emma, taking a big gulp and lighting a cigarette. "One hundred and twenty dollars."

"Your teeth look fine," said Paddles, sipping a beer.

"That's why they look fine," said Emma, "because I always have them fixed by an expensive dentist. I take care of my teeth because I want to die with all my *own* teeth in my head."

"If I had what you have," said Paddles as if he had not made almost the same remark before, "I would get my teeth fixed for nothing."

"I would rather pay," said Emma. "I hate men. They just want one thing, just one thing."

"What else is there?" said Paddles, in a smirking tone but with a deadpan face.

"I don't expect *you* to understand that there *is* something higher in life," said Emma, pained and disdainful.

"Now look, Emma," said Paddles patiently, "don't you think you let yourself in for this? You could have told the ensign that you were going to dinner just for the conversation, and then you would have had no trouble."

Emma felt caught in the toils of this reasonable suggestion. She looked bemused as if such a course had not occurred to her, but perhaps should have occurred to her.

"I am engaged to be married," she said, striving to defend herself also by adopting the tone of respectability. "My fiancé is quartermaster on the *Lafayette*. His leave was taken away because of me. He stayed up all night with me in the hotel and did not get back to the ship because he fell asleep. He kept arguing with me all night, he said, If you truly love me, you will let me make love to you. And I said, If *you truly* loved me, you would not ask me to."

"The guy would be better off dead," said Gabriel, sullenly.

"Is that so!" said Emma, enraged. "Well I will have you know that that's not love. Of course, I don't expect *you* to understand *that*."

Nowadays the f——ing begins with the engagement," said Paddles pleasantly. He had returned again after a spell with the band.

"A girl is bound to say yes some time," said Gabriel, "you just can't say no all the time."

"I can say no all the time," said Emma.

"I bet you can, at that," said Gabriel severely.

"Why don't you drop dead," said Emma, enraged all over again.

"You may be right, at that," said Gabriel. His tone was suddenly conciliatory. He did not want a scene. He did not like scenes. Besides, the Greek would be annoyed. "It may be best to sleep alone. That's the only sure way of keeping out of trouble." He spoke pensively, moved by memory.

"Oh no," said Paddles, "not to sleep alone: That *can't* be the best thing."

"It's lonesome," Gabriel admitted judiciously, pouring himself half a glass of whisky, "but I can think of a lot of things that are worse than being lonesome. When you're lonely, you're sorry for yourself, you pity yourself, but pity never killed anyone."

"The rich have company," said Tobias to himself, paraphrasing a quotation.

"I pity myself," said Emma, "and I have a right to, because I've been badly hurt."

"I pity you," said Gabriel. He did not wholly conceal his scorn.

"What are you saving it for?" asked Paddles.

"For the worms!" said Emma.

"The worms won't appreciate it," said Paddles.

"How do you know what the worms will and will not appreciate," said Emma. "You're no worm, you're just a heel," she added declaratively and stupidly, putting down her drink, adjusting her dress, and obviously about to depart.

"I am going somewhere where there is a little more refinement," she said as she left, moving with an over-meticulous effort at dignity.

"That's the way it is," said Gabriel, commenting on Emma in general. "If every night were like tonight, the Greek would go bankrupt in a month."

"That certainly is the way it is," said Tobias pensively. He had drunk enough to arrive at the reflective or philosophical phase of drinking. "Someone hurt her, and now she is going to hurt everyone else she can, if he is a man."

"Not everyone is like that," said Gabriel. "*I* am not like that."

"You are right," Tobias admitted judiciously, "not everyone is just like that and some people become kind because they have been hurt, kind and generous after being cruel and nasty. But do you know, that girl Emma made me think of how I once was sure I knew what was wrong with the world, what was really and truly wrong with the world—"

"Hey, Paddles," Gabriel called out to the trumpeter who was returning from the men's room, "this guy thinks he has figured out what is really wrong with the whole world." Gabriel was tired, his irony was forced, but he was curious.

"Let's get in on the ground floor," Gabriel said to Paddles. "Maybe this guy has something, and if he *does* have something, maybe we can get rich overnight and get out of this dump."

"I am feeling no pain," said Paddles as he sat himself on the bar stool next to Tobias, "but I am always open to new ideas and always willing to learn. So now you tell us what is really wrong with the whole world," he said in a friendly way to Tobias, "and I will listen attentively. But it had better be good!"

"Look," said Tobias, in a patient tone, "I did not say that I knew what was really wrong with the world, all I said was that I *thought* I knew one night when I was drunk."

"That's what's wrong with the whole world," said Gabriel in a tone of contempt.

"What?" said Paddles.

"You can't stay drunk," Gabriel replied, pouring himself another drink and looking toward the unhappy wives at the table near the silent and gorgeous juke box, as if their appearance might have recently improved.

'Now Gabriel," said Paddles, "keep your big mouth shut while this guy tells us what he *thought* was the trouble with the whole world: how about it?" he added, looking at Tobias.

"The real trouble with the whole world," said Tobias slowly, as if he were seeking to move back to the state of mind in which he had been illuminated by passing and false insight, "is that A is in love with B, B is in love with C, C is in love with D, D is in love with E—"

"We get it," said Paddles, impatiently. "You don't have to spell it out."

"X is in love with Y," said Gabriel who had become interested, "Y is in love with Z, but who is Z in love with? A?"

"Yes," said Tobias, "that's often the case, Z is in love with A who is in love with B—"

"We get it, we get it!" said Paddles impatient and annoyed. "I may not be a master mind, but you don't have to talk as if this were a kindergarten!"

"The older I get," said Tobias, wishing to appease Paddles whom he saw he had somehow annoyed, "the more I think that the whole world is a kindergarten. At best!" he added, sadly.

"I fell in love for the first time in kindergarten," said Gabriel, a faint fond smile in his eyes.

"Who did *you* fall in love with?" said Paddles, directing his question to Tobias.

"She had braces on her teeth," said Gabriel, thinking that the question had been directed at him, and fondly remembering his childhood ambition and lust, "and her bust was nine years in the future, but my knees shook when I looked at her and once she made me wet my pants!"

"Listen," said Paddles to Gabriel, "I'd like to hear about how she made you wet your pants, but some other time. I don't care if she grew up to be Hedy LaMarr, right now I want to know what happened to this guy when he fell in love. How about it?" he said to Tobias, looking at him sharply but sympathetically.

"Maybe it was the same girl you fell in love with! But never mind that, it's too complicated. She was very nice and very pretty," said Tobias, pain on his face. "No: she was *not* nice at all, she was a witch, and I was the only one who thought she was very pretty or nice. Everyone else just thought she was pretty and some did not think she was pretty at all, but just neat, neat and mean."

"—And she must have been in love with some other guy," said Paddles sadly.

"At first it seemed like that," said Tobias, "and that was exactly what she said, that she was in love with someone else, but maybe she would forget about him, and she said that she would marry me if she ever married anyone at all, she could not imagine being married to anyone but me, which was a very nice thing to say and had me in a fine glow for weeks. But then when the other guy divorced his wife and asked her to marry him, she refused him, and came to tell me that she now wanted very much to marry me. But I had fallen in love with a much nicer girl."

"Was she just in love with herself?" asked Paddles, reduced to a schoolboy's tone by the nature of the conversation and his passionate interest in it.

"For a while I thought that was what was wrong," said Tobias. "But I decided after a time that she was not in love with herself either. She hated herself and she hated men, just like Emma, though not in the same way."

"How did you figure all that out?" asked Paddles.

"It's not very hard to figure out something like that," said Gabriel. He was also interested in the subject, but not with Paddles' intensity.

"I figured it out by thinking about what she did almost every time I was going to kiss her: she went to the bathroom to brush her teeth! Now, how about that? It had never occurred to her that she could have had trench mouth and I would not have been any the less eager to kiss her. But she did not know that, because she did not know about being in love, and because she did not like herself very much."

"Brother, you have had it bad," said Gabriel. "Have a double Scotch on the house because *I* think you *still* have it bad."

Tobias was silent. Paddles regarded him with care and sympathy. The juke box, silent all evening, began to play a famous waltz by Johann Strauss.

"Johann Strauss was a liar," said Tobias in a low voice.

"What's that you just said?" asked Gabriel.

"Onan's house was on fire," said Tobias idly. "Onan's spouse was his lyre." He was thinking of the girl who brushed her teeth with so much awareness of her physical being's possible foulness.

"I still don't get it," said Gabriel. "This double talk stopped being funny ten years ago."

"Greater love hath Onan," said Tobias heedlessly.

"Say," said Paddles, more interested than ever, "would you mind if I asked you how this dame was in the hay?"

"She was very active and vigorous," said Tobias. "She was determined to prove that she was better than every other girl in the hay and in every other way. And when we finished, she jumped up immediately to get Kleenex or paper napkins because she was afraid the bedsheets would get soiled."

"Emma thinks about her teeth too," said Gabriel thoughtfully, "she is always going to the dentist to get them fixed."

"Teeth are important," said Tobias carefully, "and tooth-brushes are also important. I read something interesting by a Viennese doctor once about the unreasonable feelings which human beings have when it is a question of a toothbrush or the same kind of thing. He said that it was strange how so many human beings do not like to use another person's toothbrush: do they think that their own toothbrush is cleaner than another person's? he said, or he said something like that—"

"That doctor was just a wise guy," said Paddles, disgusted and interested.

"Never mind him," said Tobias, "the remarkable thing was that the same idea began to percolate in fashionable schools for girls, and one girl told me that she knew what it was to be in love. When you are in love, she said, you don't mind using the same toothbrush as the man you're in love with."

"Brother, have another on the house," said Gabriel. "You've been walking on the bottom of the river."

"How did you get out of it?" asked Paddles. "Or did you get out of it? Does anyone ever get out of it?"

"Probably yes and probably no," said Tobias, smiling a little.

"Now look," said Gabriel, impatient, "here we are having a very interesting discussion and you have to interrupt it with double talk every now and again. Did you or did you not ever get out of it?"

"I was serious; I was not talking double talk," said Tobias carefully. "I did get out of it, in a way, but in a way, I did not because I went and fell in love with another girl who was very nice and not at all like the toothbrush girl and who liked me very much, if you boys will forgive me for boasting a little."

"Boast all you want," said Paddles, "but tell us what the final score was—"

"The game has gone into extra innings," said Tobias.

"But look, if you fell in love with the girl and she liked you very much, what went wrong? That's the way all the pictures end—" said Paddles, distressed and perplexed.

"—Not any more they don't," said Gabriel. "What happened in the ninth inning?"

"The girl's father hit a homer with the bases loaded, sending the game into extra innings," said Tobias. "He swung from below the belt, stepping out of the batter's box."

"Look," said Gabriel, "are you or are you not going to tell us what happened and finish the story?"

"It is only once in a while," said Tobias, "that I think I know what happened and this is not one of my intelligent nights. How about another Scotch on the rocks? Swiss cheese is full of holes," he added pointlessly.

Gabriel poured the whisky in Tobias' glass after putting two cubes of ice in it.

"Are you hungry?" asked Gabriel, troubled. "Oh, no, you can't be hungry: first you give us a blow-by-blow description," he said, "then you clam up on us!"

"I am not trying to keep anything back," said Tobias, "but if I tried to make sense, I would have to tell you what happened when I was three years of age and you would not be interested: no one except proud parents like to hear stories about children."

"Does he want us to coax him?" said Paddles to Gabriel in disgust and irritation.

"What happened when you were three years of age?" asked Gabriel patiently. "Ordinarily I don't give a f—— about what happened to anyone before the age of consent, but you've blown this up until everything sounds important!"

"Give, man, give," said Paddles, "take us off the hook!"

"Four years ago," said Tobias, his glance growing abstracted as he went down to the past in his mind, "I took the nice girl I fell in love with to see my mother. Look, are you sure that you want to hear this story?"

"Brother, I am all ears," said Paddles, wiggling his ears a little.

"Sure we want to hear the story," said Gabriel, "but it better be good or you are going to have to explain it to us. And kindly also omit the double talk."

"I will try," said Tobias. "You can see that this was a fairly important occasion, for I was taking my best girl to see my mother. I won't try to tell you all that happened, and I don't know if I could, but anyway, during the evening my mother blew out all the lights in her apartment when she plugged in a lamp. We sat in the dark for a moment and then my mother lighted candles and looked for a new fuse. There were no fuses in the house, so I went to look for the superintendent, but he did not seem to be home, although it turned out that he was home and dead drunk. I went out to buy a new fuse and I had to walk several blocks before I came to a store. While I was gone my mother was telling my girl Isabel a story about me when I was three years of age. This was supposed to be the inside story of what I was really like, and don't forget that my mother had never before known and talked with Isabel, not that *that* makes much difference, except to me. The story was about how when I was three, she often told me a story about the oil painting on the wall—"

"A story inside a story inside a story—" said Gabriel, disappointed.

"That's the way it has to be because this is an endless story," said Tobias. "But I will try to get to the end of the endless story quickly. The oil painting was on the wall as my mother told Isabel the story and it was near enough to be seen in the slim, flickering light of the candles. It was a sentimental painting of a barefoot boy who played the violin, which he held in his hand, and he looked very pathetic, cold, and unhappy. He played the violin as a way of begging for money. When I was three, my mother would tell me that this boy whom she had named Tony was my older brother and he had died before I was born. This made me cry, I suppose because I immediately thought that if my older brother had died in early youth, I might die too and fairly soon. But when I cried, my mother just called me a cry-baby and told me that Tony had never cried, he had been a very good boy, and he had never had a pair of shoes while I had all the shoes I needed. The more I cried, the more my mother kept telling me the story and comparing me to Tony. He had been a good boy and I was not. He had been brave and I was a coward. I did not know what a coward was, but I knew that it was not what anyone would want to be. And it turned out that my mother was right, for I was a coward for a long time after that, for I believed what my mother said and I was afraid that I would die, since after all my older brother Tony had died and he had been a good boy which I was not—"

"Is that the inside story?" asked Paddles.

"It is an important part of the inside of the inside story," Tobias replied, bemused. "You cannot serve God and Mama," he added under his breath.

"Please omit the double talk," said Gabriel. "Is that the end of the story? If it is, I wish you would explain to me what it means and why you think it is so important."

"Gabriel," said Paddles, pained in several senses, "much as I respect you, you sometimes talk like a complete dumb-bell."

"All right, I am a dumb-bell," said Gabriel, "lots of people are dumb-bells. It is no crime to be a dumb-bell. But all I want is a simple explanation of the story from one of you guys."

"I can't explain the story," said Tobias politely, "not right now. And even if I could, my explanation might very well be wrong."

"Just be patient," said Paddles to Gabriel, "I will explain the story to you, but not right now," he added, looking at Tobias who had withdrawn suddenly, although he stood at the bar holding his glass.

"I guess we better call it a night," said Gabriel, responding to the mood and the silence of Tobias and Paddles. "How about one for the road?"

Tobias extended his glass and Paddles said that he had enough of a load for the time being.

One for the road, one for the sphinx, and one for the jinx, said Tobias to himself, one for the fog, one for the past and one for the future, one for self-pity and two for resentment, one for cowardice and brandy for courage, but dutch courage is better than none at all. One for love, one for frustration, and one for desperation, brandy for hope and beer for nervousness, Martinis to eat and whisky to sleep, one to be calm, two to be gay, one to be warm and a few to have something to say. A pint to make love and a case to get away from the guilt one cannot face after the great wild flower of the sunset has gone down and left one alone in the isolation and condemnation of the night, the darkness of fear amid electric light. One for the strength never to despair, one to be near the hope which is born of desperate fear, one to remember always that the greatest courage is born of the greatest danger, that courage is born of fear, one never to forget how hope is a way of being alive and living with the real people. One for Emma, one for Ethel, one for Arabel, one for the Danish girl, one for Isabel, one for the power that moves the sun, and the other stars, and the dancing daemons of heaven and hell. This is the doctrine of the master of joy: God is love. Hatred is death. The kingdom of love is within you; also the kingdom of death.

"Are you going my way?" asked Paddles who saw that Tobias had just finished his drink and who had been regarding him with curiosity and sympathy, for Tobias' lips had been moving as in unmeant prayer, and he had been looking at his own drawn face in the broad looking-glass above the long bar.

"I don't know where I am going," said Tobias, remaining at a distance, "but thanks anyway," he added absent-mindedly. "I think that I'd better walk home."

"Come again," said Gabriel, who felt that he liked the

stranger, even though he was certainly strange. "Next time I will tell you a very funny story about what the housewife did when the milkman looked her straight in the eye and said: 'Do you have the time?' "

Tobias smiled vaguely and left, saying that he would come again during the week and knowing that Gabriel wished to tell him the funny story immediately probably in the friendly hope of cheering him up and making him forget himself or forgive himself. It was easy to forgive others, it was very difficult to forgive oneself, but one had to forgive oneself or one would never be truly able to forgive others.

Tobias moved through the restaurant bar of the *Vienna Woods* awkwardly, for it was half dark. He reached the door and went out, walking toward the hope which is on the other side of despair, where one learns to care and not to care.

"What's the story?" asked Paddles, putting his trumpet case under his arm as Gabriel turned out the lights, after reaching for his hat and coat. "What does the housewife do? What does she say?"

"She pulls him through the doorway and asks him what he likes? 'My husband owns a pistol,' she says, 'but he's away all day!' " Gabriel answered his friend but listlessly and tiredly, so that he did not sound self-amused or gay.

Paddles made no comment, looking at himself in the darkened jewel of the looking-glass above the bar.

"In God I trust," he said despairingly, "and no one else!" He was thinking chiefly of his first two wives as he looked critically at his thin and balding image.

"Do you know," said Gabriel sadly, "a lot of guys are all f——ed up, a lot of guys and a lot of dames too, and the guys because of the dames and the dames because of the guys. Which reminds me. If you heard this one, stop me. A soldier is telling another soldier about what he did on his one-day leave the day before. 'First I take a f——n bus to get out of the f——n camp, then I go to the f——n whistlestop town and go to a f——n bar and pick up a f——n piece of gash and take her to a f——n hotel and get us a f——n room—' "

Gabriel paused for effect.

"Man, what happened then?" asked Paddles, interested in part by the intense harshness of Gabriel's tone.

" 'Then we had intercourse for the rest of the night,' " said Gabriel in a tone which was sweet, and tender, and soft, and immediately thereafter resumed his previous tone, harsh and contemptuous. " 'Next morning we left the f——n room, and the f——n hotel, I kissed the f——n dame good-by and took the f——n bus back to this f——n camp and now I have to wait a f——n month before I get out of this f——n concentration camp again!' "

"What's so funny about that story?" asked Paddles, bored and tired.

"Who said it was funny?" said Gabriel. "Are all stories supposed to be funny?"

Paddles said nothing.

They moved through the darkened *Vienna Woods* and closed the door and shivered a little in the dead street of after-midnight.

"Man," said Paddles to Gabriel as a way of saying good night, "some one of these days you are going to have to blow that horn!"

> *At the round sky's imagined circles, blow*
> *Your trumpets, Angels, and arise, arise*
> *Before the fission foams up to the sky's*
> *White upon white upon light and untouched snow:*
> *Now let your trumps declare, once more, once more!*
> *That love is the fulfilling of the law!*

The Fabulous Twenty-Dollar Bill

"I never liked him," said Professor Robbins to his wife, "and now I know very well why I don't like him."

"He has a hard time," said his wife mildly, "he has never had the recognition he deserves, and you know how great the strain upon painters is, these days."

"The strain is great on everyone," her husband replied, lifting his fourth highball of the evening and gulping his drink as if his irritation would be reduced by the speed with which he drank. "The strain is great on me, and this kind of an incident is a very good example of it."

It was a wet Sunday evening in early May, and the Robbins' living room was enclosed in the hush of an academic community on a Sunday when the weather is poor. For the past twenty years it would have been quite unlikely that on a Sunday evening Professor Robbins would have been doing anything other than preparing for tomorrow's lecture. Indeed he had often expressed the sternest disapproval of any teacher who drank in the evening when he had to meet his classes the next day. But during the afternoon Professor Robbins had conversed at length with Professor Anderson, another member of the committee which chose the painter who was to give the annual Winslow Homer lectureship in the history of American

Painting. One of the leading candidates was the well-known painter, Leonard Pierce. However, there were a dozen other candidates and one member of the committee had argued against Pierce, declaring that several other candidates were just as gifted, and needed the money as Pierce did not, for his wife was rich. Professor Robbins, knowing how eager and anxious Pierce was to get the lectureship, had recently told the unhappy painter that he was first on the list of the younger candidates. For it was customary to have two sets of candidates, the older men and the younger men, the older men being those who had already achieved a national reputation which would assure the university prestige and honor if they were appointed. However, it was likely each year that the older men would not want to spend an entire year in an academic community, lecturing, lionized, and otherwise distracted from their work. It was customary each year to ask one of the older men and when he refused, to turn to the younger men. Leonard Pierce had been one of the leading candidates among the younger men for three years, and he was very much afraid that he was going to be disappointed again, as he had been for the past three years. Knowing Pierce's anxiety and eagerness, Professor Robbins had sought to reassure him by telling him that this year he was first on the list of the younger men.

"You see the consequences of attempting to be kind to an insecure and gifted human being," Professor Robbins said to his wife, gulping his highball again. "If I had not told him that he was a leading candidate, I would not have been humiliated."

"You have not been humiliated," said his wife patiently. "It is Leonard Pierce who has been humiliated for years. Knowing how disappointed he has been, you ought not to be surprised or wounded by his behavior."

"But what does Anderson think of me, now that Pierce has gone to question him?" asked Professor Robbins impatiently.

Pierce had asked Anderson if it was indeed true, as he had

been told by Robbins, that he was the leading candidate among the younger men, and it was Anderson's report of this inquiry, during the afternoon when they had encountered each other in the street and spoken briefly, which had caused Robbins' state of profound irritation.

"My dear, Anderson's attitude toward you is not influenced by the behavior of unhappy artists," said Mrs. Robbins, tired by her husband's mood and the way in which his mind moved, although she loved him very much.

"Don't forget," said Professor Robbins, "that I've made a special and strenuous effort to get Pierce the appointment. I argued vehemently at each meeting of the committee, insisting that the fact that Pierce's wife owns a lily-cup factory ought not to have anything to do with our choice. Now, as a result of my efforts, Anderson has every right to suppose Pierce thinks I do not tell the truth."

"I imagine," said Mrs. Robbins, "that Anderson is not sure anyone tells the truth; and I don't see why you care very much, in any case, what Anderson thinks." Mrs. Robbins considered in her own mind the question of why Anderson had told her husband what Pierce said, but she was too experienced, by now, to waken this further suspicion in her husband's tormented mind. She felt that it was difficult enough to live life on the level of complication and anxiety which was natural to her husband; any further speculation would merely aggravate her husband's emotional plight. Moreover, Professor Robbins had often expressed a principled scorn for the kind of academic politics in which Anderson engaged for no reasonable motive whatever, except that perhaps he enjoyed academic politics for their own sake, as a kind of amusing game. Anderson had nothing to gain which he had not already secured. One could perhaps explain his behavior by supposing that he had con-contracted the habit of playing politics during his youth, before he was established.

Mrs. Robbins watched her husband go to the table where the

whiskey stood and fix himself a fresh highball. And she noticed that he had made his highball very strong again.

"I think I will have one too," she said, sodden with tiredness and wishing to revive herself a little. She felt that she must continue to argue patiently with her husband. Sometimes when he was upset or angered, he talked himself free of the emotion which had disturbed him by going to extremes in discussing the matter with his wife, by condemning the human beings involved so severely that he himself felt what an excess (what a caricature!) he had committed. Sometimes, on the other hand, his anger was merely intensified, and he became angry at his wife because of her mild effort to be judicious and just.

Robbins brought his wife a highball and seated himself in his armchair, his shoulders hunched, a sign of the tenseness his wife had come to recognize and fear during the long years of their married life.

"I do not like to be distrusted," he said, "and I do not see why I should continue to support anyone who has openly expressed his distrust of me."

"You've said that Pierce is very gifted," his wife replied, "and you know as well as anyone what men of genius have been like. They have been diseased, neglected, patronized, plagued by all the ills the creative life attracts to itself as sugar attracts flies. It is one thing to expect a genius to be a genius: why do you also think that he has to be the embodiment of moral goodness?"

"You're right, Isabel," Professor Robbins answered, touched by the strength of his wife's formulation, "it is too much to expect moral goodness in men of genius. It would be very pleasant, if it were present, but one ought not to require it. Moral perception," he added, as if he were speaking to a hall of students, "is certainly necessary, but the strength of character which marks a good man is something else again: it is a career or profession in itself!"

Mrs. Robbins had succeeded in soothing her husband by invoking the one sympathy in her husband's mind which surpassed his concern with moral probity: his admiration of genius and his feeling that the history of art was full of the persecution of great artists.

"You are right," he said again to his wife as he rose to go to bed, "the question of Pierce's behavior is quite irrelevant. He has a hard time, he is very gifted, and he should get the appointment. It may help him in his work." And he touched his wife's shoulder with affection as he left the living room and mounted the stairs to the bedroom from which he would hurl himself into the labyrinth of sleep, in which, at some turn, toward the small hours when the heart is pitiless and the mind an inquisitor, he might ask himself why Anderson had reported Pierce's preposterous mistrust of him.

2

Professor Robbins was a great man and an exhausted one. At the end of World War Two, the boom in education had increased his academic duties, and since he was a conscientious, scrupulous man, he performed them with a care and an intensity which his colleagues considered unnecessary. One of his colleagues said to his wife—no one would have dared to speak directly to Professor Robbins, and in any case, the method of indirect communication was a favored custom in the academic community—one of his colleagues told his devoted wife that her husband was driving himself too much and that it would not be impossible to pass on some of his burdens to another and younger man; nor would it be unjust to do so.

"I know," said Mrs. Robbins, "but it would be useless to tell him. He has been like that all his life and he is not going to change now." Having said this, she sighed, and silently reflected upon her sigh. The truth was that Professor Robbins did not permit other younger members of the department to take over some of his burdens because he did not think well of most human beings. In fact, it might be said that he did not trust them. At times, Mrs. Robbins thought that her husband did not really trust himself or think well of himself: what other explanation was there for the haste and the fear which she observed in him when he prepared a lecture or undertook any task, important or trivial? He seemed to her to behave as if he were afraid that he might suddenly stop in the midst of his preparation or in the midst of his lecture and not complete the work at all. The fact that he had never done any such thing and the more present and more vivid fact that he was esteemed the most brilliant man in America, in his subject, did not appear in the least to make him any the less fearful that on each new occasion something might go wrong unless he made efforts which to his wife looked nervous or hysterical or desperate, the efforts of a man who is trying to complete an invention or scientific discovery before rivals elsewhere, who are certainly on the same track, succeed in anticipating him.

Professor Robbins' fame was such that distinguished visitors to the university were flattered when he entertained them; and if he was the host of one he had to be the host of all who were equally distinguished. The entertainment of visitors was a nervous hardship to Professor Robbins, it was a distraction from his work, it was trying and forced. Moreover, as his wife alone knew, he was never at ease with strangers (although his wife knew this truth, Professor Robbins did not know it much of the time). In the same way, he was at ease with his students only after the first two months of each scholastic year, when their open admiration of him and their obvious concentration upon what he had to say finally reassured him once again. For he was, in a way, a spellbinder, so much in love with his subject and with teaching and with being clear and interesting that the students, at first perplexed by him, came in the end to admire him so much that they mistook his failings or his weak days as cunning devices and pedagogic methods.

Strangers were not students, however. During the past four years, as the number of strangers he had to meet increased, Professor Robbins had begun to drink too much. It was the only way he knew of relaxing with strangers. As a young man, he had hardly known the need to relax, he had driven himself by what he thought of as will-power, and he had spoken with contempt of those who made drinking a habitual part of their social life.

"It reduces my efficiency by about fifty percent the next day," he had said in his late youth, and arrogantly, "I believe in being conscious and drinking means blunting one's consciousness. It is a kind of cowardice, like sleeping all morning, or reading novels all the time."

His wife had dissented tactfully, saying that there was no need to be conscious all the time, there was such a thing as being too conscious, and drinking helped human beings to be friendly with one another. Her husband, in the pride and insensitivity of his late youth, had answered that such friendship was false: true friendship ought to be based upon a community of interest and not upon chemical agents. Mrs. Robbins, then as now, sighed and ceased to argue with her husband about being conscious. He merely became irritated and he regarded his unquestionable success as a confirmation of all his principles and opinions, the principles and opinions by which he certainly lived.

His opinion of drinking changed as his obligations mounted, and these obligations as a host and teacher increased sharply and suddenly when the government began to send veterans of the Second World War to school. Professor Robbins lectured to his classes on Monday and Wednesday, which meant that he had to prepare his lectures with characteristic furious meticulousness on Sunday and Tuesday night. By Wednesday he was very tired, he was unable to respond very well even to those things he cared about very much, and by Thursday, very often, there was a visiting lecturer or distinguished visitor whom Professor Robbins felt that, as an inevitable duty, he must house and entertain. Thus it was on Thursday and Friday that Professor Robbins drank too much. The physician whom Robbins visited every six months for what is known as a routine check-up, perceived that Robbins was drinking too much, but he had known his patient for twenty-two years, and he knew that it was better for Robbins to drink too much than not to drink at all, which was probably what would occur if he was given medical advice to the effect that drinking blighted his health and reduced his "working ability."

3

Two weeks after Professor Robbins had been persuaded by his wife to overlook the failings of Leonard Pierce, since he was a very gifted human being, it was Robbins' duty, and as he said to the lecture hall audience, his privilege, to introduce Pietro Tuciano, who had come to give a public lecture at the university. Pietro Tuciano came from Italy, yet to say that he was Italian would be a crude classification, however unavoidable. For Tuciano had grown up in France during the years of the Fascist regime in Italy, and he had lived in the narrow and narrowing confines of a colony of exiles who are not only foreigners, but who are further constricted by the suspicious regard of the police, a surveillance made necessary by the fact that they were political exiles. Their energy was intensified by exile and frustration, and they were compelled to be self-righteous by the very nature of their situation.

Tuciano was pleased by America, but he was also bewildered by it. This mixture of emotions was not new to him. Certainly bewilderment was not new to him, and one of his strongest resources as an author was his power to make the most of his bewilderment in the face of experience (his leading characters were often lost in a strange city). Nevertheless his bewilderment in America was something new to him (for this was indeed *the* new world and not merely a strange city), and new to his wife Priscilla too. Priscilla was an English girl who had married Pietro in Paris in 1945, and she too was bewildered, although she concealed her feelings just as much as her husband revealed them. One great difficulty for her was that she did not understand why America was not more like England, and this difficulty was complicated by her impression that some Americans were trying to behave like Englishmen and failing so dreadfully that one was left stupefied by the question: how is it possible to respond adequately to human beings who are trying to be what they are not and do not know how utterly they have failed?

Pietro was a poor lecturer, although he spoke English well. He was very nervous and he suffered from the common delusion that his listeners perceived how nervous he felt on the lecture platform, just as he was under the illusion that most of his audience was capable of understanding what he was saying and cared intensely about whether or not they understood him. Tuciano's lecture was about the influence of Croce's philosophy of art and literature upon the Italian novel since 1900. His point, in general, was that sometimes Croce was a good influence, sometimes he was not; and furthermore, he was sometimes a good influence for the wrong reasons—because the novelist had misunderstood philosophical doctrine and transformed it into something personal. And sometimes he was a bad influence because an author had understood Croce very well and let the philosopher's doctrines as to what a novel ought to be make him engage in efforts which falsified his native gift or mutilated his natural idiom and inspiration.

Before his lecture began, Tuciano thought that what he had to say was almost too obvious and platitudinous to be worth an entire lecture. As he lectured, he saw the look of perplexity on some of his listeners' faces and supposed wrongly that his nervousness and his imperfect command of English were responsible for the perplexed looks of some of his listeners. During the lecture, Professor Robbins, seated benignly on the platform, remarked to himself that the Italian was striving to elucidate a set of observations which were perhaps too complicated for a single lecture before a public audience consisting of undergraduates, old ladies who lived near the university, harassed and overworked young instructors, and idlers who came because they had nothing to do at three o'clock in the afternoon. Since this audience knew almost nothing about Croce and precisely nothing about the Italian novel, the gulf between the lecturer and his audience was huge and invisible. Nevertheless most of the listeners found the hour quite pleasant and relaxing, and some of the young ladies thought that the foreigner was fascinating—pale, thin, obviously very sensitive. In addition it seemed to some of the more advanced and deprived of the young ladies that Tuciano's eyes were "very passionate."

When the lecture had ended and the audience had applauded politely and several students had requested the novelist's autograph, Tuciano departed with Professor Robbins, rejoining his wife Priscilla, who told him that he had done "rather well," although she had scarcely listened to him, being drowsy after the train trip from New York. Besides, she had heard what her husband had to say on the subject several times before, as is natural in all interesting and interested marriages.

As husband, wife and professor moved with the crowd through the lobby of the lecture hall, Mrs. Tuciano heard two students discussing the curious fact that the novelist's name was Luciano, a mistaken impression which had been caused by the fact that they sat in the balcony, listened carelessly to the introduction, and were more interested in criminals than novelists. Since Priscilla Tuciano had no interest whatever in crime or in criminals, she had never heard of Luckv Luciano and she did not understand in the least the overheard conversation, which had to do with the question of whether the novelist was related to the famous gangster Lucky Luciano. Yet Mrs. Tuciano's lack of understanding did not trouble her, for it was just the kind of surd and perplexity which had made America a bewilderment to her, a bewilderment which she was now, in a way, prepared to encounter at every turn.

4

At the Robbins household, Mrs. Robbins prepared for the visitors. Ordinarily there would have been a reception or a cocktail party—or a cocktail party disguised as a reception or a reception used as a pretext for a cocktail party—for the visiting lecturer. But there had been so many cocktail parties recently, and so few people knew about Tuciano or wished to meet him, and the spring term was so near its end, that Mrs. Robbins had decided that a reception or a cocktail party was unnecessary. And it was. It probably would have made more trouble, for one of the habits of the academic community was not to go to the lecture but to come to the cockail pary which was being given for the lecturer, since the lecture would probably be boring and the cocktail party probably would be amusing. Those who came to the cocktail party after having absented themselves from the infelicity of the lecture made apologies about other engagements, which was of course a waste of time, and then paid little attention to the lecturer, whom they did not know very well, or did not know at all, and who was consequently much less interesting than the other guests.

Just before Professor Robbins came home with the Tucianos, Professor Anderson called Mrs. Robbins saying that he would be unable to come to meet her guests, since his wife was ill. This excuse was resented by Mrs. Robbins, but she knew that she must accept the rudeness politely, and conceal her feeling that the Andersons might have found something more desirable to do (otherwise Professor Anderson might have come by himself), and Mrs. Anderson was very seldom ill, for she had the constitution and the vitality of lady wrestlers and the cowgirls of a third-rate rodeo show.

Mrs. Robbins felt that she ought to ask some other couple to meet the Tucianos, but she was afraid that it would be rude to ask anyone at short notice. She tried to think of some couple who would be sensible enough or humble enough not to be offended by being invited at very short notice. Before she was able to decide on what couple would meet the difficult requirements of the situation, the Tucianos arrived with Professor Robbins, and if Mrs. Robbins had been less agitated by what seemed to her the probable rudeness of the Andersons, she would have perceived that the Tucianos would not be offended at all either by the lack of a cocktail party or by the absence of another couple. And yet how, in the labyrinth of misunderstanding in which this small but truly international occasion was located, could Mrs. Robbins have understood the actual attitude of the Tucianos, who, having been in America for six weeks, had come to expect only one thing: surprise and bewilderment. They were in the New World, it was very different from the Old World, it was very different from hour to hour, from place to place, and from street to street: this had been their continuous experience from the moment they had landed in the Canadian port of Halifax, and they had no reason to expect anything else.

Mrs. Robbins apologized to the Tucianos for not having been able to come to the lecture, and Professor Robbins immediately gave the Tucianos the highballs they had come to expect and Tuciano had learned to like very much because he was naturally very nervous.

Mrs. Robbins asked Priscilla Tuciano how she liked America, a question which she answered by saying briefly that she liked it very much. Priscilla thought that this question, which she had had to answer often before, was very rude. It was like asking a visitor if he or she liked or disliked the child of the family: if he regarded the offspring as a monster or a beautiful charmer.

"Americans do drink a good deal," said Priscilla, since her

answer had led only to silence. A moment after she had spoken of the drinking habits of Americans, she was shocked by the quality of her remark, which was inspired by her resentment of the question directed at her by Mrs. Robbins. Mrs. Tuciano was unaware of how impossible it was for Mrs. Robbins to know that her remark had impinged upon her guest's sensibility as rude.

"I suppose it is the press of American life which makes for so much drinking," Priscilla Tuciano added. "We did hear a great deal about that when we were in Paris, but we had no idea of what it was really like."

"We have been under an unusual strain in recent years," said Professor Robbins who was drinking his first highball too rapidly because he was eager to get the second one. "Since the war, we have all had more work than ever before, and at times I have felt that a day of twenty-four hours was not long enough for the performance of our duties in the way that anyone could regard as adequate. In fact, the old sense we had of gracious living and of the academic community as a sheltered retreat seems as distant as our grandmothers' era."

The idea that twenty-four hours were not enough struck Pietro Tuciano as very strange indeed. It was illogical, if considered literally; and lame, if taken as an irony. He himself slept until noon every day when he was working very hard on a novel, and in any case the question of time was important, so it seemed to him, only when one had to get to a train.

"Even when I am at home working on a novel, I often sleep until eleven or twelve," said Pietro Tuciano absentmindedly, bemused and self-involved.

Mrs. Robbins thought that he wanted to change the subject of the conversation and asked what book he was working on now?

Tuciano did not like to discuss any book of his own, and he certainly did not like to discuss a book on which he was still at work. Hence he shifted quickly from himself to another Italian novelist of his own generation, Guido Costello, an author whom Tuciano felt to be extremely good, in fact, first rate, and partly because Costello was very unlike him and possessed certain literary qualities which Tuciano would like to have possessed in his own right.

"He is a very fine talent," said Tuciano, "and he should be very much liked in America, although his books will suffer in translation."

"What kind of a novelist is he?" inquired Professor Robbins politely, unaware of how far this leading question would lead Tuciano.

"He writes a kind of story which is at once real life and a fable. And each fable when scrutinized carefully will contain some sharp inversion of a Biblical maxim or folk proverb. For example, he says in one of his books: 'Cast your bread upon the waters and that may very well be the last you will ever see of it.' And in another, one of his characters says, 'Turn the other cheek, but if that does not appease your bellicose opponent, punch him in the nose.' "

"He seems rather cynical," remarked Professor Robbins, hugging his highball and not in the least amused.

"On the contrary," said Tuciano, "he is profoundly religious. He has very—how do you say it?—high ideals and standards, and this makes for an ironic bitterness. I know this is true in his own life too, for when I said to him once: 'You are very modest,' he answered: 'No: just disappointed!' "

"You have a very charitable interpretation of Mr. Costello's cynicism," said Professor Robbins in a questioning, doubting tone, as if to say that he himself was not certain that such an explanation of anyone's cyncism was of necessity true. He felt vaguely disturbed by Tuciano's admiration of Costello's mind and art, for Costello was clearly so critical of everyone that he would certainly be critical of Professor Robbins.

"I do not think that I am being charitable," Tuciano replied, "and it is true enough that Costello is far from being a saintly man. But he understand his own cynicism sufficiently to be able to use it as a means of insight. Thus he believes in suspicion, but he also believes in hope, and he writes that both suspicion and hope are major modes of the imagination. And when one of the characters in his novels declares with over-emphatic irony that the only reason why anyone writes fiction—short stories or novels— is that they are afraid to gossip about other people's lives and can do so with some safety in the medium or in the disguise of fiction,—well, then it is that another character corrects him and says that fiction is written for a variey of reasons, and if sup- pressed gossip is one, another is the feeling of love for other human beings which the infatuated author has to restrain be- cause he is afraid of appearing sentimental or because he is bashful or is in love with so many human beings that if he expressed his love openly, he would seem to be promiscuous, or an exhibitionist, or a spaniel, or a Casanova."

Professor Robbins was not appeased, but only further dis- turbed by this explanation. In the back of his mind was his sense of guilt about his attitude toward Leonard Pierce, and his feeling that Costello and Tuciano were more generous in spirit than he was.

"Mr. Costello," he said in expression of his distress, "seems to be one of those intellectuals who think too much, who use their minds too much."

"When one uses one's mind, one does not use it up," Tuciano replied sharply, annoyed because he too was an intellectual novelist. But then, as he perceived that his remark had been understood as an affront by Professor Robbins, to judge by the sudden frozenness of expression on his face, he added, "That's precisely what Costello himself has said to very intelligent critics who have accused him of reducing his spontaneity by relying too greatly upon the powers of the intellect. I am sure that he would agree with you if I understand you correctly. One can be too intellectual and one can be insufficiently intellectual."

"Is he at all like Pirandello, the Nobel Prize winner?" asked

Professor Robbins, trying to change the subject on the off-chance
that irritation would be less likely.

"Not really," said Tuciano, seeking to be exact, "the only
resemblances are those inevitable to authors of the same nation
and two consecutive generations who have written during the
same period of time."

"Have you met Signor Costello?" asked Mrs. Robbins, sens-
ing the effort to shift the topic of discussion, but remaining
too curious and interested to be able to depart from Costello
entirely. She knew very well that her husband was always
disturbed by human beings, and authors such as Costello, until
they are dead.

"Yes," answered Priscilla Tuciano, although the question
had been directed at her husband, "I know him quite well. At
first I did not like him. He seemed rude and theatrical about
his feelings. But as I came to know him very well, I came to
understand that the severity with which he satirized human
beings came in some way from a very warm feeling about human beings, a genuine love of them, so to speak."

"Jonathan Swift is the supreme example of such an author
in English. Does Mr. Costello's work resemble his?" asked
Professor Robbins, who continued to drink too fast because
of tiredness, nervousness, and a vague but powerful discomfort
in the conversation and the attitudes which had been suggested,
understood or misunderstood.

"I have never read Swift," answered Pietro Tuciano, "although I hear that he is extremely good. However, perhaps you
can judge the resemblance for yourself if I tell you the leading
theme of one of his best novels. The theme, as usual, is expressed in passing by means of certain inverted and augmented
proverbs and maxims: 'Opportunity knocks but once. Oppor-
tunism, however, knocks all the time, like the beating of the
heart and the flickering of the pulse.' 'We are all scoundrels,
in the eyes of God. But those who know they are scoundrels
may repent from time to time, while the worst scoundrels are

those who do not know or admit at least to themselves that they are scoundrels at any time, in impulse or in action.' And last: 'Those who live in glass houses should be sure to have a great many stones at hand and excellent throwing arms.' Clearly it is his own feeling of guilt and dismay at being a satirical fictionist that Costello is attacking in this masterpiece. But the more he attacks himself, the more, in a serious sense, he defends himself. For he would not question his attitude of satire, if he did not possess an attitude of—how shall I put it?—desiring some state of mind superior to satire—the state of mind of love, one might say, to put it crudely and platitudiously."

"But what is the plot of this novel?" asked Professor Robbins—made curious by Tuciano's passionate defense of Costello.

"The plot is rather simple," Tuciano answered, delighted to be asked. "The hero, or rather I should say villain, is offended by the fragmentary report of a remark which has been made about him by one of his best friends. This friend has inquired as to whether the hero or villain really wants him to get the job he has been seeking. And the protagonist is so much disturbed by the suggestion that he is not entirely trustworthy, he is so vain, so self-righteous, and so severe, that he does in fact prevent his friend from getting the job he wants. Thus the attitude of unwillingness to accept human nature's nature leads to utter disaster, a broken friendship, the hero's distrust of himself."

Tuciano had spoken so rapidly and with so much absorption in what he was saying that he did not notice how sullen and distressed Professor Robbins had become as he listened. And even if he had observed his host's distress, how could he have known that as he summarized the plot of the novel, Professor Robbins thought of how cruel and vain he had been about Leonard Pierce's inquiry as to whether he himself was trustworthy?

"It's somewhat over my head," said Mrs. Robbins, "it is as

complicated as our American novelist, Henry James, who has always disturbed me by his unwillingness to admit that any person or thing is ever to be taken at face-value, as being spontaneously and genuinely what he or she or it presented itself as being. I find that life cannot be lived very well, if one makes assumptions about it which complicate it immensely."

Priscilla Tuciano did not understand a word of what Mrs. Robbins had just said. Professor Robbins understood very well and was extremely irritated. Tuciano thought he understood what had been said and answered in his own terms.

"I believe in consciousness and in unconsciousness," he remarked, "just as I believe that being awake and being asleep are pleasant, necessary, and important. And I think that just as there are certain times when we must sleep, so there are certain times when we must be awake, and in perhaps the same proportion or division, eight hours of sleep and sixteen hours of being awake, under ordinary circumstances."

Priscilla now understood what was in question, for her husband had formulated it in terms familiar to her. Mrs. Robbins, however, did not understand what Tuciano's answer had been, since she was unfamiliar with his ways of formulation and had never been subjected to the influence of Freud. Neither had Professor Robbins, except indirectly, but he understood perfectly what Tuciano had just said, and his irritation increased again, but he concealed it. If Tuciano was right, Professor Robbins had been foolish throughout his adult life in certain important respects. He had tried to be conscious at the wrong times and tried (alas!) to be unconscious or spontaneous at the wrong times too. He had been conscious and not spontaneous too often in dealing with his students and his colleagues; and he had been unconscious of his own motives when he should have been conscious of them, both for his own sake and the sake of others.

"What would Mr. Costello say about this subject?" asked

Professor Robbins, partly to conceal his ever-growing irritation partly to get rid of the subject entirely by making Tuciano speak of other aspects of Costello's life and work.

But Tuciano had a trained mind, so that even in conversation, if he was unguarded, as he was when he drank, he tended to feel that he ought to stick to the point.

"I think that Costello would agree with me. In fact, I think as he does as a consequence of his influence. Both of us have studied the work of Sigmund Freud—we call him Sigismundo Freud, conquerer of the Africa and jungle-like world of the unconscious mind—and we were both delighted by one of his metaphors, which I can't quote exactly, where he describes the ultimate purpose of his art and science of psychoanalysis. He says that the therapeutic aim of psychoanalysis is to increase the extent of consciousness, to give the consciousness of human beings the strength and power to understand all or much that is unconscious, all the ignorance, self-deception or habitual blindness which makes them sick, unhappy, incapable. He says, if I remember correctly, that where unconsciousness was, there consciousness shall be, and his metaphor is this: that it is reclamation work, like the draining of the Zuyder Zee."

"That sounds very well," said Professor Robbins, "but the metaphor is misleading. For if one follows the doctrine to its logical conclusion, one would have to believe in total consciousness, twenty-four hours a day. Total consciousness, however, is insomnia, among other disabling things."

"How very interesting," said Mrs. Robbins, "I never thought of the matter in that light, but I do agree with you, Mr. Tuciano."

Priscilla Tuciano wondered just what it was that her hostess and husband agreed about; she was English, she took such matters for granted, they were an instinctive part of her being, and hence she never had to think about them.

Tuciano agreed with Professor Robbins that total consciousness and insomnia were deplorable and to be avoided, but he remarked, politely and with an effort at not seeking to argue where there should be a discussion, that insomnia was not the result of consciousness, but the result of a variety of emotions which the sleepless human being did not understand, and was unable to control because he was insufficiently conscious of their causes.

Professor Robbins was annoyed further because his wife agreed with Tuciano and especially since he did not think that she actually did agree with her guest, she just did not understand her own mind unless she had suddenly changed her mind, which was very unlikely.

"We must watch the time, Pietro," said Priscilla who was becoming bored, as well as tired.

"Do stay for dinner," said Mrs. Robbins politely, although she naturally wished her visitors would go. "You can take a later train after dinner, and it has been such a pleasure to have you here and exchange points of view. I feel there is so much more to say and to learn from others who have come here from a very different background."

"Thank you very much," said Priscilla, 'but I think that we really must go. The later train will bring us back to New York at a very early hour in the morning."

Pietro wished to stay and he did not care, at the moment, what time he got back to New York, but he always obeyed what he took to be his wife's wishes, when he knew what they were and when they seemed consistent with his being her husband.

"We must really go," he said. "I'm so sorry. It has been so pleasant and so interesting to us."

Professor Robbins' irritation had by this time turned to suspicion of Tuciano. He disliked what Tuciano had said so much that he felt that what he said might very well be the indication of a shady character. Perhaps, he thought to himself, Tuciano was Sicilian, and he was in any case Mediterranean and European and not American, and Robbins had often remarked upon the systematic duplicity of the Mediterranean mind, which he perceived more often among immigrants than among visiting Europeans.

"I would like to give you a book of my most recent essays," Robbins said, shamed by his feelings and wishing to make a friendly gesture.

"That would be very kind of you," said Tuciano. "I do not know your work very well and I have not read your most recent volume, although I should have, but it is so difficult for me to read when I am travelling."

5

Professor Robbins departed to get a copy of his most recent volume of essays. There were six copies in his study, stashed away in his desk next to a neat folder which contained copies of the reviews of this book. Most of the reviews had been favorable, hence Professor Robbins had formed the habit of reading them, a practice which he regarded as a secret and low vice dictated by mere vanity. He was wholly unaware that other authors did not shrink from the pleasure of reading favorable reviews again and again, and these authors were human beings whom he admired and would have liked as human beings, had he known them.

As he took a fresh copy of his book from his desk and examined it to see if it was unmarked and clean of smudge or fingerprint, he noticed that there was a twenty-dollar bill in the back of the book. For a moment he was unable to remember how it had come to be there and he had acquired the habit, common among those who drink too much (as well as others who are distracted and unhappy) of putting things away in a hurry and forgetting where he had put them. Then he remembered what had happened: two weeks before, he had taken twenty dollars more than the usual amount from the bank in order to buy his wife, whom he loved very much, a birthday present which would be more expensive than she thought sensible. Mrs. Robbins was very stern about financial matters, as indeed she had to be during the first part of her husband's career, and Professor Robbins knew that her pleasure in an expensive gift would be disturbed if not spoiled if she knew the price to be extravagant. Nevertheless this was something which she had wanted for four years and Professor Robbins was determined that she should have it, despite inflation, the necessity of subterfuge, and the indignity of disingenuous concealment.

He had placed the twenty-dollar bill in the book, thinking that he would be bound to remember where it was or to come upon it when he looked for his folder of favorable reviews. Now, tired, half-intoxicated and irritated very much by what Pietro Tuciano had been saying (he was profoundly irritated by existence itself, and by the distrust communicated to him gratuitously by Professor Anderson) he was tempted to leave the twenty-dollar bill in the book he was presenting to the Tucianos and see what would happen. A pang of shame winced in him for a moment, for he saw that this was indeed a trick, and he himself did not like to have tricks played upon him in order to determine his honesty or prove his probity. But immediately he thought of Leonard Pierce's distrust of him and he thought of the fact that if indeed the Tucianos were honest, they would return the twenty-dollar bill, as soon as they found it in the book. He did not think of two other possible eventualities, that they might return the money even if they were not honest—for the sake of maintaining appearances—and they might suspect Professor Robbins of playing a trick upon them and thus be offended, for after all, as a novelist, Tuciano was used to thinking in such terms of human behavior. The unhappy professor also forgot completely that he was risking a twenty-dollar bill for the sake of satisfying his idle moral curiosity, and he forgot that his wife would be very angry with him if she learned of the entire duplicity, which had indeed begun with an effort to deceive her.

Deciding to leave the twenty-dollar bill in the book for the sake of seeing if Tuciano and his wife were indeed honest—perhaps they were not, given their admiration for the works of such an author as Costello—Professor Robbins reflected rapidly, as he had often before, upon the profound role which chance and accident played in all human affairs. If the bill had not been, by accident, in the book, he would not have thought of examining the character and virtue of Tuciano in so peculiar a way. By thus shifting his mind to the idea of chance (and touching, in his passing thoughts, upon the use of coincidence, so often unjustly criticized, in the novels of Thomas Hardy), Professor Robbins succeeded in dismissing utterly from his mind all the small qualms and scruples by which he would have otherwise been troubled under these circumstances.

He returned with the book. The Tucianos had risen and were preparing to depart. And at this point chance indeed might have played the grandiose and pointless part attributed to it by Professor Robbins, for it was hardly more than an accident that the bill remained unperceived as a result of the size of the book and did not drop to the floor as a consequence of the fact that the unhappy Professor was holding the book in his left and weaker hand, being prepared to extend his right hand in a cordial handshake of farewell to the Tucianos.

The Tucianos were very pleased by the book and they insisted that the author inscribe it to them, but a taxi was waiting outside to take them to the station and the taxi-driver was blowing his horn impatiently because his wife was in the hospital having her first child, which made him very nervous and impatient, and this collocation and crossing of human lives again produced the sad operations of chance, for if Robbins had inscribed the book, the bill would probably have been exposed to view and perhaps have dropped out. But it was not and it did not. The Tucianos left in haste at the rude urgency of the taxi-driver's horn (or, one might go so far as to say, at the behest of a child moving down the womb), and Pietro clutched the presentation copy in one hand, his suitcase in another, while his wife held the briefcase in which Pietro had kept the notes for his lecture.

No sooner were the Tucianos in the cab en route to the railroad station than Pietro took the briefcase from his wife, opened it, and slipped the book into it. But as he did so, in the agitation characteristic of him, and intensified by travel, the twenty-dollar bill slipped unnoticed to the floor of the taxi, where it would not have gone unnoticed by the Tucianos, had it been daylight and not dusk.

"He is a very unhappy man," said Priscilla Tuciano. "and I think that you may have disturbed him.'

"But how?" said her humble husband, "what did I say to offend him?"

"Perhaps it was something about Costello," said his wife; "after all, Americans do not really understand the fiction of Italy very well."

"Alas," said Pietro, "mother mine!" in Italian, and then speaking in English, he paraphrased a remark he had heard attributed to the great American President and General, George Washington: "One cannot please all the people, or all the readers, all the time."

"You mean fool all the readers and all the people, and the remark was made by Grant, who was also a great general and President of the United States," said his wife.

"Are you sure?" asked her husband.

"Yes, I am quite certain," she said. "I remember seeing it in a book which I read on shipboard, a history of the United States."

Soon they were at the station, they boarded the train, their bewilderment continued as they waited to get a place to eat dinner in the dining car of the Pullman train, and it was only after dinner, as Pietro Tuciano read with mounting pleasure the book he had been given by Professor Robbins and grunted his approval of Professor Robbins' remarks, made comments on or explained what the book contained, that the bewilderment of the foreigners diminished.

"What a pity I did not read the book before I visited the university," said Pietro Tuciano. "I might have had a very interesting discussion of it with Professor Robbins. And I would have been able to speak of Costello with more tact, in terms which Mr. Robbins would have understood perfectly. You are probably right, I probably offended him, as I can see from these essays and the attitudes he adopts towards his subjects. He does not understand that some authors can only express love by means of cynicism, or rather the rhetoric of cynicism, at least some of the time. How innocent these Americans are!"

Meanwhile the taxi-driver had found the twenty-dollar bill on the floor of his cab. He remembered that his fares had taken the train out of town and he decided to keep it and start a savings account for his child, his son as he hoped or his daughter as he expected. It was a good omen. He would tell his wife. Perhaps the child would turn out to be a great financier, a mighty tycoon who made and commanded many millions of dollars. If Professor Robbins had known what was to happen to his twenty-dollar bill, he might have concluded that some actions, however doubtful their motivation, however high, low, or evil the motive, might result in fruitfulness, goodness, joy, higher purchasing power, a sense of the unexpected windfall, the generosity of the gods, and better-humored cab-drivers.

6

A week passed, and Pietro Tuciano, having finished his reading of Professor Robbins' book, wrote to him and thanked him for his hospitality and his book, which he admired very much. He described his admiration in four closely-written pages, mentioning, however, his doubt about certain minor points or trivial issues, and suggested a further elaboration of some of the topics developed by Professor Robbins. It was the kind of a letter which might very well have led to a fruitful correspondence between two sympathetic human beings, who, whatever their differences, have a good deal to learn from each other.

Professor Robbins found the letter on the table in the hallway when he returned late in the afternoon from a faculty meeting. Before reading it, he opened it eagerly and quickly, looking for his twenty-dollar bill. Then he skimmed the letter itself rapidly, overlooking the expressions of admiration which under other circumstances would have pleased him very much and seeking for some mention of the twenty-dollar bill. He was disappointed to find no mention of it, and he surprised himself by the extent to which he was surprised.

He walked into the living-room where his wife was reading a book, greeted her, and gave his wife the letter which he had just received. Mrs. Robbins read the letter and spoke warmly of Pietro Tuciano as a very intelligent and sensitive young man. Her husband was tempted to tell her of how he had left the twenty-dollar bill in the presentation copy. But, although he was sure that a discussion would relieve his disappointment, he felt that to tell her about it at all would involve him in an endless labyrinth of explanation and self-defense.

"It is a very pleasant and sympathetic letter," said Mrs. Robbins, perceiving that her husband was disturbed. If she had known the true reason for the look upon his face, she would have been indignant. And she would have insisted that he consider all the possibilities inherent in the situation in addition to the possibility that Pietro Tuciano, being dishonest, had kept the twenty-dollar bill.

The fact that he could not tell his wife what he had done made him see with unpleasant clarity precisely what he had done by placing the bill in the book. His mind moved quickly: his disappointment in Tuciano's letter vanished in his disgust at his own action: if he had to be silent, if he had to conceal his behavior from his wife, the only being with whom he had ever been intimate, then he wished there were some way to conceal his action from himself.

Feeling, as he did, ashamed of himself, paralyzed by the need for keeping silent, Robbins glared at his wife, who despite her long knowledge of her husband did not understand that she was not the cause of his look. The reason that she was unable to understand that Robbins was in fact glaring at himself and visiting lecturers and Leonard Pierce was that Professor Robbins very seldom behaved as he had behaved about the twenty-dollar bill, and on the few occasions when he had come close to a like action, he had successfully concealed the fact from his wife.

"Why are you upset?" asked Mrs. Robbins, seeing her husband seat himself, sullen and sulky in his armchair. "Is it something in Tuciano's letter?"

"No, there is nothing in Tuciano's letter," said Professor Robbins, realizing immediately that that part of his mind which was ahead of his conscious mind had just uttered a pun.

"It is a very pleasant and intelligent letter," he hastened to add, "I must read it more carefully. The fact is, I am disturbed by Leonard Pierce."

"I thought that he had been given the lectureship for next year."

"He has," said Professor Robbins, "but I am afraid that I owe him twenty dollars or he owes me twenty dollars." By uttering this statement, he succeeded in mystifying his wife entirely, and at the same time understanding and illuminating himself.

"I am sorry," he said to his wife, "I am afraid that I have not behaved very well. But let's not talk about it now," he concluded, thinking for the *nth* time that he did not know what had been concluded which made it possible for him to speak or think with conclusive assurance. Fortunately, or unfortunately, in some part of his mind he recognized—so ashamed was he— and recognized for the first time in his life, how wrong, ugly, stupid, nasty and unfair he had been, probably many times before, and when money was not involved, directly or indirectly.

"Would you like a drink, dear?" his wife asked him.

"Yes, I would like one very much," he answered, and feeling the deepening of his shame and remorse, he took hold of the evening newspaper on the table beside him, thinking that he would distract himself and forget about himself by reading about the affairs and crimes of other human beings. His eye was caught by a human interest story at the bottom of the front page:

$100 FOUND IN OLD BOOK BY BROWSER

The person who hid three $20 bills and four tens in a copy of a novel more than fifty years ago was unknowingly helping to celebrate the Opportunity Shop, a secondhand store at 13 Court Street, operated by the Community Service Society.

Miss Amy Valentine, a retired librarian and volunteer worker in the shop, found the $100 in an envelope as she thumbed through old volumes on the shop's shelves.

"At any rate," said Professor Robbins to himself, putting down the newspaper and reaching for his drink, "I am not the only one."

The Track Meet

My only other encounter with the problem of showing a visiting Englishman the sights had been very jolly, you might say, although full of minor and trivial complexities. This first visitor was a chap named Edwin Reynolds, and he found anything and everything in American life fascinating. Indeed, he enjoyed and was excited by everything so much that he thought he understood everything, too—as if excitement were insight. In the course of showing him around, I suggested that we go to a baseball game, since it was a purely American phenomenon, and he was delighted. We went to see two excellent minor-league teams play a doubleheader. As we were going down the runway to the inside of the stadium, he said that he did not know the rules of baseball, so I explained them briefly, moving through the turnstiles, looking for good seats along the third-base foul line.

"The pitcher," I said, "is trying to get the ball past the batter. The batter is going to try to hit the ball between the infielders, or over their heads, or between the outfielders, or over their heads, or bouncing in front of them. If he can hit the ball over their heads and into the stands, it's just plain wonderful and known as a home run, or a homer for short." I saw that we had to hurry, because the game was going to begin very soon; the pitcher for the home team was already on the mound and making his last few warmup throws to the catcher. "The infielders are trying to get hold of the ball and throw it to first base before the batter gets to first base. The outfielders are trying to catch the ball before it bounces, or if it does bounce, to get to it, and throw it back to the infield as soon as possible."

"What about that chap with the mask on his face?" Edwin asked. "And the peculiar jacket or what have you?"

"Oh, the chest protector," I answered. "That's the catcher. He wears the mask and chest protector because the ball may hit him hard and injure him. He is trying to catch the ball if the batter misses it or lets it go by, and he is also trying to tell the pitcher how to throw the ball so that the batter will have a hard time hitting it well—not hitting it so hard or so far that the infielders will be unable to get it and the outfielders will be unable to catch it."

I must say, I was rather pleased with my elucidation, at first, and it took a little time for me to perceive how numerous were the shortcomings and omissions. However, I took care of them one by one as the game continued, and by the seventh inning practically everything was cleared up except for two somewhat important points. The first was the double play. For a time, it seemed that this would remain for Edwin a mystery, involving what might even be called antinomy; for he found a contradiction in the fact that if a man was on first, the infielder had only to touch the second sack to put him out, but if the batter hit a ball to the outfield, rounded first, and tried to make it a double, then the infielder had to tag him out. Edwin thought it rather unfair that he should have to tag the runner in the second instance but in the first only had to touch second base. Finally, I said to him that this was one of the rules of the game, and light shone immediately in the darkness. I still don't know why this was so utterly and quickly illuminating, except that perhaps if anything is a rule, and, moreover, a rule of the game, it is as lucid to an Englishman as trial by jury. However, this did not entirely dispose of the difficulty, for Edwin had no little trouble understanding why a base runner must tag up before running if a fly ball is caught but is allowed to run if the ball is not going to be caught. This, too, seemed unfair to him; so, after other attempts had proved vain, I just said that it was one of the rules of the game, and that settled that. Lastly, Edwin would not believe that the game was played with passionate seriousness by the players and regarded with equal seriousness by the spectators. He thought that the roar of the crowd and the booing at the umpire was either a kind of ritual or the fulfillment of an obligation. Nothing I said dissuaded him, and it was useless here to invoke the rules of the game, for he mistook emotions for rules.

As we left the ballpark, moving among disgruntled and downcast fans (the home team had been beaten), Edwin declared that it had been a most refreshing and charming experience, and "quite typically American."

Because he was the kind of person he was, his gazing politely at America was very pleasant, and interesting, in a mild way, and did not bring about any emotional strain. Thus I was not at all prepared for what happened when I was visited a second time by a touring Englishman. However, it is difficult, if not impossible, to conceive of how anything would have served to prepare me and help me to behave with propriety and dignity during the painful incidents that occured during this second visit. Perhaps if I had been sent to a concentration camp, or if I had lived my childhood and adolescence in a jungle, I would have been less innocent and better prepared; but perhaps not.

The visit was curious from the very beginning. The doorbell of my apartment woke me up. I did not want to answer, but the ringing was persistent, and it stopped but started again, as if my visitor had paused to make sure he was ringing the right bell.

I answered at last, annoyed and feeling sure that this was the only way to stop the ringing. It was just six, and although it was spring, a chill drizzle was falling. I heard the little dripping and the sliding sound of a passing car. And when I opened the door, my visitor told me that his name was Reginald Law, and I asked him to come in. He did not apologize for his persistent ringing. He sat himself down in an armchair and explained that a mutual friend whom he had encountered in Japan had suggested he look me up when he came to New York. The mutual friend was Hippocrates Pappas, and I was astonished to hear that he had been to Japan, for he was the kind of person who did not even like to leave his house. But perhaps during the war . . .

Reginald Law did not respond to my effort to make conversation by discussing the friend we had in common. I thought I recognized in him a type—the kind of person who makes no effort to sustain a conversation and who appears to be not at all disturbed by the painful silence that occurs when strangers meet and find that they have little or nothing to say to each other. In these circumstances, I have often said foolish, and indiscreet, or intimate, or tactless things, merely to revive conversation, being made panicky by painful silences and feeling wrongly that the responsibility is always mine.

This time, I decided immediately that the responsibility was equally his and that I would not say anything, if he did not. We glanced at each other, and I thought he was regarding the fact that I was in my dressing gown and pajamas.

"You *are* Frank Lawrence?" he said at last.

I said that I was, and he told me that he had two tickets for a track meet, which was to begin in half an hour. I argued mildly with him that it couldn't start so early in the morning, and I had no desire to go to a track meet. It all seemed quite strange to me; it was as if I were dreaming. There was a curious lack of sequence in what had occurred since I had been awakened, although the cloudy spring light that appeared in the windows was real enough.

The telephone began to ring, and I was astonished again, for it was extraordinary for anyone to call me at that hour in the morning. I answered the telephone, which was in the bedroom, and heard the receiver at the other end being placed back on the hook. I thought, It must be that crank again. . . . I had been for the past year an editor of a new encyclopedia, and a hack who had been fired, after turning in several poor and inaccurate articles on subjects he knew worse than nothing about (he cribbed from older encyclopedias, and even his cribbing was mixed up, inaccurate, and disjointed), thought that I was the person who had been the cause of his losing his job. So he had called me at three o'clock in the morning, and attempted to hold a genial and intimate conversation, and when I told him I was trying to sleep, he wanted to know if I had a woman with me! I hung up in anger, and he kept calling, night after night, until at last I told him how unkind he was to wake me up at that hour, and he replied, "My hatred of you has turned to pity," but he had continued to call and then hang up without speaking. That was why I thought it was him again, although he had been silent during the past two weeks.

Anyway, I got dressed and decided to go with Reginald Law and see whatever there was to see. Outside in the street he hailed a cab, and then explained that he was travelling on an expense account.

"I say, do you mind if I call you Frank?" he said, as we sat back in the taxi.

"I wish you would," I answered, but I was struck again by how curious his behavior seemed. It was quite natural for an American to use my first name immediately, but it was not at all natural—at least to me—on the part of an Englishman.

We were soon at the high-school stadium where the track meet was to take place, and again, when I saw the crowds entering the stadium, which looked like a small or diminished version of the Polo Grounds, I really thought that I must be dreaming.

I pinched myself as we went down the runway, and then I asked Reginald to shake hands with me. He did, raising his eyebrows, and his hand, slightly moist, was real, not imagined.

"Do you·want to be sure that I don't have a gun or a knife up my sleeve?" he asked.

"I just want to be sure I am not dreaming!" I replied, troubled by the irony and dislike in his tone.

As we moved to our seats, I was sure that something was wrong, for I saw in the distance, in a box seat, my mother. What was she doing at a track meet? And I was displeased that she was present. I did not want to greet her, and I hoped that she would not see me.

Around the baseball diamond there was a cinder track, concentric with the stands, and with a starting line, hurdles, a finish line, and the like. And yet the field still seemed very much a baseball diamond and not a track.

An official who looked like a baseball umpire was firing a gun idly into the air. He's practicing, I thought, to start off the runners. But it occurred to me that this was not the kind of thing which required practice. All over the field, young men in track suits were jogging up and down, limbering up, stretching, and turning somersaults. The crowd, as it continued to increase, became more and more tense with excitement.

And then among the track men I saw my five brothers, Edward, Nicholas, Leopold, Alphonse, and Carolus. We had been named after the crowned heads of Europe (my own name was actually Franz Joseph, not Frank) and this not only affected us all very much but showed the infinite and foolish hope our parents fixed upon us. And I knew then that something must be wrong; something must be very wrong. If I was not dreaming, certainly I was in a state of hallucination, for this was not the real world.

"You see those young men jogging up and down near first base?" I said to my English visitor. "They are my brothers. We were named after the crowned heads of Europe." Now, if I am not dreaming, he will not reply, I told myself.

"Really?" said Reginald Law. "I was informed that you had no brothers, and were an only child."

What was I to make of this? I shrank from asking him who said that I was an only child, knowing that it might have been Hippocrates Pappas, who had often told me—but in a friendly way that kept me from becoming angry—that I was a hardheaded egotist. The idea seemed to amuse him; he seemed to think that I enjoyed being a hardheaded egotist.

I called out to my brothers, and they stopped, turned, and looked at me and then looked blankly at each other, as if they did not recognize me, or as if I were some crackpot who was pretending to be a friend of the performers.

I yelled again, and they turned to look up at me again, but they just shrugged their shoulders. I thought of going down to the field and insisting that they speak to me, but then it occurred to me that perhaps this was some gag they'd thought up. One of them—it was Carolus—waved finally. It was the vague gesture one makes to a stranger.

"Everything happens to me," I said to Reginald Law, letting the sentence slip out before I knew what I had said, and then I was ashamed of myself.

"You're all right," said the reticent Englishman. "You're doing very well. As you Americans say, you have no kick coming."

"How do you know?" I said to him in anger. "What do *you* know about me?"

"I judge merely by your appearance," he answered. "You're looking very well."

"Appearing is not reality!" I shouted at him. "How do you know what is happening to my head, or beneath my shirt, in my pounding heart?"

And now I saw that my shouting had made people turn and

look at me, among them my mother. She, too, looked at me coldly and without recognition; then she looked back at the field.

"I don't care," I said to myself. "What difference does it make, anyway?"

I shouted once again at Nicholas, whom we all called the Czar, and who had once been very devoted to me.

"Nicholas!" I shouted. "I am one of the Lawrence boys. I'm Frank. What is going one here, anyway? Why won't you say hello to me?"

He looked at me and then turned away, jogging.

"Hey, Nicholas!" I cried out, when I saw that he was not going to answer me. "You used to like me very much. When I die, you will be silent," I said desperately and passionately.

Silence except for the murmur and excitement of the crowd, munching peanuts and gazing avidly.

"Really, the advertisements are quite charming," said Reginald Law.

I looked at them. A billboard on the outfield wall advertised the overwhelming merits of an ale. A tarpon, swordfish, or some kind of fish leaped from the sea, as if to show his eagerness. A spiral of words declared the Purity, the Body, the Flavor in every glass.

"Look," I remarked idly, "fish don't drink beer. Or do they?"

Reginald Law ignored this facetious remark. I recognized the mood I was in, of trying to work off my uneasiness and shake off my nervousness by making poor jokes.

Another billboard boasted about a cigarette—"Travels the smoke further, further" (I did not know for sure what this meant)—and showed a smoker's fat and grinning face.

Still another billboard showed a scene at a masquerade party. A sad-looking, frowning young man was by himself in the foreground, dressed as a clown. His mask was up, and his face showed his humiliation. Behind his back, a girl dressed as a peasant was laughing at him, and a character attired in the red tights of Mephisto was holding a pitchfork toward our hero, and gloating and sneering. A foursome near the punch bowl, one wearing a horse's head as a mask, were also staring and laughing at him. The pretty girl was saying to Mephisto, "Maybe it's something he did not eat." Elsewhere, in neat paragraphs, the prose elucidated the theme: "It's nothing to clown about. Maybe that dull, logy feeling comes from a diet lacking in pep. Why not try America's super breakfast food?" The panacea for every form of melancholia and social failure, this matchless cereal is represented by a vivid box that ascends at the edge of the poster, while under it is a little poem which expresses incontestable insight: "LIFE IS SWELL—WHEN YOU KEEP WELL."

"At least it's not his teeth, his tooth powder, or his lack of an expensive automobile," I murmured.

Nearby, a poster showed a girl looking lasciviously at a man who had a well-combed head of hair. She was a very pretty girl, I thought, and dressed as if she were rich.

"A wise jury," I said to Law, "would convict her of fornication or adultery for a look like that."

"You make too much of these matters," he said in an offhand, deprecatory tone. "You are too serious. What difference does it make, anyway?"

"What difference does anything make?" I replied in irritation. "You can prove anything or doubt anything. Some people think that nothing exists, or that the earth is flat. Just try to prove to them that they are wrong."

I realized that I was jumping about foolishly, so I turned back to the billboards. The fact is that, to be honest about it, I knew very well how many of my comments were expressions of personal disappointment.

By the right-field foul line was a big garish billboard that showed a young man standing in back of a beautiful young lady to whom he has just given a radio. She is smiling sweetly, her blond hair is set in an upswept hairdo, and she is wearing a low-cut gown. His right hand, as he stands behind her (his smile is an innuendo), is resting on her shoulder, and his fingers point down, as if he wanted to touch her breasts—as if he would soon touch them. In flowing letters the poster broadcasts the big phrase "My Own *Personal* Radio," and she holds her small set as if she were holding a little child.

"The radio draws upon the empyrean just like the oversoul," I remarked, "or am I wrong?"

"Righto," said Law.

"You know about Kierkegaard, don't you?" I asked.

"The Norwegian playwright?"

"You are thinking of Sibelius, the Lithuanian general. Kierkegaard is the George Washington of Denmark. At least, that's what he seems to be to the Danes I encounter in New York. They admire him very much as a national hero and never read anything he wrote, although he is just as entertaining as Bob Hope and perhaps more so. But anyway, what I wanted to tell you was this: He thinks there are three fundamental attitudes to existence—the aesthetic, the ethical, and the religious. Probably as good an illustration as any other would be a situation in which you wanted to kiss the wife of a friend. If you were aesthetic, you would kiss her without compunction, and like it very much. If you were ethical, you'd take a sedative, an aspirin, or a barbiturate, and, by thus pacifying yourself, free yourself from the desire to kiss another man's wife. If you were religious, you'd neither kiss the lady nor take the sedative!"

"Yes?" said Law. "At what point, if any, would the husband's feelings be considered, or the wife consulted? Look here," he continued, "these things are in the end a question of taste."

"Righto," I said. What was the use of talking to him? I did not know why he felt as he did, nor did I know why I said what I did. Meanwhile, one of the runners had jogged up to the last billboard and was kissing the handsome girl who had just been given a radio. He was kissing with the intensity of one who drinks water after five sets of tennis in July, his throat pulsing, his Adam's apple bobbing.

"How foolish," I said. "What good does that do him? The girl does not exist. And New York is full of real girls."

"Perhaps he prefers the poster image to the difficult actuality," said Law. "He cannot be rejected, and he does not have to take much trouble to win her favors."

"But that's ridiculous," I said, and then became silent, thinking that since everything was utterly ridiculous, it was pointless to harp on any one thing.

Two umpires were now firing pistols repeatedly. The sharp sounds were like thin pieces of wood being split.

The hundred-yard dash was about to begin, and ten runners crouched tensely at the starting line. Two of my brothers, Leopold and Carolus, were in the race, and appeared just as tense as the rest. The pistol cracked out, and they leaped forward, obsessed. As I had expected, Leopold and Carolus were very fast, and ran almost even with the first runner, a tall, gangling young man. As they came toward the tape, the first runner moved ahead, his legs kicking up at the knee, like pistons. But then Carolus threw himself forward and knocked the tall young man aside, making Leopold the winner of the hundred-yard dash.

The crowd rose to its feet and went wild, clapping and roaring as when, in the ninth inning, with two men out and the bases loaded, the home-town slugger hits a homer, bringing his team from behind and winning the game with one powerful swing of his shoulders.

"That's nepotism," I said, rising to my feet to see what was happening. "I mean that's not fair—that's against the rules of the game."

"Nature is unfair," said Law, "and existence is also unfair. There is too much pointless pretense. That fellow who you seem to think is your brother behaved according to the dictates of his heart, clearly. Most human beings behave like that and don't admit it—not even to themselves."

As for me, I must admit my feelings were mixed; I was touched by Carolus' brotherly action, however unfair.

The amplifier in center field announced the winner and cited Carolus for conspicuous honesty and distinguished action, which struck me as a most curious choice of words.

Leopold, the winner, was led, like a horse, to the box where my mother was seated, and Carolus came with him. She congratulated Leopold, but she kissed Carolus fervently twice upon his cheek. "You have brought honor to the family," she said, and she looked tearful with pleasure and happiness.

Whether this is dream or hallucination, I said to myself, something is certainly wrong with me.

The drizzle had long since stopped, and now the sun was trying to break through the cold, cloudy light. Reginald Law bought two morning newspapers from a vender of pop, peanuts, score cards, and other forms of reading matter.

He read the news to me in a soft, indifferent voice. A housewife had killed her husband after finding two letters from another woman in his pocket. He had given her a mink coat that cost five thousand dollars for her birthday two weeks before, but she had stabbed him to death with steak knives, recently purchased. The couple had two children, twelve and nine. The husband had been very devoted, the neighbors said.

"She shouldn't have done that," Reginald Law remarked. "Now he's dead. Is she better off now?"

He then read a story about a husband who had killed his wife, a bride of two months, because she had come home fifteen minutes late. Insane jealousy, the newspaper explained. "I killed her," the husband told the police. "Boy, how I loved that gal!"

Law's next choice was the story of a bus that had crashed through the railing of a canal bridge, drowning the sixteen children in it and the driver.

"Somewhat pointless," he said. "Don't you agree?"

He continued to read aloud. A Chicago schoolgirl had admitted that her accusation of rape was false. She had entered the youth's car willingly, she told the police captain. A girl in Massachusetts had committed suicide because she had no date for the weekend and had had none for four previous weekends. She had left a note which said that she was sorry for the trouble she had caused everyone. A faulty gas heater was responsible for the death of three persons in a suburban two-family house.

"You're making a selection," I said, "and it's extremely one-sided."

"Perhaps it is one-sided," he replied, "but these things did in fact occur. You would not be able to console any of the victims by telling them that what had occurred was not by any means representative."

He looked at me with a faint smile. Then he took from his pocket a small volume, which I saw was the Book of Common Prayer, and read aloud, but softly:

"Keep me as the apple of thine eye; hide me under the shadow of thy wings,

". . . mine enemies compass me round about, to take away my soul.

"They are inclosed in their own fat, and their mouth speaketh proud things.

"They lie waiting in our way on every side, watching to cast us down to the ground . . ."

The mile run—the feature event—was about to start, and I saw that my five brothers were in a huddle, as if they were playing football, near the starting line, and I wondered what underhand trick they were planning now.

As the starter's gun cracked out, the crowd uttered a low roar. A runner broke forward, ahead of the rest. I would have been surprised by what happened then, had I not exhausted the surprise in me, for a very pretty girl dressed only in a bathing suit climbed over the railing (low whistles accompanied her, but the runners jogged patiently and indifferently, as if they did not see her) and crossed the path of the pace setter and tried to stop him, and when he would not stop, she hit him over the head with a pop bottle.

This action was received with a kind of studied applause— the polite but vigorous handclapping the hometown crowd awards the pitcher for the visiting team who has been shutting out the home team.

"That kind of thing is the kind of thing which is not done," I said to Law, using the phrase "is not done" in an effort to appeal to the English mind.

"What makes you think so?" said Law, without turning his eyes from the track.

"It spoils the game," I said weakly and without conviction. "There is no contest if you do not play fairly. And the winner does not feel pride but guilt."

"You are interested in platitudes," said Law, "but I am interested in reality."

The reality that interested him at that moment was the sight of the stricken runner stretched out on the grass of the infield and coming to consciousness as the pretty bathing-suit girl kissed him with tenderness and sympathy. A moment after that, they were sprawled out on the grass.

"All the world loves a lover," I remarked, but Law paid no attention to my feeble essay at irony.

Meanwhile, the runners who had been holding back were now moving forward with determined energy. I saw that my five brothers were among them and that they were close to each other, and I hoped that they would not try any tricks again. A spectator threw a pop bottle and hit one of the leading contestants on the head, and this time the applause was unanimous, full-throated, and full of conviction.

The race, as it came to the final quarter mile, had become a contest between seven runners, and I was struck by the fact that all five of my brothers were among them. Just then a fight broke out. Leopold hit Carolus, slapping him hard in the face, Edward turned and knocked Leopold flat with a quick left hook, Carolus kicked Edward in the groin, and when Leopold rose and tried to continue in the race (although he no longer had any chance of winning, barring more interventions), he was tripped up by Nicholas, who in turn was slapped hard by Alphonse, who had just stopped and watched until then, and who was himself knocked down by a hard blow to the head delivered by Edward. In a moment, they were mixed in a scrimmage, as if the runner had just been tackled in a football game, trying to break through the line, and the crowd was roaring and I stood up.

I told Law that I couldn't sit by when this family riot was going on, and started making my way down to the field. He followed me. The bell that marked the end of the mile run clanged, and some of the spectators rushed out to congratulate the winner and carry him on their shoulders, but he darted away from them like a clever halfback and kept on running, as if the race were not yet over. The crowd was very much moved and pleased by this, and they applauded him, but their applause turned to laughter as he continued in deadly serious-ness and ever-increasing speed. At last, an official who looked like a senator or the governor of a state—florid, heavy, and histrionic—signalled with a limp hand to two policemen with rifles, and they raised their guns and shot the winner down.

I halted when I saw this. "I don't want to be killed," I said to myself, drawing back.

"Don't you want to join your brothers?" asked Law, for the boys were still struggling on the ground, kicking and punching, and straining to get up. "Don't you think you should?"

"No," I said, in answer to everything.

Five girls dressed as drum majors pranced forward, shaking

their hips, and came to attention in front of the wrestling heap. The girls, who now looked like a chorus line in a musical comedy, drew forth pistols and shot my brothers to death, as if they were shooting horses with broken legs. The struggle subsided immediately, the boys collapsed like punctured balloons, and I was terrified, and started to run away. Law caught up with me, seized me by the shoulders, and punched me in the nose, knocking me down.

I cried out, "What have I ever done to *you?*"

At first he didn't answer. When he saw that I was going to get up and try to run away, he said to me that it would do no good, I would not get away, and I said to him that I knew this was just a dream, nothing more than a dream, and I was running away to awake into the ordinary day, and the little things and small actions of early morning, since this was just a dream, as he knew very well.

"What difference does it make if it is a dream or it is not a dream?" he said coldly and sternly as I burst into hysterical, grotesque, and unmanly tears. "It is worse for you—it is far worse for you if it *is* a dream. I should think that by this time you would know that."

He stood above me, glaring and looking as if he still intended to keep me from getting up from the ground where I sprawled. The dusk was growing above the empty stadium, and the cold sky looked like a distant lake ringed by black and leafless trees.

"How is it worse for me if it is a dream and only a dream?"

"I detest explanation," said Law. "Do you insist on one? Are you really sure that you don't understand?"

"I often feel that I know little or nothing," I said, in a pleading voice, fearful that I would soon awaken, and that the moment of awakening would occur just as he began to tell me what I wanted to know so much.

"The things I read you out of the paper were, if anything, more shocking than what has just occurred down there on the field. You don't escape from nightmare by waking up, you know. And if what occurred on the field were merely imaginary and unreal and merely your own private hallucination, then the evil that has terrified you is rooted in your own mind and heart. Like the rest of us," Law said scornfully, "you not only know more than you think you know but more than you are willing to admit. Look at yourself! *Just look at yourself!*"

I tried once more to stand up, and awoke, and found myself standing up, staring, in a sweat of confusion and dread, not at the sky but at the looking glass above the chest of drawers next to my dishevelled bed. The face I saw was livid and swollen with barbarous anger and unbearable shame.

An American Fairy Tale

This is a fairy tale. And it is a success story. It is a story which is not only full of goodness and beauty, but it is also a true story. It is full of purity, innocence, and happiness. Since it is the kind of experience which could only occur in America and the kind of a story which has and must have a happy ending, it shows that America has to be discovered again and again by everyone in America, for America is always new and always full of the unknown and undiscovered.

Melvin Smith was a prosperous businessman. He was a manufacturer of scholastic jewelry and thus his prosperity was comparatively stable because whenever a young boy or girl was graduated from high school or college, the parents felt that it was a matter of pride to congratulate their progeny by presenting them with a scholastic ring or some other form of scholastic jewelry as a reward and as a token of their progress in higher education.

His wife, Naomi Smith, was a strong and domineering woman who had helped her husband in business from the very start, when he was very poor; and she had become an equal and far from silent partner, as soon as the business became successful.

Melvin Smith wanted his son to be his junior partner as soon as he was graduated from high school. But Paul asked his father to give him just one year at college. And since so many other boys were also going to college, it was difficult to deny Paul's desire. The father's feeling for his son was a very strong one, for he thought of him as a part of himself, refreshed, renewed, youthful once more. He felt almost as intensely about his son as he felt about his own body when he had a toothache, or an upset stomach. There were two other children, Mildred—but she was a girl and thus did not satisfy the father's need—and Howard—but he was just a little boy, and the father was only able to think of him as the baby of the family.

Paul went to a Midwestern university, for it was only by going out of town that he was able to believe that he was really going to college as he had fondly imagined it. He was unhappy there, since he was afraid of girls. This was the one remaining dreg or drag of his shyness. In all other things he made his voice heard, but he thought that he was too plain for girls to like him very much. He was plain, but not repellent, as he supposed, and when he asked a dormitory friend if any girl would ever really love him, the friend thought that Paul must be joking. Then his friend perceived that Paul was not joking, that he awaited an answer fearful that his doubts would be confirmed. Hence the friend sought to explain to Paul that most girls were not really interested in good-looking men, they wanted something else, a sense of power, or a sense of importance, for the sake of their unborn children. But Paul would not believe him. He thought that his friend was just trying to reassure him.

"You just like to cheer up your friends," Paul declared, self-convinced and self-dismayed. Some three years before this time, having been told that one grew to look like the objects one looked at a great deal, he had purchased a bust of Apollo, placed it in his bedroom, looked at it as much as possible for the next few months, and obtained no results.

Paul did not know that his exuberance and his bouncing, exciting, delightful vitality made him attractive to girls. What happened on dates was that he rushed to make amorous overtures, he rushed for fear of rejection, and when his haste was criticized, he concluded that was an absolute judgment and refusal.

During the first year at this Midwestern university, Paul became known to the other students, and in fact he was loved as a delightful fantast who did many hilarious things. He was arrested for drunkenness and he argued with the policeman and the judge that they had no right to judge him because they had studied neither Plato's *Republic*, nor the works of D. H. Lawrence, where the necessity of spontaneity and wholeness of being was shown to be an imperative of nature, an imperative blocked and frustrated by our industrial civilization, thus forcing all who were intelligent and sensitive to take up hard liquor and sprees. No one really knew what he was saying, but it seemed to some charming and to some hilarious.

And when he walked up the steps of the library with his crony Sylvester, who like him came from New York, and when Sylvester asked him to speak in a lower voice, if he used four-letter words (Sylvester was more sensitive than Paul to conventional mores), Paul responded by denouncing the conventions and the squeamishness of gentility, of academic institutions, of the entire middle class.

"I face the facts," he shouted to Sylvester, "I use four-letter words because existence is full of four-letter facts and phenomena! I refuse to be an ostrich! And I don't care if all the nervous prudes shudder when they hear FOUR! FOUR! FOUR! As for me, I like it very much, I find it delightful. It is delicious. It is most enjoyable. FORE! FORE! FORE!"

When, during the worst part of the great depression and during the year before the New Deal began, Paul Smith began to become very much interested in Marxism, he became a member of the student political group which was called YPCL, or Young People's Communist League. Voluble and dogmatic as ever, Paul argued with his friend Sylvester about Marxism and Communism and the Soviet Union and he had like arguments, when he went home during holidays, with his father.

Sylvester infuriated Paul by telling him that he did not understand his own motives for being interested in Marxism or joining the YPCL's. Even when Paul was elected president of the YPCL's, a post he desired for its own sake and in the hope that it would make him more attractive to the girls who were his comrades, Paul refused to admit that his reasons for being a political radical were purely personal and sexual and artistic.

"How about you?" said Paul, irritated and triumphant. "What reason is there for your hatred of Marxism and Communism except the fact that you are a serf of the lower middle class and lack the courage to emerge from your class and place and join the brotherhood of the human race."

Sylvester told Paul that he would change his mind again and again, but Sylvester did not suspect that in twenty years' time Paul would be an ardent and self-righteous defender of Senators McCarthy and Jenner, arguing as violently about their political rightness as he argued in defense of Josef Stalin, Karl Marx, and the Soviet Union.

"You can't tell me that the one hundred fifty million people of the Soviet Union are all wrong!" Paul cried loudly to Sylvester.

"Many millions of human beings have been wrong again and again and will be wrong again and again," said Sylvester hopelessly.

"What egotism!" said Paul, "You think you're right and yet you're only one among millions and millions of human beings: a guy like you ought to want to be something more than a lackey of the lower middle class."

"I just want to be a human being," said Sylvester, hopelessly and hopefully, "a human being and an American: I was born in Brooklyn and thus I was fortunate enough to be born a native of the United States, an American; but what I want now is to be permitted the right implicit in the Constitution, the right to the pursuit of being a human being and not the hypnotized puppet of an economical interpretation of history and of human nature."

"Chauvinism, pure chauvinism!" said Paul, stalking off in ideological indignation.

During school holidays, Paul had arguments of a like kind with his father. Melvin Smith told his son with pride that since he was the son of a capitalist, he ought to be a capitalist himself, and join the family business as junior partner, instead of joining the traitors and revolutionists who were trying to destroy capitalism and take over the family business.

"If I were not a capitalist," said Melvin Smith, "you would not be going to an out-of-town college. You would be a shipping clerk in the garment center and a parlor socialist on Sundays and holidays. You can't have your cake and eat it too unless you want indigestion and constipation or unless you are a capitalist and can afford to buy more and more cake."

In reply, Paul denounced him as a vicious and shameless sentimentalist as well as a petty bourgeois blinded by capitalist lies.

But Paul did not remain a Communist for very long. He had become interested in music and in making music and he decided to be a great musician like Bach, Beethoven, and Brahms. For a long time he had been delighted by jazz music and he had played the piano very well with a small jazz band on Saturday nights. But now he decided that he was against jazz, he detested it. Jazz was a debased expression of the anxiety and frustration of the creative, progressive, and revolutionary working-class.

His interest in studying classical music came into conflict with his political activity very soon, and he quickly decided that he was through with Communism, a shift which was made the more rapid when two factions of his party unit sought to win his favor by denouncing the other faction as in the pay of the police, an accusation entirely untrue of both factions.

"Something quite theatrical," Paul told Sylvester, "theatrical

and histrionic about their behavior. It is as if they were acting
out the scenario written for them by previous revolutionary
movements. The police are called the Cossacks, not the cops."

At the music school where Paul now went to study harmony
and counterpoint, he denounced anyone who seemed to be conscious of the trials and crises of society. He said that they really
hated art and tried to deform it. And he studied very hard, amid
his denunciations, and he fell in love with an extremely pretty
and extremely self-conscious girl named Dorothea. Dorothea
was also an ambitious musician and she responded first of all
to Paul's extravagant vitality and forthrightness, even though
she sometimes was shocked by his foul language. Dorothea not
only admired Paul very much, but she was sure that he was a
genius: she thought that she was a genius too, but said nothing
about this certainty to Paul or anyone else.

In a short time, Paul and Dorothea were very much in love
with each other, and when Dorothea introduced Paul to her
parents, and told them she intended to marry Paul, they were
horrified. Paul's preoccupation with the writing of great music
was set to one side when Dorothea told him of her parents'
refusal to accept Paul as her husband and their son-in-law. He
recognized for the first time that Dorothea was not only very
intelligent but that she was very much in love with him: hence
he became even more in love with her than he had been all
along, and he proposed an elopement, immediately. Despite the
poverty which troubled Paul so much, since his father refused
to do more than pay his tuition fee, Paul insisted that Dorothea
elope with him immediately. Paul was in a hurry and Dorothea
was thrilled by the idea of an elopement, and even more thrilled
because her parents prohibited her marriage to a genius. She
was also thrilled because Paul was in a hurry, he was always in
a hurry; he kept saying that either the elopement occurred
immediately or he would live a celibate's life, just as Beethoven
had. After six weeks of disputation and impatience, Paul and
Dorothea eloped and were married. Neither of them had any

money and Paul had to take a poor job with sheet music publishers, and the newly wedded couple had to live in a seedy rooming house.

Soon enough Paul was writing arrangements for jazz bands. Soon he was leading his own jazz band. But he did not in the least surrender or forget his desire to be a great composer. He began his second symphony and Dorothea, who had voiced her suspicion that the dean of the music school was jealous of Paul, encouraged him passionately.

"I know I am right," said Dorothea. "You will prove that I am right and that you are a great composer."

And she supported her hope and admiration for her husband by drawing forth her inexhaustible fund of examples of unrecognized genius in music and in the other arts as well.

"How can it possibly be otherwise, dearest," she argued. "How can genius as original and unique as yours be clear to everyone from the very start?"

"But dearest," said Paul reasonably, "you know that you are my wife and that you love me, that's why you see me the way you do."

"I would not love you," Dorothea answered, "if you were not what you are. When you love a person you know him better than anyone else does. Think of the late quartets of Beethoven, of Cézanne, of Van Gogh, of Keats, and Emily Dickinson. No one knew how wonderful they were. And Shakespeare did not know that he was Shakespeare! If he had, he would not have let some of his best plays remain unpublished during his lifetime."

Paul was somewhat consoled by these remarks. And he found himself resorting to declarations of despair just to elicit reassurance from Dorothea, a reassurance rich in examples and praise which compared him with immortal masters.

Paul became a very successful jazz band leader and he played once a week on the radio also. He earned a very handsome salary, and he lived very well. His parents and his wife's parents were now very proud of him, bragged about his early success.

Paul and Dorothea began to move among the famous and the rich, and they acquired a taste for expensive living, and they took an apartment in a fashionable neighborhood. Paul tried hard to save enough money to be able to stop conducting for a time, so that he might finish his second symphony, but this desire was contradicted and denied by their ever-increasing desire to live well and to know interesting and gifted people who were in the limelight, or the public eye, as Paul said.

Paul's success as a jazz band leader was secure. It depended upon effervescence and vitality more than upon his musicianship, but Paul strove to ignore this dependence whenever he became conscious of it. Finally, Paul secured six months of leisure, finished his second symphony, and persuaded a major orchestra to perform it.

The performance was to occur in the fall; during the summer Paul saw his friend Sylvester who was now a lawyer, none too successful, but quite content with his lot. Paul told Sylvester that he had really accomplished something new in music.

"I have augmented the world of sound in a fundamental way," he declared.

Sylvester was used to such declarations and he was pleased to hear them because he knew that it meant that his friend, of whom he was very fond, was feeling very good.

During their meetings of recent years, the friends had argued long and in vain about the possibility of being a serious composer and yet a popular one.

"Shakespeare did it," Paul insisted in a clamorous way. "If he did it, there is no reason why it can't be done today."

Sylvester felt that the Elizabethan age was different from the present. The analogy was wrong, and the whole character of modern society seemed to him to make it very difficult for a serious musician to be popular, except by some freak or accident.

"You are a melancholy Lear, howling in the wilderness," answered Paul.

But when his symphony was performed that fall and praised

politely and quickly forgotten, Paul was full of dismay. He felt that he was right back where he had started. Dorothea's reassurances were again necessary, and now they were more extreme, more exaggerated than ever.

Paul returned to conducting a jazz band at a fashionable hotel, and he played once a week on the radio. He was determined as ever to be a great composer, and he began to think of his third symphony and his fourth—perhaps if he produced the two at once, he might win the acclaim he desired so much. But he also desired and enjoyed the pleasures and comforts of his standard of living, and this desire was encouraged in him by Dorothea just as much as his ambition as a composer. Husband and wife still denied to each other and to friends that there was any real conflict between the two desires.

The year before, Paul's sister Mildred had married a likely young man who was nothing if not willing to take Melvin Smith's place in his business. Melvin Smith retired and the business continued to prosper, just as before. Since he had nothing to do with himself, Melvin Smith began to go to all the art shows in New York City, and then he began to paint himself, and in a comparatively short period of time, he was a primitive abstractionist. He showed his canvases to various art dealers, and to Claude Vermont, the brilliant critic of modern art, who told him that his primitive abstractionism was far superior to the primitive paintings of Grandma Moses. This sufficed to secure Melvin Smith a one-man show and one of his paintings was purchased by the Museum of Primitive Modern Art.

Melvin Smith gave two of his paintings to his son and daughter-in-law, and visited them frequently without announcing his coming to be sure that they kept his paintings upon the wall of their handsome Bauhaus living room.

When Paul told his father that he did not care for primitive or abstract art, he infuriated his fond father once again.

"You have sold out," said Melvin Smith to his successful son. "You have sold out to Tin Pan Alley. Why don't you be like

Bela Bartok? Money is not everything: I will be your patron, if necessary! I will support you for at least two years if you write the kind of music you really want to write instead of writing tinkle and tom-tom for Tin Pan Alley!" Melvin Smith became aware that he was shouting and he lowered his voice, "Don't you see that you will be much more satisfied with yourself, in the long run, if you stop wasting your time on pleasing the public? If you would just follow Stravinsky, Bartok, Schoenberg, and Prokofiev, you would enjoy the most important feeling in life, self-respect. You are just as good as you want to be! I knew that this was true when I was a boy and I know that it is true now."

Paul was silenced for the first time in fifteen years. He did not know how to reply to his father. He felt sure that the world was coming to an end, or at least the world as he had known it. He had tried to remind his father how much parental resistance there had been to his becoming a musician at all, and how much family pride there had been when he was a popular and successful composer listened to on the radio and frequently in the public eye.

But his protestation was quite in vain. And in the depths of his heart in all truth Paul himself was unable to disagree with his father or possess any strong conviction that his father was wrong and he was right.

How beautiful this success story is, how good, how true! It is the equal of any fairy tale, it is full of purity, innocence, and happiness. It is like a newborn child. It is as if one were to say, believe, and hope that America were going to be discovered again.

The Gift

It was something special. Mother had said it was, father had said so too, and dear Vera too. It was an honor like the gold paper stars the teacher gave for excellent deportment and 100% in arithmetic.

Once before Toby had been sent downtown to Macy's department store to return a package and get back the purchase price. And he was very proud then, in the subway and the grown ups had looked at him: they must have known that he was being trusted to travel by himself all the way downtown in the subway and back to bring a purchase back to Macy's department store.

And once before, long ago, dear Vera the servant maid (who came from Poland and wanted to go back to Poland as soon as she had enough money for a husband and to buy a farm) had put him on the train of the Long Island Railroad to the seashore where Grandma lived in the summer when it was too hot. But he was not big enough to be trusted because Vera spoke to the conductor who smiled at him when he passed on the way to the seashore, picking up tickets, clicking them.

This time was different and more important. He jingled his coins in his pocket because some one might hear and know he had money and was big enough to be trusted with silver, and brave enough to travel by himself in the subway where it was always roaring. He was going all the way to Brooklyn, the borough where he was born so long ago he could not remember: Vera said that no one ever was able to remember that, but she might be wrong. All the way to Brooklyn, under the river into the tunnel where it was like going up in the elevator in Father's office building which was a throbbing in his ears until the express elevator reached the 44th floor.

It was Martha's birthday and Isabel would be there too who liked him very much, he knew for sure, and Buck Thomas too, who hated him because Isabel liked to play post office with him and did not like Buck Thomas at all. If they played post office, he would get a kiss from Isabel and another one if he went to the kitchen with Isabel to bring back more ice cream and cake.

He saw the subway kiosk ahead, it was just like the German helmet Uncle William had brought him back from France, except it had a spike in it, and he saw the big clock next to it and the little wooden newsstand. He walked down the steps and carefully thrust his nickel into the turnstile, afraid it might get stuck and pushed the gate too soon, and felt panicky but then when he pushed a little more slowly it gave way, swung and clicked and he stood on the platform, near the pillar, as the train came roaring in like summer thunder in the upstate mountains.

Mother and Vera had told him to be sure he took the train which said New Lots Avenue or he would not get to Brooklyn and the birthday party.

The only thing wrong was that he had no birthday present and he didn't because they had decided that it was all right for him to go to the party alone only in the morning at breakfast time and it was a Sunday, so no stores except the stationery store were open and there he could buy something which mother thought would be improper as a birthday present for a girl, a toy baseball game which he had looked at for a very long time in the plate glass window, but Mother said that baseball was only for lunatics and fanatics.

He looked up at the advertisements above the seats on the other side of the aisle and began to feel more and more ashamed that he had no present. All the other children would have presents to give to Martha, it would be just like that time in school last year when all the other children gave Miss Swenson Christmas presents, but he had no present to give because Mother had allowed him to give Miss Swenson the Thanksgiving candy father had sent him when he was on the road or coming back again from Chicago: so he was ashamed twice, because he saw the look on Miss Swenson's face when she opened the box of candy and saw it was all children's candy, chickenfeed, black licorice, gumdrops, lollipops, and taffy and then he knew he should not have given her a present of children's candy. He was more ashamed then than when he had nothing to give her at Christmas because at Christmas Mother said that he had already given teacher a present, one gift was enough, which was not what father would have said if he had not been on the road again.

One of the advertisements was about God and his army and he might try praying to God, but maybe it was not right to ask him for a present now that he was already on the train on the way to Brooklyn. Mother said that there was a God and father said when he asked him that he would have to decide for himself and Vera went to Church every Sunday morning and she was sure that there was a God and she spoke of God as being very kind, not like mother who kept saying that God would punish him for being a bad boy.

Once mother and father had an argument about whether or not there was a God and father said that mother had only a personal God just for herself. God was supposed to give you what you prayed for if you were a good boy but you could never be sure about being good and only God himself knew whether or not you were good.

"Dear God," he prayed, moving his lips and almost speaking until a lady next to him looked at him, "please give me a present for Martha, even if I am not a good boy I know that Martha is good, at least I think she is a good girl."

Isabel told him the last time he was in Brooklyn that Martha had been sent to bed without supper twice in a row but sometimes Isabel made things up and did not know she was making them up. Even if God did not answer his prayer and give him a gift for Martha, it would not show that there was no God but it might mean that Isabel was right and Martha was not a good girl. Also it was so long since he had seen Martha, it was more than five weeks, it was before Christmas, so Martha might have been any old way and he would not know about it.

He was probably being a dumbbell just like the boys in Junior High said he was but one of them said to another that maybe this dumbbell might turn out to be one of those sharks. Of course he kept being skipped and promoted into Rapid Advance classes.

God would have quite a lot of trouble in getting a birthday present for him now that he was in the subway with the train racing and roaring on the long express run from 96th to 72nd to 59th and Columbus Circle. Isabel was a Catholic girl and she always promised to tell him secrets of the church and then when she got what she wanted—candy or a toy—she would refuse to tell him because she said it was not really a promise, she had taken it back under her breath.

Isabel would say it was a dumb idea to ask God for a present when he was in the subway but it was like God opening up the Red Sea and dividing it in half so that his chosen people could get away from the Egyptians who were chasing them in chariots, the Sunday school teacher said, but lots of the boys in Sunday School said it was just a fairy tale.

It was easy to get mixed up about God and about the things the Sunday School teacher told the class and once it started an argument when he came home from Sunday School for the first time and Uncle Robert who was a banker and Aunt Anne were here from Chicago and they asked him what they had taught him in Sunday School. He told them that he did not remember very much but Uncle Robert kept asking him just as everyone began on the soup, so he said that the teacher told him all about what God does, God protects everyone who is weak and helpless and poor. Uncle Robert looked disgusted and father began to choke on his soup and mother said, "Toby!" which meant "shut up." That was when he was six years old and just a baby, he would know better now. But how could he know that he was saying something peculiar which one ought not to say to a banker? Uncle Robert kept after him and became angry and asked him whether the teacher had taught him that God made the earth and waters. Then Mother said, "Robert!" and she was angry at Uncle Robert and father laughed so much that he thought it was like when father took him to the pictures where they saw Charlie.

God was like being born, it was very hard to understand anything about God. When he was a baby still and went to kindergarten he thought it was the stork that brought the baby and he looked out at night to see if storks were flying in the sky over where Dr. Young lived. Vera had been born on a farm and she said babies grow like the trees from the earth and then there are flowers in May and the bees come and then there are fruits in August and September. But this was not the way that city babies were born because they were born all year long. He asked his father once when there was company and father said he always thought it was the stork who brought the flowers of spring. Everyone laughed but Toby. He did not like jokes which he could not understand. He asked father if storks did not bring babies too and father said that there were not enough storks to take care of all the babies of all the married couples, and there were more marriages than storks and everyone laughed again but Toby and father said, because he seemed to be enjoying himself, that a new baby arrived every six seconds in the city of greater New York and there was no evidence that there were any storks sufficient for the growing population. But that must have been a joke too: if there were enough ambulances for all the babies there might be enough storks just for the babies especially because the grown-ups need ambulances too.

Vera said that there was a God and Vera was very smart too and she never told lies, she was not as smart as Mother and father but mother and father did not always tell the truth to him or to each other. Vera taught him arithmetic quicker than the teacher taught the class in school. Vera prayed for her family in Poland and she told him how to pray, you must get down on your knees and close your eyes and you must mean what you say because no one can fool God. He could not get down on his knees in the subway or else everyone would think he was sick but maybe it would make no difference if he just prayed with his lips. Father and Mother did not pray or if they did they kept it a secret but still they had everything they wanted without praying while Vera who prayed all the time did not have enough money to go back to Poland and the farm she came from and she said she would not have enough for at least three years and sometimes Toby heard her cry in her room because she was so lonesome.

He was sure he was making a mistake about Vera's prayers because God knew best, Vera said. He always made mistakes because he thought too much and did not get things straight like the time Father and Mother took him to the moving-pictures because it was Vera's night out; on the way they passed the Deaf and Dumb Academy and he read the name on the sign and he shouted out: "Deaf and dumb! Deaf and dumb! deaf and dumb!" at the top of his voice until his father stopped him.

"They can't hear me, they're deaf and dumb," Toby said to Father. "How could they hear if they're deaf and dumb?"

Father said: "The people who run the Deaf and Dumb Academy can hear you yelling and bellowing." Father smiled but he was angry.

"But they're not deaf and dumb, so why should they mind?" Toby said to Father.

"What a logical monster we have spawned!" Father said, turning towards Mother. Then he said, "Just don't yell, Toby, if you don't mind," and then he said to Mother, "I suppose he'll grow up to be a shyster lawyer."

Mother did not like that. She said to Father that he was being mean to Toby so Father said to Toby in a nice voice, that there was a proverb, a very old saying, that anyone who was wholly clever was half a fool. Just before they came to the theater Toby asked Mother what was logical and mother told him that being logical was like arithmetic and that he was being logical when he said that deaf and dumb was something which would not make the doctors and nurses in the Deaf and Dumb Academy mad when he shouted out the way he had just shouted out. It was logical that they should not be mad but that was not the way people's feelings worked. They became mad whether they had any logical right to become mad or not. Father said, "Your mother is right. Being logical is also being someone who loves to argue all the time." So Toby said, "You and Mother argue all the time, don't you?" So Father said, "You see what a logician he is! What a logical rascal!" Then he said to Toby, "The reason most people are logical is because they get mad and are trying to hurt someone's feelings. Now no more discussion of the topic for several days to come."

He still did not know what logical was but from the way father said it, it was not a very nice thing to be and he did not like it when Mother and Father would argue even though they did so behind closed doors most of the time.

Bedford Avenue was the next stop. Toby got up and got out of the train when it stopped and walked up the steps and looked for the taxi he had been told to take to get to Martha's house. The taxi driver asked him if he had the money and Toby showed him the dollar Father had given him. Then he got into the taxi and the taxi was soon going down the big street where the streetcar ran. Another taxi turned in suddenly and hit the taxi's fender in front and it all happened so quickly that

Toby did not have time to get scared. The taxi driver got out
and looked like he was going to get into a fight with the other
taxi driver.

"Guys like you ought to be in jail," the taxi driver yelled at
the other taxi driver. "I'll beat the living daylights out of you,
you little draft dodger. I'm a veteran. I was taking potshots at
the Germans when you were cleaning up." They stood like that
yelling at each other, getting closer all the time, their eyes
bulging. "Just say that again," said the taxi-driver to the other
taxi-driver, "just say that again." Toby burst into tears and got
out of the taxi. He was afraid he would get lost although he
had the address of the house where Isabel lived. "Just look
what you've done to this kid," said Toby's taxi-driver to the
other one. "Oh, I did that too, I did that too," said the other
driver and just then a few people and a cop came along and
when Toby saw the cop he thought he would never get to the
party on time and he began to cry again.

"Which of you guys made this kid cry?" the cop asked the
two taxi-drivers. Both of them said nothing at all in answer.
Toby felt he couldn't stop crying anymore.

"Look, kid," said the cop, "you see this box I have? It's a
present for one of my own kids. I'll give it to you if you want
it and if you stop crying. You might not want it because it's for
a little girl, but maybe you have a sister." Toby stopped crying
and started to gulp and hiccup.

"I would like to have the box, officer," said Toby.

The cop gave Toby the box and told the two taxi drivers to
take each other's license numbers and beat it. Toby got back
into the cab, holding the box and wondering about his prayer.

Soon the cab-driver stopped at the brownstone house where
Martha's birthday party was and Toby gave him the dollar he
had been told to give the taxi-driver.

"Thank you, kid. That was a pretty nice cop, wasn't it?" the
driver said.

As he got out of the cab he was afraid that it might have been wrong to take the box because then the cop's little girl would not get it and she might have been praying for it. He would ask Vera because she would really tell him whether it was wrong to take the present even though he prayed for it. He would tell Vera about how God had answered his prayer and had made the box a present for the little girl and not for a boy. He wanted to open the box and see what was in it but that would spoil the fancy wrapping-paper. He stopped in front of the door of the brownstone house because he suddenly remembered that his prayer had been answered only after a taxi had bumped into another taxi, and a big fight had started and he had started to cry like a big baby and a sissy. It might be dangerous to pray for presents but anyway he was sure now that there was a God. He rang the doorbell and began to think of how proud he would be when he gave Martha her present and he told Isabel all the things that had happened when he had been allowed to go by himself to the borough of Brooklyn where he had been born so long ago.

A Colossal Fortune

For Marshall Allan

During the long idle pleasant luxurious summer of 1935, Monroe Lawrence added to his other scholarly attainments a new one, singular indeed for him. Although he had never seen a horse race, nor had ever wanted to see one, and was certain that he would never want to see one, he became an expert on the horses who raced in horse races all year long all over the country, in the United States, in Mexico, in Cuba, and in Canada.

He studied the horse sheets, as he called them, at Atlantic City, where he had gone with his parents after getting his degree of doctor of philosophy at the precocious age of twenty-one. In only two weeks, he felt that he had acquired all the knowledge necessary to betting on the races and winning all the time. He did not actually bet on them, partly because his parents would have been shocked, for they disapproved very much of any form of gambling; but there was another and more important reason for not betting: what interested him was the correctness of his choices and predictions, and he was not concerned in the least in gambling as a way of winning money quickly. Monroe's parents would have been astonished to learn that their only son was devoting himself to the horses; he had never followed any sport or game, except for chess, which required calculation and judgment also. And it was not that Monroe was disdainful of the sport of kings or of any game and sport as wasteful preoccupations unworthy of him. On the contrary, his preoccupation with every form of learning and with the powers of his mind was so complete, and excluded everything else in the world to such an extent, that the question of whether any interest was low and vulgar or exalted and noble was a question which would never occur to him.

By making private bets every day after studying the horse sheets, Monroe soon found himself in paper possession—which was entirely sufficient possession, from his own point of view —of a large theoretical fortune. His hypothetical bets on the horses who raced every day all over North America had resulted, within less than a month, in the acquisition of more than two hundred thousand dollars.

Monroe was gratified by his success in winning this large amount of money, but he was not in the least surprised that he had won it, for he had always been very successful in everything he attempted. He had no way of knowing, and he did not know, that he had never attempted anything in which he was likely to fail. He had been an infant prodigy, a boy wonder, a prize winner, a quiz kid. He had also been, as he still was, an adored only son. He was not surprised that he succeeded in getting his doctorate in philosophy at the unprecedented age of twenty-one, nor was he particularly impressed or delighted with himself. It was the sort of thing which he took for granted. He wanted to be a teacher of philosophy, but his extreme youth and his boyish appearance seemed to be the reason that he had not been asked to teach. Monroe took it for granted that at the proper time he would certainly be asked to teach philosophy.

At first when he strolled on the boardwalk and looked at the ocean, the breaking waves made him think of his studies in metaphysics, and he asked himself: what is Time? what is Change? what is Movement? But soon the enchanting, enthralling, fascinating, entrancing activity of betting on the horses took his mind entirely, and as he strolled, he thought only of the races on which he had bet with himself: he was blind to all the vividness of the seashore resort which surrounded him, he looked impatiently at his wristwatch to see if it were time to go again to the billiard parlor where at the ticker tape the results of the races came over the wire and over the radio: there he would find out how he had made out in all the day's races all over North America wherever the sport of kings excited human beings.

In the middle of the summer, his father asked him if he wanted to go to law school. So far as his father could see, there was little else for Monroe to do except to continue to be a student, even though he had received his Ph.D. degree. Anyone who looked at Monroe saw that he was a student, he was still a student, he had been a student for a long time now, since he had entered kindergarten at the age of four.

When Monroe agreed that it was indeed sensible for him to go to law school, when he agreed with perfect aplomb as if he had thought of the possibility for years, Monroe's father was perplexed as well as relieved. Monroe had often induced such a mixture of feelings in his father. There was something about Monroe which his father was unable to fathom, something which did not fit into previous patterns of his experience of human beings. Or perhaps the something was nothing, perhaps it was the absence of some quality of being, not the presence of something which was positive. Monroe responded with clear and complete calm to many things which would excite most human beings—but then Monroe was in so many ways a remarkable young man. In the past when Monroe's father had felt the same vague but painful doubts about Monroe, he had discussed them with his wife, who reassured him, and often went on to criticize him for having any doubts about Monroe.

"No matter how good a doctor is," she said, "he cannot understand a metaphysician." Monroe was a perfect student, she reminded him, and he was very successful in whatever he attempted: he would continue to be, as he had always been, very successful. He must not be judged by ordinary and average standards. Monroe's father was a doctor, he was a specialist in ear, eye, nose and throat diseases, he did not know the world except in these special ways, but nevertheless he was not reassured by his wife's attitude. Hence he concluded that perhaps law school as a practical training for the real world might make Monroe less unworldly. For he sometimes thought he heard an indescribable and nameless pulse or vibration in Monroe—it was like coming upon an alarm clock, ticking, in the wilderness of the northern woods, while hunting: Monroe seemed to be disconnected, or unconnected, with the real world; although he obviously existed and functioned in the real world, at the same time—and this troubled Dr. Lawrence very much —he was also utterly lost in some private dream, and did not know it, untroubled and apparently certain that everyone else existed in the same dream. Yet Dr. Lawrence was uncertain about his anxiety; he was not sure that he ought to be troubled; perhaps it was his own narrowness of mind and of experience which made him doubtful about Monroe who, all his teachers agreed, was remarkable and brilliant.

During the pleasant lounging loitering summer, Dr. Lawrence did feel that he ought to question his wife about the fact that Monroe showed no interest whatever in girls, although there were many girls of all kinds at the seashore resort. But the mother saw nothing strange in this lack of interest. She felt that Monroe was a superior, elevated, dedicated young man. Concerned with objects of the intellect, he soared above the average concerns of the flesh: he was a student of philosophy, and he had written his doctor's thesis on a metaphysical subject. Mrs. Lawrence knew nothing about metaphysics, except that it was very important and unknown to most, like relativity physics. But she knew how rare a mastery of it was—perhaps Monroe would be an Einstein of philosophy, a Freud of metaphysics.

Dr. Lawrence was not convinced by his wife's lucid explanation: it was too lucid. Perhaps, however, his son's shyness was the reason: it was certainly true that Monroe was shy, although his good manners did much to conceal this fact from most people. Monroe did not have any close friends of his own sex either, and he did not appear to mind being without cronies or chums. He always seemed to be able to find enough—more than enough!—to do with himself. Anything, something, and everything fascinated him. He was never bored; the doctor had never known any other human being free of the pain of boredom; there were others, however, who, like Monroe, were never unhappy.

Dr. Lawrence did not find out the truth about his son's being and character, for he died suddenly of a cerebral hemorrhage during the winter of Monroe's first year at the law school of Fairfield University. Monroe was no more disturbed by his father's death than by most of the events, occurrences, and episodes of life. He was sorry, for he had liked his father very much. But his concentration on whatever interested him in the immediate present prevented him from feeling any acute or extended grief. Yet death had made a serious difference in his future, for his father's estate provided only enough to assure his mother a modest livelihood, and Mrs. Lawrence wrote to tell her son that he would have to think of making a living for himself as soon as he had finished law school, getting along until then on a sharply diminished allowance. Monroe replied with much sympathy. He knew that she found it very painful to deny him anything, and he declared that he could certainly get along very well on the curtailed allowance.

Monroe made a new budget for himself: the effort was as

exciting as a game of chance, a puzzle, or a new subject of study. He devoted himself to the problem with the intense concentration and playful ingenuity which he had always enjoyed so much. Moving from an expensive rooming house to an inexpensive one, he began to be careful in the most precise and detailed way, calculating the cost of each meal. Within a week—and once the pleasure of calculation was past—Monroe's curtailed allowance proved annoying and unpleasant. Accustomed to eating well, the need for economy depressed him, sometimes before and sometimes after his dinner. And the inexpensive rooming house to which he had moved was a very unpleasant place. His room was small and uncomfortable: it was a hall bedroom: the closet was dark and did not provide enough room for his suits, about which he had always been very careful. His books, too, crowded the room, had to be doubled up on the shelves, and many important books packed in cartons and shoved under his bed.

Worst of all was the middle-aged and irascible drunkard who lived on the same floor and shared the bathroom with Monroe. He went to the bathroom all evening long, drinking and quarrelling through bouts of beer with his middle-aged girl friend, going to the bathroom spitting and coughing like a choked-up motor, disturbing Monroe as he tried to study, not always closing the bathroom door, and slamming it when he did close it and sometimes slamming his own door too in the midst of his absorption in drinking and arguing with the choice of his heart, a lady who made Monroe remember that love was blind, or blinded by beer. Finally Monroe knocked timidly at the drunkard's door and asked him very politely but tensely and nervously if he would please try to be more quiet and would he make a point of being sure that he shut the door whenever he went to the bathroom. The middle-aged drunkard told Monroe that if he wanted that much quiet he ought to go live in a lunatic asylum, in a hospital, or in a cemetery, and if he did want that much quiet, there must be something wrong with him.

Then he slammed the door in Monroe's face, insulting Monroe as he had never been insulted before, and leaving him helpless to do anything about the humiliation. Monroe's helplessness was also something utterly new to him.

After the assault of the insult and the shock of helplessness, Monroe became extravagant and self-indulgent. He broke the rules of his budget and he spent so much money on his meals that his monthly allowance was exhausted and he had to borrow money from one of his law student friends.

It was natural and inevitable that Monroe should think of how to make money and remember how much money he had won for himself on paper by betting on the horses. He had not forgotten about the horses, he had continued to follow the races during the fall and winter season, despite the arduous law school courses in which he soon excelled just as he had always excelled in all his studies. The more he thought of it, the more Monroe saw no reason why he should not make as much money in actuality as he had made on paper by betting on the horses. If he applied himself when it was a question of genuine necessity as he applied himself to his studies, he would certainly succeed just as before.

Monroe now had more friends and acquaintances than he had been accustomed to have in the past, for he went to dinner as well as to lunch with other law school students where everyone talked passionately, cases were argued loudly, points of law were struggled with and struggled for as if the young men were playing football, or were already practicing law. Soon Monroe had a close friend, Sidney Prince, a dark, tall and handsome man, who was different from Monroe in most ways, and different perhaps most of all in being very much interested in girls. Monroe had been attracted to Sidney by his obvious warmth and good nature, his quick, intuitive, rapid-fire method of arguing. Sidney liked Monroe most of all because he felt supported by Monroe's precision, his learning, and his marvelous memory.

Sidney was brash, but in such a good-natured way that no one was offended, and some were charmed; he was shrewd, but he mocked his own shrewdness; he delighted in himself, but he delighted almost as much in others. He was full of optimism, overflowing with confidence, sanguine about himself and his future, and about the future of everyone else. Sidney had come to Fairfield for the first time two weeks before the beginning of the fall term, and announced to one of the famous professors, whom he knew of through his writings, that he wanted a scholarship. All scholarships were awarded in late winter and made public in April, this was September, the famous professor had been summoned from the depths of the university library: hence this was a most extraordinary request. It was a Saturday afternoon and Professor Reynolds had tried to gain time by asking Sidney to wait until the weekend was over—when he would be able to consult colleagues in the department. Sidney candidly explained that he would not wait, he did not have the funds with which to stay in town for more than a few hours, he had to get the next bus back to the city in which he lived. Sidney spoke clearly and without haste, with so much aplomb, frankness, and charming self-confidence—he seemed at once to be so self-possessed and so deprived—that the famous professor, feeling that there was no reason to be at all suspicious of Sidney and being a very kind man who was always afraid that he must be doing something wrong unless he exerted himself wholly to doing the right thing, expedited the matter of getting a scholarship for Sidney immediately. Sidney did not work hard because he was very quick and very clever. What he did, he did with a genuineness and a flair which made his superiors and his peers feel that he was a young man certain to make good, to make his mark, to make his way in the world, and to bring honor and satisfaction to his friends and his family.

When Monroe called Sidney and told him that he wanted to speak to him about a very important and private matter, Sidney thought that Monroe must want advice about an affair of the heart. Sidney had tried several times to get Monroe interested in going out with him on double dates, and he was curious about Monroe's silent and withdrawn attitude, supposing that Monroe concealed some fascinating and rare peculiarity or perversion beneath his indifference to matters of sex and his bemused attitude when the other boys talked about their amorous adventures.

They met in one of the most expensive restaurants of the town, and Sidney was very much amused when Monroe suggested that they have dinner in the cocktail lounge of the restaurant, where they were not likely to be disturbed or overheard. This seemed to Sidney to confirm his guess that Monroe wished to discuss a love affair with him. Cocktail lounges and secret confidences were always associated, for Sidney, with sexual adventure: perhaps Monroe had taken up with a married woman, was afraid of the lady's husband, and did not know that a wife was the best kind of a girl for an affair.

Swearing Sidney to secrecy, Monroe outlined to Sidney—in a low voice, almost a whisper, which was all the more marked because Monroe always spoke in a low and soft tone of voice— his scheme for getting rich very quickly, a scheme which he felt sure was infallible, provided the necessary capital could be raised. On certain days, Monroe explained, it was possible to pick seven winning horses, if one calculated properly. Horses, he reminded Sidney, were much more predictable than human beings, and by studying their past performances on the horse sheets one could be absolutely sure of making a killing. The only drawback was that the horses who were certain to win raced at very low odds, so that the gambler could not make much money by betting on any one of them. But Monroe was convinced that this difficulty might be wholly overcome by betting large sums of money throughout the country, among the many bookmakers throughout America, on the horses who were sure to win: and a real killing could be made by betting on one horse after another, parlaying the sum won on one race by betting it on the next one and thus pyramiding the sum. The stupendous coup of a seven horse parlay was not only possible, it was a certainty, if one made an effort to be intelligent, and sensible, and, above all, patient.

Sidney's native scepticism, a habit of mind spontaneous in him, made him say that all this was too good to be true, and if it was true why had no one thought of it before among the many who bet on the races all the time? Monroe was prepared for this query, which he had examined briefly and scornfully the summer before; he replied that most gamblers did not possess the patience to wait for the right combination of races: all of them were too eager to win on long shots, on horses who paid off at heavy odds: they did not bide their time and make a big killing by betting on horses who were sure to win although they paid off very little. The only real difficulty was to secure the large sum of capital which would make a bet which paid very little pay very much because so much money had been bet upon it. Monroe had a pad and pencil at hand, and he showed Sidney how, if one wagered ten thousand dollars on a horse who was sure to win, then even if the odds were one-to-three one would win three thousand dollars.

Sidney still felt that the scheme was too good to be true; nevertheless he was impressed with it. The idea of getting rich rapidly, of making a fortune, was all the more attractive to him because, unlike Monroe, he had passionate longings for expensive things: girls, however eager and amorous, were always expensive. Monroe added that the reason the scheme would work for them was precisely because they were not professional gamblers, they were free of all the preconceptions and prejudices of ordinary horse players; and it was then Sidney's shield of prudence was penetrated. It seemed quite plausible to him— it happened so often, in so many pursuits—that the intelligent outsider might very well be apt to transcend the entire situation just because he was an outsider.

For the next few days, Sidney followed the horses with Monroe and saw how Monroe's choices, if they had been backed by large sums of money, would have yielded large returns. Sidney's scepticism, intelligent doubt, and hesitation vanished, and Sidney turned with the practicality which was characteristic of him to the question of how they were going to get the necessary capital. First, he decided, he would canvas his friends among the law students: there was Nathaniel Burke, but he was very poor; Ellsworth Clark, who had a small amount in the bank which he might be willing to put into the venture; Eli Ford, who was parsimonious but whose parents were very rich; Cyrus Jones, who seemed to have an income; Newland Cameron, who was being subsidized through law school by his rich uncle, Stewart Cameron, a manufacturer; and Ernest Robinson, although he was also probably too poor to be of much help. Sidney also supposed that he would doubtless be able to borrow at least a thousand dollars from the dean of the law school, if he concealed the purpose for which he was borrowing the money.

Sidney conferred with his law school friends. He assumed, with utter sincerity, that he was doing them a great favor, an attitude he believed in so completely that others were utterly convinced. When each of them suggested one of the doubts that had troubled Sidney, he answered that he himself had thought just that, he too had wrongly entertained that objection. Nevertheless, none of them, whether tempted or not, had very much money to contribute to the necessary sum of capital. Elssworth Clark, who did have several hundred dollars in the bank and was the most sceptical of all, was tempted to put in two hundred dollars just for the sake of going along with his friends, and because two hundred dollars more or less would not make much of a difference to him, one way or another, so far as his financial problem went, since it was a question for him of having enough money for an entire year at a time until he finished law school. Sidney was too kind and generous, however, to take advantage of Ellsworth's bemused willingness to go along as a matter of camaraderie, and he told Ellsworth that by the coming fall, when he returned for the new term, Monroe and he would be so well-fixed financially that they would set up Ellsworth in an apartment of his own and take care of all his financial problems until he was done with school. Sidney made this generous offer with characteristic sincerity and unqualified certainty, for he by now was sure that the scheme would work perfectly and make all of them rich.

Meanwhile Newland Cameron had been persuaded so overwhelmingly of the practicality of the scheme by Sidney's arguments, that he went to his rich uncle Stewart Cameron and, in an unprecedented intensity of enthusiasm, after much effort, succeeded in persuading his uncle that the scheme was at least worth examining. The uncle was a cautious and toughminded businessman, and it took a whole week of very careful predictions—which turned out to be true—on the part of Monroe to make Stewart Cameron feel that he might venture to put twenty thousand dollars into Monroe's money-making scheme. Hearing hat Stewart Cameron had invested that much money in it, Cyrus Jones, who had been tempted but afraid, became very excited and got on the bandwagon, as he called it, withdrawing from the bank five thousand dollars which were intended to assure his completion of his course at the law school. Cyrus Jones felt that if a canny business man were willing to put so much money into the project, it was bound to work, and he thought too of how miserable and foolish he would feel if the whole scheme succeeded and he had been deprived of his part of the good fortune by mere caution and good sense. Sidney also borrowed the thousand dollars he had expected to be able to borrow from the dean of the law school, and he felt so jubilant, so confident, that in delighted revery or fantasy he began to spend his winnings in advance.

It had taken little more than a month to accumulate what Monroe called a stake. And although the process of getting together all the capital had been frantic, rushed, desperate, as if everything would go wrong and all would be lost if the money were not secured immediately, once Monroe had the necessary sum he paused, he was moved to proceed slowly. He studied the horse sheets, he did not lay any bets, and he waited, waited for the right horses and the right races, the right combinations of horses and races, for the big killing which he was sure he would be able to make.

Monroe did, however, permit now himself the modest luxury of finding new quarters where he would not be disturbed by the middle-aged drunkard. The new rooming house to which Monroe moved was owned by a brother and sister, John Duncan and his sister Cordelia Duncan. John Duncan was a ne'er-do-well who barely managed to support his drinking on the meager income of the rooming house. His sister Cordelia was ambitious and studied law and was very plain and very intense. When Sidney visited Monroe in the evenings at this rooming house, he brought with him his latest girl friend, Gloria, who was blonde, and who was, Sidney announced, just what you would expect a dizzy blonde to be like. Bringing along his girl friend when he visited friends was a custom of Sidney's which had always been dear to his heart, for he never was sufficiently involved with any young lady to find her company and companionship sufficient unto itself, apart from the physical process and reality which, after all, did not occupy a very great deal of time. Gloria came with Sidney to visit Monroe, and listened as the two young men discussed their money-making venture, their courses, and sometimes the ancient and profound problems in philosophy, in which Sidney was also interested. Gloria stretched out on Monroe's great big bed, chewed gum and smoked cigarettes, and wondered in God's name what on earth

Sidney and Monroe were talking about and if they were really interested, if they were not really just showing off?

One night when Gloria was there, John Duncan knocked on the door of the room, and when Monroe said come in—for the door was open—John Duncan appeared to be angry and embarrassed. He asked Monroe to step into the hall with him for a moment, and when Monroe had come to the other end of the dimly lighted hallway, he whispered to him.

"I don't know how you fellows from other parts of the country feel about it," said John Duncan in a whisper of anguish, "but I would not want to be left alone in a room with my own sister."

"I am sorry," said Monroe. He was perplexed, and he told John Duncan that he would not have female visitors again, but when he returned to the room and told Sidney and Gloria what John Duncan had said, he was dumbfounded when they laughed and then had to explain that John Duncan's remark was hilarious.

"Monroe may know all about philosophy and all about horses," said Gloria as she went home with Sidney, "but that's all he does know. He is just a lamb, he is just a sweet innocent lamb."

As the spring term drew to a close there was a general relaxation and abandonment in the university city where for so many months through the fall and through the rigors of a northern winter there had been a disciplined, systematic, determined, and virtually musclebound effort to study and to be efficient and to resist temptation of all kinds, if only the temptation to be with one's friends and to converse. Monroe himself, the upright young man, surrendered to the erratic, passionate season by going for long walks along the river near the university city. He was very happy, for he felt that his scheme was certain to succeed, and on his walks he rehearsed the stages in the realization of the money-making scheme and fondly murmured the names of the horses who were promising.

On one of these walks, on a wonderfully radiant blue and gold day in May, he paused and permited his delighted revery to be interrupted by ditch diggers who were digging up sewer pipes which had to be repaired.

"Heavy exercise must be a good way of keeping from being too nervous," said a tall pretty blonde girl who was also regarding the labor of the ditch diggers and who spoke to Monroe as if she had known him for years.

"Yes, I suppose it is," said Monroe, feeling very shy when he saw how very pretty the young lady was. He had never been addressed before by a young lady without being introduced to her, and he was scared as well as delighted. Nevertheless, he moved toward her and discussed the question of daily exercise as a means of keeping in trim, and soon found himself walking her home to the girls' dormitory in which she lived. She was an undergraduate, she was in her third year, and her field of concentration was music. Her name was Kitty Deutsch and she came from Schenectady, New York, where her father was an electrical engineer; he was also, Kitty added regretfully, a Swedenborgian. Monroe in turn described himself in a like way: he was a law student, he had taken his doctorate in philosophy, and his father, who had died during the winter, had been a physician who specialized in diseases of the eye, ear, nose and throat.

"Oh, I am sorry to hear that," said Kitty.

"What?" said Monroe.

"I am sorry that your father died," said Kitty.

"Oh, yes, I am sorry too," said Monroe, who was preoccupied with Kitty's dazzling prettiness, and had mentioned his dead father in an absent-minded way, and merely because Kitty had spoken of her father with a regret which perplexed him.

Monroe, seeking a subject, broke into a description of how

he had given a brief talk at the Philosophy club on the nature of probability and chance, going into detail about what his thesis had been, the objections to it, and how he had answered the objections, telling Kitty all of these things as if nothing in the world would be of more interest to her, and then suddenly interrupting himself.

"Say, Miss Deutsch," he said suddenly and in an uncertain way, as if the question were very difficult to answer, "do you suppose you can have dinner with me this week?"

"I'd be delighted," said Kitty, hurriedly, relieved to hear something she understood, a little startled by the abruptness of the proposal, but looking with a new interest at Monroe, looking at him up and down, and deciding that she was pleased by his looks.

"Then I will call for you at six on Saturday," said Monroe, "I will look forward to it very much." And he made a hasty departure, so great was his pleasure in the acceptance of the invitation, and so fearful had he been that the very pretty girl would not want to have dinner with him, since anyone so pretty as she was must be tied up by all sorts of engagements with the many active young men of the university city.

Departing from his new-found friend, Monroe hastened to seek out Sidney. He was convinced that he was in love and he wanted to discuss the matter at length with Sidney. He had never taken out a girl before, he had never thought of going out with a girl before this day, he had been bored, as by a discussion of the Ubangi or of Australian bushmen, whenever he had heard a discussion of dates, and he knew that Sidney was an expert in all affairs of the heart. Sidney would advise him on how to behave and where to take the girl to dinner.

He did not find Sidney at home; hence he left a note for him, and went to sit on a park bench by the river where the college crew toiled back and forth and the coxswain barked importantly and the sunlight danced an electrical dance on the surface of the sliding waters. Staring at the river, he thought of Kitty, and it was inevitable that he should think of when they would be married, although they had just met, for to be in love and to get married were identical for Monroe. He would marry Kitty as soon as his money-making scheme was set up, or as soon as the horses racing at the racing tracks brought him the substantial fortune he was sure would result in reality, just as at had on paper.

Monroe soon found that he was unable to think of anyone or anything other than Kitty. Sidney was annoyed with him because whenever he called to converse with Monroe on the subject of their money-making scheme Monroe invariably converted the conversation to the subject of his relationship to Kitty. He saved the cigarettes which Kitty had smoked when she went out to dinner with him in a tobacco pouch purchased for the purpose, and he showed them to Sidney, as if they were holy relics or precious manuscripts, mooning over the marks of lipstick upon them. Sidney was quite disgusted, particularly when he learned that Monroe had not yet kissed the lady of his heart. And he stood on the street near her dormitory and waited until she put out the light every night before being able to go home to sleep himself. The idea of sleeping with Kitty had not occurred to Monroe, although, in 1936, when the depression, although stabilized, seemed permanent, such practices had begun to be taken for granted. The idea of spending the night— or weekends—asleep with Monroe had occurred very often to Kitty, and she wondered how soon he would make it possible for her to consent immediately to his first proposal. If Sidney had known that Monroe never thought of what Kitty thought of constantly, he would have refused to believe the truth, or suspected Monroe of an inconceivable sadism of dalliance, a monstrous pleasure in not taking or giving pleasure.

The relationship between Monroe and Kitty was set, poised in a state of transfiguration, in motionless, unbroken ecstasy.

Monroe adored her, he worshipped her, he cherished, treasured, and contemplated with a sacred joy everything she touched and came near. Kitty, although certainly aware and mildly pleased that Monroe adored her, was also extremely disappointed. She expected excitement, she expected activity, wrestling, kisses, and she felt the need to be touched, not adored, but Monroe did not touch her at all, except to take her arm when they crossed the street, and he had not even held her hand when they went to the theatre.

Her disappointment was lessened when she returned to her family at the end of the spring term, for Monroe wrote her special delivery letters every day and he called her up long distance every night, and these tributes had some of the effect of actual love-making because Monroe was not present to show that love for him had very little to do with physical togetherness or biological activity of any kind whatever. She was flattered also because her mother and father were impressed by the ardor and long-distance hour-long telephone calls of her suitor. But despite all this, she still felt that there was something wrong, indeed there was much that was wrong with Monroe as a lover who sought her hand (her *body* as well as her soul), and when she went to the motion pictures and saw the passionate kisses of the hero and heroine, then, more than at any time, she felt the absence of something very important, and carried this feeling home with her as she passed parked cars in which other couples were making love.

Sidney had also left Fairfield. He had taken a job as a waiter in a summer hotel, since all his funds had been put into the so-called pot, which was to make a fortune. Monroe, left alone in the university city, studied the horse sheets absent-mindedly at whatever time was available to him after composing his special delivery letters to Kitty and making long-distance phone calls to her. He wrote to Sidney that the right time had not come to begin to plunge. Sidney mistook his absent-mindedness and his preoccupation for a sensible caution, and was delighted to be reassured.

In the summer hotel where Sidney worked as a waiter, he was at first the same invincible success with the ladies he had expected to be and had always been wherever there were wives somewhat dissatisfied with their husbands and with their lives, interested in variety, and exposed to freedom, free informality, the freshness, the heightened vitality, and the warm radiance of a country summer. But after Sidney had enjoyed what was, for him, the customary number of conquests and was ready to run through the summer ladies a second time (for what during past summers had been called, by one needy but sardonic young matron, a return performance by request), he suffered humiliating and inexplicable repulses. It turned out that a sensational newcomer had appeared, a chauffeur who, because of some physiological abnormality which gave him remarkable prowess and efficacy, became the favorite of all the ardent, necessitous ladies: some wives bragged about what they called his secret weapon. Sidney was welcomed only by those young women who had been turned down by the gifted chauffeur, or put off to some other night, or already used and cast aside. Sidney felt that his rival was like a god, masked in a chauffeur's uniform, and he resented him as any human being would resent the erotic descent of a supernatural being.

On top of this unexpected humiliation, Sidney was unable to make head or tail of Monroe's letters, for they were couched in such abstract and high-flown terms that it was impossible to make out how the scheme was going. His astonishing rejection by the ladies and the infuriating and bewildering obscurity of Monroe's letters made Sidney return to Fairfield in the middle of the summer.

Monroe, when Sidney returned, was in an utterly despondent state: so despondent that he was nothing else, no other emotion seemed to be present. He hardly listened to Sidney and he showed no signs of being pleased that Sidney had returned. What he had to say about the scheme was as vàgue as his letters had been obscure. What had happened was that Kitty had asked him not to write her special delivery every day and not to call her up every night; not only that, she was going to Maine for several weeks, and when Monroe suggested that he visit her there (although this would have been impossible unless Monroe drew upon the money raised for the scheme), she had replied that it would probably be better if they were not in touch with each other for the brief period of a few weeks. This seemed to be a complete rejection to Monroe, and he felt that he was going insane, he was losing his mind. Sidney was not interested at all in Monroe's love affair, he was not his kind and characteristic self sufficiently to point out that Kitty had not *completely* rejected him: if indeed she had rejected him at all. It all seemed weird and foolish—nothing but puppy love— but after a time he did try to cheer up Monroe by remarking that young girls were always fickle. Monroe, beyond consolation of any kind, told Sidney that he did not know or understand Kitty, otherwise he would not think of her and speak of her as if she were just an ordinary young girl and just like all the other young girls, and particularly the tramps with whom Sidney consorted and played house so casually and superficially.

Sidney remarked bemusedly that Monroe's blessed damosel might be better off if only she had a little more of the tramp in her, and Monroe felt so indignant that he turned his face away and stared out of the window, unwilling to speak to a human being who would make such an infamous remark about the angelic woman he loved.

Sidney, tired and vaguely troubled, sought to appease Monroe; he apologized, he even went so far as to say that he hoped he would be in love some day in the way that Monroe was in love—not, however, for several years to come—and that perhaps he did not understand how Monroe felt because he himself had not been fortunate enough to be in love with as wonderful a girl as Kitty. Sidney felt sure that Monroe would detect the falseness and laboriousness with which he spoke, and the half-smile he was unable to suppress, but Monroe was too far gone in despair to notice anything except that there was in Sidney's tone a shift to friendliness and patience. But he did not want to go out to dinner as Sidney proposed, he had been eating at home to save money. He explained to Sidney that a chocolate bar was excellent to kill one's appetite, and he showed Sidney how he had purchased a great deal of canned food—it was really a remarkable bargain—in order to tide him over until they had made their killing.

Looking at the canned goods and seeing that much of it was canned fruit, Sidney was alarmed, and since he knew something of diet he asked Monroe if he had had any stomach trouble. It turned out that Monroe had had diarrhea off and on since purchasing the canned goods, but he reported that he did not mind it very much, he was far too unhappy for another reason, and in a way he thought he was feeling better except for the fact—the all-important fact—that it had become clearer and clearer that Kitty was not in love with him. Sidney was immediately moved to action and Monroe was too despondent to stop him. He packed all the canned goods in cartons which he had extricated from the dark damp cellar of the rooming house in which Monroe was living, and insisted that Monroe tell him the name of the grocer from whom he had purchased so many cans. Undeterred when Monroe kept saying, fearful of the grocer, that he had been given a special discount because he had purchased so many, Sidney went off with the packed cartons to the grocer. The grocer was not unwilling to take back the canned goods, and he told Sidney that he had been under the impression that the purchase was being made for a boarding house; although Monroe did not look like the kind of a person who ran a boarding house, still you never could tell about people in a university town like Fairfield.

Returning with the money he had regained, Sidney insisted

that Monroe come with him to get a good solid meal such as he had not had for several weeks. And when Monroe ate voraciously, Sidney was unable to check himself, he felt that— given the way he had just put himself out for Monroe—he had a right to work off a little steam by making a short and ironic remark, as Monroe gobbled up another helping, on how the desperation of Monroe's love did not seem to have interfered with Monroe's appetite. This brief and passing and idle remark was a catastrophic error, for Monroe immediately stopped eating, his fork midway in air between the plate and his mouth, looked at his wristwatch, checked his wristwatch time with the restaurant clock, paused, put down his forkful, stopped chewing, and announced to Sidney that even though evening rates were not yet in effect, he was going to call up Kitty in Schenectady. Sidney sought to stop him, arguing that Kitty had told him not to call up so frequently and a little pretense of indifference might awaken or revive Kitty's interest. Monroe could not have been stopped by anything less than an earthquake in which he had been a victim along with all the citizens of Fairfield. His face became active and voracious. He cheered up immediately and enormously at the idea of calling up Kitty, and also influenced by the first solid meal he had eaten in weeks.

He went to the phone booth of the restaurant and was gone for twenty minutes; during this interval Sidney amused himself by ogling the young lady at an adjoining table whose young man could not see what was going on, nor that Sidney was making a charming flirtatious impression, immediately terminated by Monroe's return and his announcement that he was going to commit suicide.

Sidney would have taken Monroe's declaration that he was going to commit suicide less seriously, had it not been for the wild, distraught and weird look upon Monroe's face. The deliberations which flashed through his mind were rapid calculations; he did not really believe that Monroe was going to commit suicide, but he felt that anyone who would say that he was going to commit suicide was in a very disturbed, virtually diseased frame of mind. Anything might happen, once a human being said something like that.

No one had ever said anything of the kind to Sidney, no one had ever before avowed a determination to commit suicide, and although he had heard stories about false and true suicides, nevertheless his lack of first-hand experience left him at an absolute loss, as if someone had addressed him passionately in an unknown language.

Monroe sat silent, his face hard as a stone, and otherwise expressionless. He did not seem to desire any sympathy nor to expect any effort to be made to deter him from the act of desperation and destruction to which he had pledged himself. He was merely waiting for the waitress to come with the check. The pause and delay was occasioned by the crowded dinner hour.

"Did you tell Kitty that you were going to commit suicide?" Sidney asked, to break the silence in which Monroe had enclosed himself as in armor behind a visor, or behind the wall of a fortress.

"Yes," said Monroe, a grudging answer.

"What do you mean, yes?" said Sidney in sudden irritation, for he felt that Monroe was mistreating him for reasons which had nothing to do with him. "What did she say?"

"She said that if I really loved her," Monroe replied, "I would not commit suicide. And if I did, that showed I did not love her! I did not care that she would go through life suffering from my suicide."

Sidney admitted to himself that this was indeed a clever and ingenious answer, however ineffectual and self-involved or one-sided. And Sidney was not entirely sure that it was ineffectual. He decided to make no comment on what Kitty had said to Monroe.

The check arrived at last, Sidney paid it, and the two young men departed from the restaurant, Monroe hurrying as if he had some serious reason for haste, some urgency or emergency which would place death beyond his reach very soon.

"Do you mind if I stay with you tonight until you commit suicide?" Sidney inquired, very shyly for one who was not shy, feeling that it was his duty as a friend to stay with Monroe, however foolish he might be or however false his threat of suicide. And as he directed this query at Monroe in as gentle a tone as he could summon up in the immediate impact of the situation and with a physical sense of how fast Monroe was walking on his way to his house and eternity, it occurred to him, as it had not occurred to him before then, that Monroe had said nothing about the method by which he proposed to commit suicide.

"You can stay with me if you like," said Monroe curtly, as if Sidney had injured him, "but you will not dissuade me, and you may find yourself in the middle of a great deal of unwelcome publicity."

Sidney saw the lightning of photographers' flash bulbs as he heard this sentence, and the hubbub of neighbors, reporters, the police, and an ambulance, a midnight scene suggested by motion pictures and his casual daily reading of newspapers. He said nothing and he wondered again how Monroe meant to commit suicide, what method he had in mind. His curiosity, although acute, did not prevent him from remaining silent.

They arrived at the rooming house in which Monroe lived, and went down the hall to the room at the back of the house, Monroe's room, which looked out on a small garden. They entered the room and Sidney noted with pleasure the French windows, which opened upon the garden and which eliminated gas as a method of self-destruction, or thus it seemed to Sidney, who found suicide, in the news, boring, hectic and barren, no matter what method was used.

The room was small and Monroe's bed was a studio couch. There was no place for Sidney to lie down, except the floor. He pointed out this fact to Monroe who replied that Sidney did not have to stay at all, implying that his stay was entirely a favor on Monroe's part, a generous permission granted to a troubled friend.

Monroe neatly disrobed, folded his coat and his trousers with habitual care, garbed himself in an elegant pair of pajamas, brushed his teeth and washed his face, turned back— with the same neatness—the counterpane of the studio couch, and without saying a word to Sidney, who had been regarding these actions from an armchair, smoking, and seeking to be silent and unresponsive—got into bed and went to sleep.

Sidney, who believed that since his intuitions were sometimes correct they were always correct, was possessed by an intuition as to what Monroe had in mind at the very moment that Monroe turned his face to the wall. Sidney was certain that Monroe was waiting for Kitty to call him and beg him to reconsider life and death. And when he saw and heard (for Monroe snored softly) that Monroe had immediately fallen asleep, he thought that sleep was for Monroe a way of being patient, a way of waiting, for thus he would have felt himself had he been waiting for something which he desired very much: he himself would have sought in unconsciousness the luxury of patience.

Since there was no other place for him to lie down, Sidney put the extra pillows of the studio couch upon the floor and stretched out, seeking some repose for himself. Once upon the floor, he remembered that, in the emotional chaos caused by the threat to commit suicide, all thoughts of the infallible money-making scheme had been forgotten. And he felt alarmed as he had not felt before, for he had not believed that Monroe would kill himself, but he could see that in the midst of so much amorous preoccupation Monroe, the one key to the colossal fortune and the sole master of the scheme, would not be very likely to give much time or thought to what, from his present point of view, was at best a side issue.

An hour passed as Sidney permitted these considerations to torment him, and he began to feel very uncomfortable because the floor of the room was hard. The late summer twilight had turned to black night, the room was dark, Monroe was fast asleep, Sidney felt very foolish and, what was in a way worse, he felt very uncomfortable, he felt more and more uncomfortable, he felt that he too would like to fall asleep and forget all trouble and anxiety for the night at least, just as Monroe had. It would not be right to leave a friend in such a state of mind, however irrational and self-indulgent he was, and Sidney told himself that he would never forgive himself if anything happened to Monroe, but the floor was certainly hard, and it was certainly hard to believe that anything would happen to Monroe when one heard him sleeping and breathing so softly and so peacefully.

As soon as Sidney had persuaded himself for the tenth time that it would be wrong and it would be unwise to leave Monroe alone on such a night, he arose to go home. His concern with Monroe, his feeling of responsibility towards a close friend, had exhausted itself by the eloquent arguments he had made to himself to persuade himself to stay, and the sheer physical discomfort of lying on the floor, near the carpet, which was dusty and unclean, made him get up and go home, leaving a note, however, in which he asked Monroe to call him about something important which had to do with Kitty as soon as he awoke. The ingenuity of this note was wasted, for it would have had no effect on Monroe, nor would he have noticed its calculated cleverness.

Sidney slept until noon in his own room, waking up anxious and guilty. He dressed quickly, he did not shave, he hurried to Monroe's room, afraid that something might have happened. But Monroe was not there, and his dissheveled bed suggested complete disaster to Sidney. He had had no breakfast, the pangs of hunger ached in him, but he dismissed his need, telling himself that he had behaved very badly in leaving Monroe alone, and seeking expiation by denying himself breakfast. He could not think of where to go to look for Monroe, nor what else there was to do, apart from notifying the police, which was surely unwise and at best a last resort, for it meant, probably, publicity all over the college town, and in the three daily papers.

He looked for Monroe in the library, he looked for him in the college cafeteria, he returned to Monroe's rooming house to ask the landlady if she had seen him, and when she reported that she had not, and that he had not picked up his morning mail, Sidney concluded in a panic that perhaps Monroe had thrown himself into the river, from which he would be dragged up three days hence. The more he thought of it, the more he believed that suicide by drowning must have been what was in Monroe's mind and must have been the reason why he had been unconcerned about the method of his suicide. Sidney suddenly remembered then, appropriately, relevently, and fearfully, that Monroe did not know how to swim.

He told himself that his mind worked in an utterly frivolous, shallow, and trivial way, for he had not been aware in the least —or he had not taken seriously—something which was a matter of life and death. He had regarded Monroe's state of mind as a child's tantrum, he had not been sufficiently intelligent to see that he walked in the midst of life and death, no matter what he did, nor where he was—on land, on sea, in city and country, in solitude and in society.

As he said this to himself, he passed the Versailles, the most expensive restaurant in town, glanced through the plate glass idly, saw Monroe seated at a table there, eating, and casting a superior eye at the morning paper. With the immense relief of a convalescent who has been very ill, he rushed in, shook hands with Monroe delightedly, as if he had not seen him for a long time and as if one of them had won a prize! Told him how glad he was to see him, grinned at him, so great was his pleasure, and refused to allow his conscious mind to consider the sumptuous meal which Monroe was calmly munching.

Monroe offered no explanation of anything whatever. He said nothing of why he was where he was, nothing of the suicide he had contemplated the day before, nothing about his future failure, so to speak, to commit suicide. Had Sidney been less relieved to find Monroe still alive, politeness would not have prevented him from questioning Monroe about his present plans for the immediate future. Despite the emotion of relief, Sidney, looking at Monroe, had difficulty in believing that he gazed at the friend who had been so desperate, stone-faced, wild, and distraught the day before.

Monroe had dined on shrimp cocktail, tomato bisque, a tenderloin steak. He was topping it off with a frosted chocolate sundae, peppermints, and coffee. There was a certain unconscious but unmistakable satisfaction—almost complacency —upon his face, the look of one who has been enjoying himself with a clear conscience in a way to which he is entitled. Sidney ordered a pot of tea, thinking that tea might calm him down. He was not hungry; his appetite had been destroyed by the emotions from which he had suffered while looking for Monroe. Then, remembering that he had had no breakfast, he also ordered toast.

"The food is quite good here," Monroe asked in a tone of gentle tact, "don't you feel well?"

Taking this as a comment on his meager order of toast and tea, Sidney felt that he was faced by a maniac and a monster.

"How do you feel?" he asked by way of answer.

"Just fine," said Monroe, "and I hope you don't mind if I rush off, there are several important things which I must attend to immediately."

Sidney was dumbfounded again. He had known Monroe for almost a year, but he had never behaved with *this* lack of connection, *this* degree of unrelatedness—a would-be suicide in the evening, but then, a mere twelve hours after, a preoccupied, self-satisfied man of the world. Sidney was too baffled to say anything whatever as Monroe made his departure.

Sidney returned to his own place and sought by reading a work expounding the nature of relativity physics to forget about the chaos of perception and response into which he had been plunged by Monroe's behavior. Often before he had reached for and grasped forgetfulness, consolation, and new strength by reading works of this kind, which, having nothing or very little to do with what chiefly concerned him and meant the most to him in relation to his hopes, his desires, and his future, he could regard with a free and serene mind—or rather, this was the freedom and serenity of mind which he gained as he strove to fathom the book in the way that some play chess or try to solve cross-word puzzles. Moreover, there was also involved in such reading what Sidney was wont to call "the hidden dividend," or which he sometimes termed, when he wanted to be amusing and colloquial, "the unexpected gravy." These works were full of information which others did not expect Sidney to possess—their expectation was quite natural—and he knew the joy of schoolboys who throw snowballs at adult pedestrians when he sprang his unexpected and often esoteric knowledge at others, delighting perhaps more than anything else in the smiling deprecation of his possession of that knowledge (this was one of the ways in which he enjoyed the surprise), or at other times taking pleasure in assuring and doubly dumbfounding his listeners by maintaining that there was nothing strange, out of character, or learned in his knowing about such matters. "After all, I am a baccalaureate, I did matriculate for four years," he said, when he felt drawn to the superior attitude that it was quite natural and to be taken for granted that he knew about these difficult and recondite studies and sciences.

This method of self-consolation and self-escape was useless throughout the summer afternoon, as Sidney sat in the window-seat of his small room. The afternoon darkened, the summer sky clouded over, Sidney hardly noticed that this was happening until the darkening affected his reading of the page, and then suddenly, there was a blowing in the leaves of the trees in the garden in back of his room, there was a sharp chill, and in a few moments, thunder and lightning, the thrashing of the rain and dashes of wet against the screen window. The entire environment in which Sidney had seated himself to read and forget this immediate problem had changed profoundly, and Sidney looked up from his book as if from a terrifying dream to a strong apprehension, an anxiety as painful as an ache in his side after running too much. Where was Monroe? What was he doing? Nothing had been said of the money-making scheme, and nothing above all, about the money. He felt as he did when he was afraid of missing a train, and he rushed downstairs to the phone next to the hat-rack and the mirror in the hallway of the rooming house, called up Monroe, dialed the number wrongly, heard the empty ringing of the wrong number in a house in which as it happened, no one was home, thought of trying again just in case—though it seemed unlikely to him he had dialed the wrong number, just as he was always astounded when he was wrong in any way—and as he dialed remembered that the landlady was almost invariably at home at Monroe's rooming house. He got the right number, talked to Monroe's landlady, and learned from her virtually nothing: she had not seen Monroe all day, she told him what he already knew and was now of no help to him, that Monroe had slept in his bed that night; and he hardly listened when she suggested in response to the urgency in his voice that she leave a note for Monroe to call Sidney as soon as he returned.

Sidney felt foolish and weak: his knees knocked against each other as he put the receiver back upon the hook and returned to his room. How, he asked himself, could he have been so foolish as to let Monroe depart after what had occured during the past twenty-four hours? How could he have permitted himself to forget that Monroe had in his possession a very important twenty-four thousand dollars which was supposed to transform the immediate future of himself and several other extremely interested people? Thinking these thoughts, Sidney forgot that the day before he had been naturally very much troubled by the suicide Monroe meant to commit, and he also forgot that he had been sufficiently concerned and aware to return from a distance of two hundred miles to Fairfield for the sake of finding out just what Monroe was doing or not doing.

He had an overwhelming sense of his own unawareness, helplessness and deviceless inadequacy. For where was one to look for Monroe? He might be anywhere. He might very well merely have gone to the motion pictures, of which he was very fond, of which he had said the previous winter: "in our kind of work, that kind of relaxation is invaluable." It would be rather ridiculous to go and look for him at the university theatre, although Sidney recalled the relevant fact that doctors of philosophy had been paged there, including Monroe himself. Perhaps Monroe had decided to commit suicide after all. For a moment Sidney entertained, with a logic intensified by his own alarm about the money in Monroe's possession, the conclusion that *if* Monroe had committed suicide, the situation could be liquidated or resolved in a way that was not entirely disastrous to him, for the money would be intact. He was immediately ashamed of himself for thinking such thoughts and for not being more concerned about Monroe: Monroe, to be just, had done nothing whatever to deserve death. He did not merit capital punishment, even if he had condemned himself to death.

Sidney's panic came and went in waves like an attack of acute indigestion, or like an attack of colitis. On the one hand—he thought suddenly that now he was thinking just as Monroe wrote letters, in which repeatedly he wrote "on the one hand," but never arrived at whatever was on the other hand—what could happen, what could Monroe do?—apart from killing himself—what conceivable move could he make which would be disastrous or catastrophic? But then again, with Monroe's recent behavior in mind, one could not help but have the vague yet extremely intense conviction that Monroe was bound to do something wrong.

At nightfall, after calling up Monroe's rooming house twice again and annoying Monroe's landlady by his pointless and prolonged persistence, Sidney went to Monroe's room to see for himself. Under the landlady's suspicious gaze, he inspected Monroe's room, seeking to find evidence that Monroe had departed. His dresser was full of shirts, his shaving things, his comb and brush were in their appointed places, his shoes and shirts were there, no drawer had been emptied, and there was no sign that Monroe had left town. Sidney withdrew, at a loss and in unconcealed dismay, murmuring inaudible regrets and senseless apologies to Monroe's landlady. He went to the motion pictures himself, largely for their own sake, yet partly too with some small, intense, irrational last straw of a hope that somehow in the darkness of the theatre he would encounter his absent, missing, wayward and erratic friend and partner.

Sidney did not hear from Monroe for three days. During those three days he moved through dark, distressing recesses of actionless immobility and nameless fear.

Soon after Sidney had left Monroe to his own nameless devices and the profound, serene isolation of sleep, on the night that he had proposed to commit suicide, Kitty had called Monroe long distance from Schenectady. She dreamed that Monroe had killed himself, awakened in a state of terror, and called him to find out if he were dead. "No, I am not dead," Monroe said in a drowsy voice, garbed in his pajamas and dressing gown. Reassured but afraid that she must be near Monroe if she were to avoid the repetition of the fear he had induced in her, she told him that she was returning to Fairfield as soon as the next train would get her there and she would stay there for the rest of the summer, until school began again. It was with this delightful prospect in view that Monroe had been dining in serene joy at the Versailles when Sidney found him there; he had expected Kitty to arrive within two hours, at about three o'clock in the afternoon, and he was very happy; he was sure that Kitty was going to marry him very soon, if she were so concerned about his well-being, his survival, his life and his death. But Kitty had changed her mind, and Monroe found a telegram waiting for him when he returned to his rooming house to prepare himself to go to meet Kitty at the railroad station. In the telegram Kitty said only that she had to make an unavoidable change of plans. Monroe had called her long distance again, disappointment like a bitter taste in his mouth, and tried to persuade her to come or at least to explain to him why she had changed her mind. He was too excited to renew his threat of self-destruction, he merely begged her, and when she refused, he proposed that he come to see her in Schenectady, and when she refused to see him if he came, Monroe was more desperate than ever, convinced that all was over, and although he summoned up one more convulsion of persuasion—declaring that he would come to Schenectady and stand in the doorway of her house—she then replied that she would see to it that the door was not opened. Monroe stopped, silenced by his image of rejection and repudiation, imagining his terror of embarrassment if he stood at the door of her house and no one answered the bell. He wished Kitty the best of luck, shifting his tone entirely from intimate desperation to polite resignation, and speaking as if Kitty were about to marry another man or he were about to go forth to war in a foreign country.

Monroe's resignation did not last very long. He felt the need of action, any kind of action; the more bold and daring the action, the more it would serve to free him from the emotions caused by Kitty's quick changes of mind. He went to the bank, secured as much money as he could, and then went to a bookmaker's establishment, where, in the course of the afternoon, completely forgetting all his careful and elaborate plans and promising himself—chanting to himself—that he who was not lucky in love would be lucky at cards, he splurged and lost all the money which had been laboriously gotten together: he bet on one long shot after another, and he lost again and again, and the more he lost, the more he felt that it made less and less difference if he lost again, so that it turned out to be not at all difficult to lose all the money on which so much had depended. The downward path to the abyss had been as rapid and sudden as a bolt of lightning.

Returning to his room, Monroe had slowly been overtaken by a sense of what he had done. And the realization made him want to tell Kitty what he had done as a way of confessing that he was, in all truth, wholly unworthy of her, he had violated the trust of his friends, he had acted wantonly, foolishly and at the mercy of his own disappointment, he was without question a wholly worthless human being. He called Schenectady again and he told Kitty these things in a low tone and in a voice of resigned sincerity, and said again and again, as he described his sudden debacle, that he was obviously unworthy of her. The effect upon Kitty was tonic and electric, the opposite of his conscious intention and precisely what he had hoped to hear when he had said he would kill himself. She immediately declared that it had all been her fault, for she had made Monroe desperate: if she had not changed her mind he would not have "splurged" (the word Monroe used repeatedly in describing his actions). Monroe's abandoned leap and fall had the effect upon her of a shock (as, upon some girls, four-letter words, verbal violence, a twisted arm, an overt sexual move), and an intense drama to which all that was eager and passionate in her responded. Hours of careful seduction would have had far less effect than the tragic drama of Monroe's losses, which Kitty referred immediately, directly, and solely to herself, which pressed against her virtually as if Monroe had been pressing against her in a rough, demanding, confident, imperious embrace.

Moved by this new emotion, Kitty told Monroe to come to Schenectady as soon as he could, she would take all her money from the bank and they would go to New York to get married unless her parents consented to an immediate marriage. Monroe was overjoyed and at the same time stupified by the very rapid shift in events: but he knew that what he wanted most of all was to marry Kitty, and he feared that something might occur—Kitty might change her mind again or his partners might find out what he had done with all the money and take some serious action against him—something might occur, something probably would occur to keep him from what he wanted so much: the possession of Kitty. Hence, he hastened to Schenectady, chanting under his breath all the way "unlucky at cards, lucky in love," where Kitty had been arguing vainly with her parents to permit her to marry Monroe immediately using as an argument the sorry straits which Monroe's love of her had brought him to, an argument which made her parents believe with greater conviction what they had believed all along, that Monroe certainly was not the most desirable husband in the world for Kitty. The parents perceived Kitty's overwrought urgency, but the entire situation had descended upon them so suddenly (as if a plane had crashed in their backyard garden) that they merely suggested weakly and in a state of shock that Kitty become engaged and wait the mere nine months until graduation before marrying Monroe, or at least a mere six months, to which Kitty replied that this was just what all parents proposed, as she knew from what the girls said at school, when what they really wanted was to stop a marriage entirely.

Monroe entered Kitty's household and met her parents in the midst of the increasingly irritated exchange of the discussion of an immediate marriage, interrupting them by his arrival. His serene appearance at first put off, surprised, and distracted Kitty's parents, who had expected a young man who looked like the younger brother of Dracula, Lon Chaney, Dr. Jekyl and Mr.

Hyde, Caliban, and Henry the Eighth or Charles Laughton. And when Monroe, moved by politeness and his natural tendency to yield to strangers and those who were older than he was, explicity entertained the idea of a delay and a postponement, Kitty's parents were very pleased and Kitty was furious. She had reached that point in the passage and travail of her passions where any pause or change of direction, however trivial, was complete frustration and loss; she insisted that Monroe come with her, she would not stay with a father and mother who did not understand their own daughter, she was going to elope! Monroe awkwardly and constrainedly — his hesitation informing the movements of his limbs—followed Kitty to her bedroom where she packed a few things quickly. He looked back at the father and mother as if to say that if they would only do something, a new set of actions might be set in motion to alter the juggernaut course of events, but the parents, looking at him and shamed by their daughter's behavior, for which nothing in the past had prepared them, could think of nothing whatever to do. Monroe shook hands sheepishly with Kitty's father and slowly followed Kitty from the house, feeling guilty and carrying with him the image of the silenced, offended, bewildered parents, wounded us never before by their only child's vivid and silent departure.

Once Monroe and Kitty had boarded the train for Maryland, where they could be married without any delay whatever, both became aware of shifting emotions. Kitty began to feel a little sorry for her parents, and she sought to soothe herself by telling herself that she would make it all up to them in a sweet reconciliation soon after the marriage was a reality, and besides they had not shown any real sympathy for her sufferings, they had not understood her at all, in any way whatsoever. Monroe forgot about Kitty's parents, forgot his sympathy for them, began to be more and more exhilarated until be became exalted, telling himself that here, next to him, was Kitty, the girl he wanted so much—wanted more than life itself! His exaltation was broken and interrupted now and again by the thought of the money he had wasted, plunged, and "splurged," but he was too intensely happy not to be able to put aside his remorse, such as it was, telling himself that nothing is as useless as regrets, why cry about spilt milk, nothing could be done now about the money, it was too late, he would pay it back as soon as everything was settled and straightened out as it was surely going to be now that he was going to be married to Kitty. Monroe had seen many motion pictures since the age of four come to a happy conclusion at the moment of marriage: surely it would be the same for him. Once Ellsworth had said that Columbus had discovered not only America but Hollywood. In his mounting happiness, Monroe forgot Ellsworth's wry comment that Columbus was entirely self-deceived and unaware, and closer to Hollywood than to the Indies in 1492.

Monroe and Kitty were married in Maryland and returned the next day to Fairfield, where Monroe, determined to be prudent now that he was married, and moving as he had always, feeling that he must, from extreme to extreme, found the least expensive room in town, a room which cost just two dollars and fifty cents a month.

Sidney rushed to see Monroe when he heard that he had returned to Fairfield, wondering and angry that Monroe had not called him and thinking that perhaps now, with the collapse of the money-making scheme, Monroe was going to try to avoid him.

Monroe greeted him warmly and without any sign of guilt or misgiving, introducing Kitty as his bride with a pride which seemed to Sidney to imply that he had invented marriage. When Sidney arrived, they were engaged, like typical newly-weds, in fondly tidying their small and miserable room, and Monroe was helping to put up the curtains which Kitty had just made. Sidney saw that Monroe was so happy he did not even remember the great scheme to make a colossal fortune. And although Sidney was very angry and very disappointed and desperately troubled about what would have to be done about all the money that had been lost, nevertheless he liked Monroe so much and the mood of happiness and self-delighting domesticity was so intense and so contagious that Sidney was caught up into it, forgetting his anxiety about the money and the depressed impact which the small, narrow, grim and dreary room had made upon him when he had first entered it.

In the midst of mutual pleasure and conviviality, Sidney forced himself to think of his duty, which was to ask Monroe what was going to be done about all the money which had been thrown away so quickly. Thinking that probably Monroe would not like to discuss the calamity before Kitty, he tried to be tactful by telling Monroe that he wanted to speak to him privately. But Monroe declared with pride, love, and rhetoric that he neither had nor would he ever have any secrets whatever from Kitty, placing his arm around her shoulders, and then adding that he had no secrets in any case, he was not the kind of a person to have secrets. When Sidney succeeded in interrupting his eloquent pronouncement long enough to raise the question of the lost money, Monroe announced blandly and with the utmost assurance and confidence—as if no problem was involved and no difficulty—that he would pay back every cent out of his own pocket as soon as possible.

Sidney wanted to know how. Monroe elaborated a scheme which obviously delighted him and seemed to him to answer all the needs of the situation. He was going to become a tutor; he was going to tutor the rich undergraduates who wasted money in going to tutoring schools which did not help them in passing examinations as much as Monroe might—in fact, surely would, being a Phi Beta Kappa, and a doctor of philosophy. He would pay back the money in weekly sums, he explained, and he showed Sidney an elaborate chart and schedule which explicitly organized every waking hour of the day and the week so that he would be tutoring as much as possible. He also showed Sidney a budget which demonstrated to Monroe's satisfaction the easy practicality of his scheme for returning the money, and a list of unfortunate investors, among whom, as Sidney silently noted, he himself was not included.

The more Monroe explained, the more pleased he was with himself, until he was so pleased that he suggested that they all go out and get some coffee. In the face of Monroe's calm of mind and contentment with the future, Sidney found it difficult to remember what had disturbed him so much. They went to the Versailles, for Monroe insisted that they go there, and drank coffee and ate cheese cake—"Kitty is an excellent cook," Monroe remarked in passing—and when Sidney finally made his departure, he was so much a part of the joy of the newly maried couple that only after he had been by himself for an hour did he begin to think of what had happened, and to be aware that, in departing, he had escaped two creatures made insane by joy: he had left a fool's paradise which Monroe's comprehensive, ingenious and indestructible optimism conjured up like a summer balloon or a Mardi Gras.

Not all the participants and investors were as easy to appease as Sidney had been (partly because he was full of good nature and he was very fond of Monroe): Newland Cameron was very angry when he heard the news and he said that his uncle, Stewart Cameron, who had put up the major part of the cash was very angry too. When Newland heard how the money had been lost, how the foolproof system had been ignored, he was so angry that he wanted to hit Monroe for being so complete and so untrustworthy a fool, and only Kitty's unexpected return from shopping halted Newland, who grew more and more infuriated as he became more aware of Monroe's bland serenity amid catastrophic bankrupcy. He was unwilling to look at Monroe's chart and budget, and Monroe's declarations that he would pay it all back, week by week, seemed quite implausible to Newland, while Monroe sought to seize upon Newland's unwillingness to look at his chart and budget as a way of putting Newland in the wrong. Newland paid no attention to this diversion, and only when Kitty burst into tears did he stop uttering threats which, as they became more physical, became more unreal. Kitty's tears made him leave with one final threat which was more serious because it was more practicable than the others, the announcement that his uncle had said that he would go to the dean and tell him what had happened, a threat which made Monroe afraid that he would be expelled from law school.

As a result of this interview, Kitty proposed that a reconciliation with her parents be effected as soon as possible, for her father was wealthy enough to be able to help out, and besides she very much wanted to be reconciled. It was necessary to borrow the train fare from Sidney to go to Schenectady, but the enterprise worked as well as anyone could have hoped or expected: Kitty's father gave the newlyweds half of the sum which Monroe had lost, and he gave Kitty a weekly allowance which would be enough to enable both of them to live comfortably until Kitty was graduated at the end of the year. He attempted to prevent the couple, who had been exalted, lifted into a new stratosphere of bliss by his generosity, from becoming dependent upon him by warning them—in a tone which sought but failed to be grim, for he was unable to take seriously a course of action which was incredible—that he would not help them at all after the year was over and Kitty's schooling had been completed. But neither Kitty nor Monroe were in a state of awareness or of being in which it was possible for them to be concerned about what their problems would be at a time so distant in the future as nine long months: Newland Cameron's fearful visit had isolated them in the immediate present. They left Schenectady in ecstasy, an ecstasy of feeling free suddenly and absolutely of terrifying problems, a bliss of feeling free to enjoy all the newness and all the new arrangements and routines of married life. When they returned to Fairfield, they took Sidney to dinner—the best dinner in town— and Monroe kept telling Sidney that all was well which ended well: Sidney remarked to himself upon the good fortune which guards the foolish and the innocent. It seemed to him that probably Monroe and Kitty were so happy because they were having so much fun in bed, an explanation which occurred to him because it would have been true of himself under the same or like circumstances. Perhaps there is a great deal to be said for marriage, after all, he said to himself, questioning his own resolution not to marry until he was thirty-five at the very least, and thinking of the girls he might marry, if he but wanted to, a survey which changed his mind quickly since the very process of thinking of the absent girls made many of them seem very desirable to him and no one of them made him forget about all the others.

Monroe's bliss brimmed over during the following week, when, by paying them back in part, he made his peace with the Camerons, both nephew and uncle, and received a grateful apology from Newland, who went so far as to say that he hoped the unfortunate incident would be entirely forgotten and they would be good friends as before. Monroe's joy passed into action: he decided that they must get a good apartment, and when they went looking for a new apartment, nothing but one in the best and most expensive apartment house in Fairfield suited Monroe in the least. Kitty suffered from misgivings and compunctions, but after voicing them briefly, she yielded to Monroe's superior judgment, to his governing dictatorial tyrannical and Napoleonic emotion that the world now belonged to him. No sooner had the apartment been rented (with a lease for three years—Monroe assured Kitty it would be easy to sublet the place if they went to live elsewhere) than Monroe went to look for furniture with an increasing drunkenness of delight and exaltation: with a sense that life was just beginning or beginning all over again and with the feeling that existence would always be joyous, now that he was married.

Monroe was not in the least satisfied by any of the furniture he saw—Kitty was pleased by everything she looked at—and only by a long luxurious survey of the catalogues of furniture companies did he find what he really wanted, which Kitty too liked very much, understanding—as she thought—why Monroe had been so critical of the furniture they had seen. But the furniture which Monroe wanted had to be made to order and would take three months to be delivered. Kitty did not like to wait that long, but Mouroe argued convincingly that they were buying objects which they would be using for life, or at least for twenty years, or if not for so long a period of time, then it would be because they had become rich and could afford even better furniture, and thus they would not have to be disturbed by the expense of the furniture they were now buying. They did, however, buy a bed, an unavoidable necessity (Monroe did not care very much for the bed, but recognized that he could not be without a bed unles he wanted to sleep on the floor), and, as a concession to Kitty's desire for some of the necessary instruments of domesticity, Monroe permitted Kitty to buy a kitchen table, kitchen chairs, pots, pans, dishes, knives and forks, all on the condition that they would be replaced with more appropriate ones when they had the furniture they had ordered.

It was with no little pleasure and pride that Monroe invited Sidney to visit him in his apartment, inviting him to his home as a married man for the first time, and surprising himself by the pleasure which the invitation gave him. Sidney asked Ellsworth Clark, whom he had come to see more frequently now that Monroe was married, if he wanted to come with him, and Ellsworth, who did not know Monroe very well, nevertheless did want to go, for he had been made very curious by what he had heard of all that had occurred since the previous fall as a consequence of Monroe's scheme, ideas, aspirations, and adventures.

Strolling after dinner toward the apartment of the newly wedded couple, Ellsworth expressed his feeling of perplexity about Sidney's attitude toward Monroe—for the friendship had

continued as warm as ever—and asked him how he now regarded the money-making scheme. Ellsworth had been more
sceptical than anyone else invited to participate in the scheme.

"I still think it is an excellent scheme," said Sidney, "it is
just that we did not give enough weight to the human element,
a foresight which was really impossible: *just how could anyone
know that Monroe would fall in love?*"

Ellsworth did not argue with Sidney, feeling, as he often
had felt before, that nothing was ever proven, nothing was
ever established as true or false, since the human mind was
always able to devise some formula, some formulation, explanation or mystification, which blurred or denied the fact that
one's judgment had been wrong.

"I like Monroe anyway," said Sidney, feeling the criticism
in Ellsworth's silence, "I can see how impractical he is, but
he has many redeeming qualities. It is foolish to give up all
that is good in a friend just because of his faults."

They discussed this delicate and difficult question until they
arrived at Monroe's apartment by the river.

Both young men were taken aback by the bareness or nakedness of the apartment—it was like an empty warehouse's interiors
—and by Monroe's garb when he opened the door and greeted
them. He was in a dressing gown, slippers, and pajamas, and
looked as if this was precisely the attire anyone would expect.

Monroe explained that there was very little furniture in the
house; their furniture was being made to order and would not
arrive for three months. Consequently, he and Kitty had to
receive their guests in the bedroom. If they wanted chairs,
Monroe would get the kitchen chairs and bring them into the
bedroom, but most people did not mind sitting on the floor
and there was a theory that it was good to sit on the floor, and
now that he thought of it, the Greeks and the Japanese did not
have chairs and did not seat themselves, in our sense of the
word, but sat on the floor.

Ellsworth sought to exchange glances with Sidney, but Sidney would not look at him, and besides it was too dark to see any-one's face clearly. When the visitors entered the bedroom, they were astonished again. Kitty was in bed, sitting up, backed up by two pillows. They greeted her and made light, polite, facetious remarks, and seated themselves on the floor, against the wall, while Monroe returned to bed—it was a very big four-poster bed—next to Kitty.

The circumstances were too remarkable, from the point of view of the visitors, to permit of easy conversation, but Sidney tried hard, forcing himself.

"This is just where one would expect to find a bride and a bridegroom—in bed," he said, grinning grimly.

Monroe looked disturbed by the remark as if it had been licentious, salacious, pornographic, indeed one might go so far as to say obscene. Kitty, however, giggled, she giggled so much that Sidney wondered if his remark had been far more comical than he had supposed. Then he perceived a movement under the covers—the movement of a hand—and he saw that Monroe had been tickling Kitty. A moment after, Monroe had begun to giggle in a way which seemed very strange to the visitors. It was a giggle like the neighing of a horse, or at any rate the giggle of someone who was not used to giggling very much. Kitty had retaliated by tickling Monroe with much more vim and energy than Monroe's, and he in turn increased the range and tempo of his tickling.

Soon Sidney and Elsworth were seriously embarrassed and now they did exchange glances dimly, the glances of the un-married when they are confronted—in fact, trapped!—by the explicit affection of those who have just been married and who believe that the whole world participates in their joy, and enjoys beholding a prolonged and explicit demonstration of it.

"We can't stay very long," said Sidney suddenly, feeling his embarrassment had reached the point of torment as the mutual tickling not only continued but reached new phases of hilarity, squirming, upheaval, uproar, and convulsion.

Kitty, more sensitive to others than Monroe, was immediately aware that something was wrong. She stopped tickling her husband, and he stopped because she had stopped.

"Would you like to have some cocoa?" Kitty inquired. "We really are not being very good hosts." Some memory of the good manners of her parents' household had moved her to speak, though her parents did not serve cocoa.

The visitors refused the cocoa, but Kitty's trembling tone, the slight quaver in her voice, made the two young men feel that a departure just at that moment would be precipitate and offend Kitty. Monroe dismounted from bed, a tortuous operation since Kitty and he had become a little entangled and mixed up while tickling each other, and went to get the family schedule to show to his friends. Ellsworth and Sidney looked at it together, fascinated by its minuteness, comprehensiveness, rationality, and insanity. Only six hours were left for sleep, and—as the visitors looked at the carefully-ruled and annotated and timed blueprint of twenty-four hours—Monroe explained that six hours were enough, perhaps more than enough for sleep, once the foolish habit of sleeping longer than necessary had been overcome, though he had not yet persuaded Kitty that this was true: that Thomas Alva Edison had slept only four hours a night made no impression whatever on Kitty, who replied that she was not a genius. But what troubled Sidney most of all was the apparent fact that Monroe and Kitty seldom saw each other, according to the detailed plan. Monroe had decided that Kitty's dedication to music was important and should continue, but it was equally important that she should know enough philosophy to share her husband's intellectual interests. Since she had only a year more at school, she had to engage in a speed-up program, which Monroe had carefully worked out for her, and which was intended to bring her up to date in philosophy within six months: this was to be accomplished by Kitty's "sitting-in," or "auditing," of every course in philosophy she could attend when she was not taking the courses in music which were required for her degree. Meanwhile, it was clear that Monroe was even more engaged than Kitty, he was booked up for fifteen hours a day, every day of the week, except perhaps national holidays. Despite his father-in-law's generosity, he had not abandoned his career as a tutor; he tutored all day, or attended courses which would help him to extend the span of courses in which he could tutor, and then used the entire evening until three o'clock in the morning for his own work.

"When do you see each other?" asked Ellsworth, unable to suppress his curiosity.

"Oh, we manage," said Monroe. "We manage," added Kitty and they broke into a new giggle, embarrassing their visitors all over again, and making them determined to leave immediately.

As they closed the door behind them, Ellsworth thought he heard the rising glee of giggling again, but he was not sure that this was not just his imagination and merely suggested by what had already occurred. Ellsworth made no comment, aware that Sidney had been very much disturbed by the visit.

"Let's go and have a drink," said Sidney. He did not want to go back to his own solitude and self without interposing some different passage of consciousness between himself and the visit he had just made.

Ellsworth assented, though he had wanted to go home and prepare for the next day's labors. He had been more amused and astonished than disturbed, being less involved—hardly at all involved—with Monroe.

"He is a noble fool," said Sidney when they arrived at a bar and ordered their drinks. "He is foolish, but he is as noble as he is foolish. There is something exalted, romantic, heroic about everything foolish in Monroe and all his foolish actions, schemes, schedules, theories, and opinions."

"I know what you mean," said Ellsworth, who wanted to be sympathetic to Sidney. "You mean that the foolishness of most human beings is mean and disgusting and that Monroe's is a relief, in a way." There was no conviction in Ellsworth's tone, and the last phrase, "in a way," expressed his true attitude, as Sidney immediately recognized.

"It is perfectly true," Sidney added, responding to Ellsworth's unexpresed doubt, "that the world would collapse very quickly if everyone were like Monroe. But since that's not very likely, since it is really inconceivable—and since, if many others were like Monroe, and thought and acted as he does, he himself would not be the noble fool that he is—I can't help feeling that I like him very much."

Sidney's conclusion was so lame that Ellsworth was only able to repeat in different words what Sidney had just said, and add that the old saying was true: "God loves fools, drunkards and the United States of America."

During the first week of the new school term, Sidney encountered Kitty on the steps of the university library. She seemed to be loitering there, books under her arm, sunning herself in the warm September afternoon. She seemed to want to talk to anyone, and not to Sidney in particular.

"Why don't you ask me to have a cup of coffee with you?" said Kitty in a way which, had it not been the wife of a friend, and of Monroe at that, would have appeared to Sidney to be extremely flirtatious. They went to the usual drugstore, and then, hesitantly and yet at the same time, with intense determination, Kitty began to question Sidney about how a husband and wife made love. Was there a long period before they *really* made love? Was it mostly hugging and kissing and tickling and affection for a long time?

The questions became more pointed as Sidney sought to evade them by judicious generalities, remarking awkwardly that there was a good deal of variation among individuals, and it depended upon the temperaments of the husband and the wife.

"What kind of a temperament would you say Monroe has?"

asked Kitty, unwilling to be put off, although Sidney was clearly becoming more and more uneasy.

"You must know better than I do," Sidney answered, standing up as a way of suggesting an end to the conversation or at least the subject.

"I don't know," said Kitty, "but then I don't know much about men, or about being a wife either." She looked disappointed at not finding out more from Sidney. But she rose to go, recognizing that Sidney felt that a point of honor was involved in not discussing Monroe intimately with her. She had been on the verge of asking Sidney whether he had ever taken Monroe along when he went "wenching"—a term used by other girls in her dormitory, which Kitty remembered, rather than some other word with the same meaning, because it sounded like "wrenching" (and because love-making had looked to her like wrestling)—but Sidney's look prohibited the question.

After he had gone back to his own work and tried to dismiss the whole matter from his own mind as being none of his business, Sidney—unable to concentrate on his book—realized what he had been trying to keep from thinking: it was extremely probable that the consummation of the marriage had not occurred. There could be no other explanation, no matter how ingeniously Sidney tried to find one, of the leading, penetrating, more and more intimate questions which Kitty had asked him, selecting him not only because he was a close friend of Monroe's bus also because he was known as the Don Juan of Fairfield, in the girls' dormitories.

Sidney was shocked. He was, reflecting upon it, surprised that he was shocked, and surprised by the intensity of his feeling. He would have supposed that there were many other things which would have disturbed him much more, particularly in the region of sexual relationships. It seemed on the surface implausible to him that he would have a feeling about masculinity which included a concern about the behavior of his friends when they married, but it was incontestable that he suffered intense dismay and felt implicated in Monroe's failure—much more implicated, now that he thought of it, and strange as it certainly seemed to him, than he had been by Monroe's foolishness in managing the money-making scheme.

Resistance was of no avail, he could not free or remove his mind from the subject of Monroe's conjugal delinquency, unawareness, patience, absent-mindedness, ignorance, or whatever in God's name one would call it, and he could not down the need and impulse to goad and spur Monroe on to the proper fulfillment of his part as a husband.

"Monroe may be insulted," he said to himself, "but if I don't do something about the whole business, I will probably spend most of my time thinking about it."

Monroe was not at all, not in the least, insulted when Sidney, with the delicacy of one who is walking on eggs—on swans' eggs—and on knives—razor-sharp and taut as a tight rope—and on fire—the boiling fire of a volcano just before eruption—broached the subject to him, apologizing, qualifying each remark, using the most formal and general words such as conjugal responsibility, speaking of his duty as a close friend, pleading with Monroe to tell him to keep his big trap shut if he felt that he was intruding upon the intimacy—the sacred privacy—the—well—bedroom of his marriage. On the contrary, Monroe was entirely delighted, pleased that his dearest concerns were the subject of the most concentrated attention and vehement partisanship—it was as if he were the star player of the football team and his fellows were questioning him about a sprained ankle which might keep him from playing in the big game of the season. Monroe basked, glowed, beamed—and then he blushed, so intense and immense was his pleasure.

It was true that the marriage had not been consummated, he told Sidney. Kitty was a very young girl, after all, and he had at first been afraid of hurting her. There was no longer any reason to fear that, but he did not want to be greedy, sensual, a swine like other fellows—too many husbands had ruined their marriages at the very start by being insensitive to their wives' feelings.

Sidney marveled at the way Monroe had converted an important truth about the clumsiness, impatience, or brutality of bridegrooms on the wedding night into a complete falsehood. But he was puzzled about Monroe's remark that he was not afraid of hurting Kitty any more.

Monroe smiled with the satisfaction of one who has just learned to use an electric razor, acquired a deep freeze, and solved, with ease, and modern, up-to-date efficiency, an age-old problem of mankind. He explained that Kitty had had her hymen removed by a physician. It was her own idea and it was an excellent idea—she had the makings of an efficient wife. It had cost twenty-five dollars.

Sidney groaned in the depths of his being, wept at the sublime, unique waste, told himself pointlessly and passionately that he would have done it for nothing. He guessed immediately that if it had been Kitty's idea to have a surgery performed upon herself, the reason probably had been Kitty's hope that in this way the consummation of the marriage would be hastened.

Poor Kitty, Sidney said to himself, something must be done about this: what a trite thing to say, but what else is there to say? And what can be done?

Sidney arranged to meet Monroe that evening. He refused to let Monroe postpone the meeting by speaking of the urgent tutorial obligations he had. Sidney told Monroe that this was more important, this was as important as anything which was not an immediate question of life and death could be.

Sidney went then to consult with Ellsworth Clark who, as soon as he had heard what the situation was, said that he felt just as Sidney did; although he seemed to feel that the matter was, in a way, comical too, he agreed that action, immediate action, was necessary.

"It is strange how peculiar Monroe's behavior, or lack of

behavior makes one feel," said Ellsworth, "I never would have supposed that I would be disturbed by something like this. After all, everyone's sexual behavior is a private and personal matter. But this is not sexual behavior: this is not really something unconventional and abnormal which is condemned by bigots, puritans, and others who hate life and fear their own instincts and desires. It is the intensity of the unawareness, I mean, the failure to do anything, the—if you know what I mean—the cruelty of unawareness and the appalling innocence! It's like the very beautiful woman Lewis Arthur told me about when he was at the medical school—until she spoke, neither Lewis nor the other internes knew that she was a moron."

"Yes," said Sidney, with uncharacteristic formality, "there is something peculiarly disturbing about it: perhaps we feel that the honor of the male sex is at stake, although I would never before have believed that I gave a hoot about some guy's— any guy's—copulating or not copulating (what a disagreeable word that is!). Maybe we ought to use Latin just to keep everything pure and impersonal and upon the same high level as pure Monroe and poor Kitty do, in that empty apartment: tickling! Twenty-five dollars to get rid of something unique and irreversible, irreplaceable, which most girls fight like mad for the best part of their unmarried lives to keep for—" He broke off, unable for the first time in a glib and fluent lifetime to describe his feelings! He had encountered the indescribable.

Ellsworth suggested that they both go and speak to Monroe immediately if Sidney was sure that Monroe would not be annoyed at his intervention and Ellsworth's participation, since Ellsworth was not, like Sidney, a close friend. Sidney assured Ellsworth that Monroe's attitude was such that one might be discussing the Council of Trent, the secret vices of the Sioux Indians, the nature of the canals on the planet Mars, the private parts of protozoa, the belly and bosom of a fish, or the interior of an atom. But, Sidney added, Ellsworth must be careful to keep a straight face, no matter what Monroe said. He might use clinical terms as if he spoke of a menu, neckties, or a new suit; he might refer to Kitty's pudenda, mammalia, clitoris, or vagina, for Monroe had read books on the subject of female anatomy and "ideal marriage."

"Speak of sexual connection," said Sidney in unprecedented disgust, "the conjugal rite, the act of procreation: call it concupiscence—agh!—what a coarse vulgar bounder I am—or should I say, what an unmitigated mucker?"

The troubled young men took Monroe to a bar. Monroe did not like to drink, but Ellsworth urged him to have just one, until a drink became a question of being courteous to Ellsworth and Monroe consented since he was always concerned about being polite. Ellsworth persisted in urging him, with the feeling that, however remarkable Monroe might be about the act of making love, still Eros and Bacchus must unite in him as in most (whatever went on in his platonic mind, he was, after all, a part of the chemical universe), and liquor would help to make the conference itself relaxed, free, explicit, and concrete; and any future developments impulsive, impetuous, and spontaneous!

Sidney began by explaining how he and Ellsworth felt the subject to be a point of honor, of friendship, of male solidarity in which they were all involved. He then said that it was a question of Kitty's health and well-being, and he gave Monroe a brief and tactful account of how Kitty had questioned him, and how her questioning could mean only one thing. Monroe at once looked troubled and devoted as if he had been told of Kitty's sudden, serious illness.

"By the way, where is Kitty tonight?" asked Ellsworth.

"This is her night at the symphony," said Monroe, "she will be back at the apartment by eleven." He looked at his watch. "The program is excellent."

Ellsworth and Sidney looked at each other, each affirming that the other had interpreted Monroe's answer in the same way—Kitty would be back at eleven and Monroe's mind had already begun to move in the direction which both friends desired.

Sidney took up the burden: he proposed that Monroe, if he wanted to perform his conjugal duty, begin by telling Kitty stories which were slightly risqué. He asked Monroe if he knew any.

"I used to know several," said Monroe, "but I've forgotten them."

Both Ellsworth and Sidney spoke at the same time, both wishing to provide Monroe with stories of that genre.

Neither Ellsworth nor Sidney were sure that Monroe understood the slightly risqué stories which they told him. Monroe smiled throughout a story instead of smiling at the punchline. Yet this might well be because the whole subject of sex amused him very much, or made him tense, a tenseness he coped with by smiling. Monroe is an enigma; he is truly obscure: he is a mystery even to himself, said Ellsworth to himself. Sidney, however, began to think less of Monroe and more of himself, for as the stories were told sexual desire arose intensely in him, and he wondered if there were any girl he could call upon at this late hour of Saturday night.

The two tutors of Venus continued, they moved forward, they came to closer grips with the subject.

"Oh, I remember one off-color joke," interrupted Monroe suddenly. "Funny the way that one's memory awakens. Do you want to hear it?"

"Not right now," said Ellsworth, looking in sudden fear at Monroe, and then with a look of deepening alarm, questioning and requesting direction, at Sidney.

"The less said the better," Sidney hastened to say. It had suddenly occurred to him that Monroe might tell Kitty a joke which she did not understand and which Monroe, supposing that he himself did, would expound in detail until the dawn's early light.

"Pat her on the head lightly," said Sidney, "when you get up to go to the john or to get a glass of water."

"Use a dirty word here and there," said Ellsworth, "unless Kitty is very squeamish, which I doubt. Ask her if she would like you to tickle her catastrophe. She may like it. Stop unless you're sure she likes it, stop any particular thing you try—but *never stop entirely*—try something else immediately."

Monroe did not know if Kitty was squeamish or not—the question had never arisen in his mind—but he announced that she was not, for it was clear to him that in this company squeamishness and prudery were undesirable and despised.

"Pat her belly gently—very gently, you can't possibly be too gentle. Each stroke—and I mean *stroke*—should be a snowflake, very delicate: the blizzard comes later," said Sidney. "And then kiss her on the forehead to show that you respect her and that you are not just lustful."

"Don't forget to go slowly," added Ellsworth, "the big mistake of the inexperienced man is to go too fast and not to understand that slowness is an aphrodisiac to the fair sex!"

"Slowness is an aphrodisiac: an aphrodisiac—like Spanish fly," Monroe said pensively, thinking aloud. "I must remember that: your metaphor is excellent; may I quote you?"

"No," said Ellsworth, "please don't: Kitty will think I am a Casanova, a Spanish—" He was about to say *flier* when Sidney kicked him hard under the table. The word sank in his throat.

Monroe arose. He was inspired. His two friends were hardly halfway through their disorganized and passionate exposition, but Monroe was too excited to wait any longer. Sidney, feeling painfully interrupted, reminded Monroe that Kitty would not be back until eleven o'clock, to which Monroe replied that she sometimes returned during the intermission, when the second half of the symphony program did not interest her.

"You don't know how grateful I am to both of you," said Monroe as he left his friends, his eyes shining. He looked as he strode away, like a knight who has just dedicated himself to a crusade or to a daring coup in which he will rescue the oppressed and beautiful maiden.

"Probably everything we said was senseless," said Ellsworth to Sidney, after Monroe had made his eager departure.

"He was certainly moved in some way," said Sidney.

"Yes, moved: but moved in what way? We probably accomplished nothing. I have the feeling that he was simply encited, as he would be if he had been finding out how to construct the engine for a motor-boat."

"Monroe does not care for motor-boats," said Sidney, "he has never mentioned them. But then he does not care for girls, either, and before he saw Kitty he never mentioned girls."

Both friends felt frustrated by the abrupt conclusion which Monroe had imposed upon their difficult and painful instruction.

The next morning was a Sunday, and Sidney, accustomed to sleep late on Sundays, was annoyed to be awakened and summoned to the telephone by his landlady. It was Monroe, who wished to tell Sidney that all had gone very well. Kitty and he were in a state of bliss, and it was virtually all his doing. Kitty had returned from the symphony feeling too inspired by the music she had heard for any amorous innovation, too exalted by Mozart's sublime emotions; and although Monroe had faithfully attempted in a curtailed form all that Ellsworth and Sidney had suggested, she had been immovable, obdurate, adamant, deaf; she had also been quite tired. Monroe had, in the end, before resigning himself, mentioned Sidney's and Ellsworth's advice, which had quickened Kitty's curiosity: she questioned him about exactly what his friends had said and if that was all that they had said. Then, after looking pensive and bemused, turned to her pillow and fell asleep quickly.

In the morning Kitty had awakened in a passionate state, awakened Monroe, and now, at last, the marriage was consummated, and the consummation had been not only quite fascinating but it had also been great fun, Monroe asserted, adding that he would enjoy describing how interesting and delightful it had been, except that Kitty had asked him to say nothing even though he and his friends were unconventional, sophisticated, and believed in the utmost candor. But Monroe wanted to ask one more important favor of Sidney. Neither he nor Kitty knew how to take the proper precautions against conception. Would Sidney mind meeting them at the drugstore in the square and telling them what to get? Sidney sighed and insisted on giving all the information on the phone, annoyed because he had to spell some of the words for Monroe and had to wait for Monroe to get a pencil from Kitty, who was standing by the telephone booth. Sidney went back to sleep after the conversation was concluded, and awoke in an hour in a state of horror: he had dreamed that he was making love to Kitty while Monroe looked on and encouraged him, cheered him, applauded him, congratulated him as a virtuoso, a paragon, a true friend, and a Spanish flier.

Thenceforth, Sidney saw less and less of Monroe, and it was only after a time that Sidney became aware of the reason: he saw less of him because he did not want to see Monroe at all. Monroe was too little of this world for Sidney: he was too distant from the real world in which Sidney wanted to play an important part; he gave Sidney the feeling of being part of an unreal comedy or masque.

He saw less of Ellsworth also, for no particular reason, he supposed, unless it was Ellsworth's knowledge of the innocence in which they had all been involved. The first time that the two did meet after their tutoring of Monroe, Ellsworth had looked immediately at Sidney with a silent and overwhelming question upon his face, and Sidney had nodded and at the same time gritted his teeth, grinned, and grimaced, but said nothing more of what had occurred. Instead of going into detail, he said only that the consummation had been sticky but successful and one could hardly discuss it much further without making Monroe's libido and marriage a kind of life-work in itself, a vocation, indeed an obsession.

"Do you know," he said to Ellsworth before concluding all conversation on the topic once and for all, "if we told anyone, we would not be believed. I would not believe you, nor would you believe me, that in 1936, in the United States of America, a brilliant young doctor of philosophy, trained by some of the best teachers in the world—" He stopped: it was too much to formulate without becoming extremely dismayed: without feeling lost in a peculiar and new way.

"That's right," said Ellsworth, "no one would believe the story and certainly neither of us would. But that's the way experience is and always has been: experience has always been and will always be far more incredible and improbable than any of the fantasies of the imagination and—"

"Did you say *experience?*" Sidney said, "what experience? there was no experience. Monroe is prior to experience, he is a living example of what the philosophers—and their brilliant student Monroe—call the *a priori*. So am I. What Monroe needs is a visa to reality. He has confused it with the Irish Sweepstakes. And I have confused it with the gambling tables at Monte Carlo, the Belmont Race Track, and the bull market of 1928. Do you know what a jackass is? I will tell you: someone who believes in the jackpot and thinks that a Ph.D. in philosophy knows what he is talking about. Monroe does not know the difference between a horse race and a horse show, a race horse and Pegasus, a sure thing and horse-shoe. And I don't—or did not, until I went to great expense—know the difference between being intelligent and getting a Ph.D. *summa cum laude*—(in metaphysics, mind you, the study of the ultimate nature of reality)."

"Take it easy," Ellsworth said, "and don't forget that a hardheaded successful businessman lost a lot more than you did."

"He didn't know Monroe," said Sidney, inconsolable, full of self-contempt, unwilling to deny himself the inexpensive luxury of condemning himself, "I did, or thought I did.

"For a year I had every chance to know Monroe, to observe all that he not only does not know but all the important things which he would deny existed, insisting in his goodnatured lambie-pie way that you were pulling his leg—or perhaps I should say, limb—when you mentioned them."

Ellsworth was astonished at Sidney's wrath and remorse. He wondered if the dean had found out about the reason Sidney had borrowed the money: it was unlikely; it was, in fact, impossible; it was possible, however, that one or another greedy victim was after Sidney as well as Monroe, since not all the victims had been paid back or paid back in full.

"Don't forget that Monroe fell in love," said Ellsworth, thinking of these possibilities and deciding it would be best not to question Sidney, who certainly would have told him what had happened if he had wanted to tell him. "Anyone might fall in love, some day even you may fall in love. And when you're in love—"

"Do you know what love is?" asked Sidney. "Of course you don't, so I had better tell you. Love is a dark horse—"

"Look," said Ellsworth, "it's all over now, and besides, your aim in life, if you will forgive me for coining a phrase, was not and is not to become a millionaire, and very quickly at that —or was it? I mean, is it? And besides, if I may coin still another phrase, money is not everything."

"So I have been told again and again," said Sidney, looking elsewhere, "but I would like to find out something like that for myself. Experience is the only teacher, and do you know what experience teaches us: it teaches us not to make the same mistake more than five or six times."

Ellsworth, convinced that something must be very trying and painful and troubling to Sidney, told Sidney he would be glad to deal with any of the investors in Monroe's gold rush if they became difficult, and Sidney, thanking him, told him that no one had blamed or troubled him at all: every investor realized that love in triumph had undone them. As they parted, Sidney feared that Ellsworth might have guessed the reason for his anger, and if he had not guessed it, he probably would whenever he next encountered Kitty alone, as Sidney had several times, until he was not sure that any encounter was accident or coincidence.

Sidney heard from others of some of Monroe's new ventures. He had purchased ninety-six coat hangers, declaring that they were a bargain and would never again be as inexpensive. He had a scheme for buying 1400 acres in New Hampshire near the Canadian border and starting a summer colony (he argued that since so many teachers and students at the university had no congenial place to go during the summer certainly this venture was bound to be a success). Hearing of these projects, Sidney was relieved to think that by seeing little of Monroe he was free of pressures which would otherwise have existed, whether or not he participated in these schemes; if he did not, so much energy would be exhausted in criticizing and arguing that the result would be almost the same as participation.

Sidney heard also that Kitty's enchantment with Monroe's mind suffered bewildering interruption now and then: she had supposed that whatever Monroe's defects as a husband, he was a great intellect. But when he arrived one evening with eight dozen shoe trees, although they hardly had enough money for food until the end of the month, Kitty burst into tears. When he questioned her, she became hysterical. And when, after her explanation, he remained sympathetic but unmoved, remarking in a calm and reassuring tone that all sorts of foods were inexpensive enough to enable them to survive, and they could save money by using margarine instead of butter, eating meat only one a week and fish six days a week, Kitty ran out of the room and shut the door. Monroe felt that it was pointless to attempt to make an irrational female rational while she was sobbing hysterically. He decided to wait until morning and resume his explanation. He took a book from the shelf and began to make notes criticizing and contradicting the point of view of the author.

Fifteen minutes passed: Monroe was entirely absorbed in reading and criticizing what he read when Kitty came out of the bedroom and saw what he was doing. She stared at him in amazement and recognition. He finally looked up and saw the strange look upon her face.

"You are looking very strange, my dear," said Monroe gently, his mind still preoccupied with the book he had been reading.

"I am looking at you for the first time," said Kitty coldly, and in despair.

Then Monroe noticed that she had put on her hat and coat and applied lipstick to her lips.

"Where are you going at this hour?" Monroe asked.

"I am going to go out to a restaurant and get a real meal," said Kitty, turning towards the door and leaving Monroe, once again confirmed in his belief that all women were irrational, fickle, and impractical gluttons.

By the time Kitty had slammed the door, Monroe was peacefully absorbed in his reading again: he was entirely undisturbed.

During the next hour his concentration was interrupted only once by the passing thought of how little understanding the female sex possessed of the essential nature of reality.

Towards the end of the academic year, the head of the department of philosophy at another distinguished university visited Fairfield for the sake of finding a new instructor of philosophy. The head of the department of philosophy at Fairfield had come to know Monroe and to like him very much; despite the fact that he was at the law school, he was included among the dozen young men at the university who had Ph.D. degrees and who were to be interviewed by the visitor. Each of the twelve young men was interviewed briefly—in less than half an hour—but Monroe perceived in the first ten minutes that he was not making a good impression at all, since the visitor glanced at his wristwatch repeatedly. The reason was that Monroe's remarks were too complicated and involved when he spoke of questions of philosophy, while the visitor was looking for a teacher who would be brisk, simple, and direct, who would dramatize his subject to undergraduates instead of making philosophy seem immensely difficult. When the visitor glanced at his wristwatch for the fourth time, Monroe was not offended at all, and he thought of Nathaniel Burke, who seemed to him the most gifted of the young men who were being interviewed.

"If you don't think that I would be suitable for the appointment," Monroe said simply and spontaneously, "I'd like to recommend a friend of mine, Nathaniel Burke. He is very good, indeed, he is first-rate and far superior to me, and I feel fairly certain that he will make original discoveries in his special field, mathematical logic."

Nathaniel Burke had, in fact, already made several original contributions to mathematical logic, but he was not a good teacher: he was not only impatient, but self-conscious and shy to an extreme degree, and although this self-consciousness wore off during the course of any class period, it was succeeded very often by an overly excited exposition often interrupted by uncontrollable, unpredictable stammering, and during his own interview with Professor Wilbur he was shy, self-conscious, excited, and he stammered.

When Professor Wilbur had interviewed the last of the candidates, he told the Fairfield department head that his choice had been made during his meeting with Monroe, and that Monroe was precisely the kind of young man he had come to find.

"Just think," Professor Wilbur explained, "in the midst of being interviewed for a job which he wants very much, and which he has spent four years of study to prepare himself for, he has the generosity of mind, the goodness of heart, to suggest and recommend one of his rivals: Monroe Lawrence is precisely the kind of young man—the kind of human being—we want on our staff!"

Monroe was summoned soon after to the office of the department of philosophy and told the good news: he was also told about what he had said which had convinced Professor Wilbur that he was the right man for the post. Monroe was unmoved by his success in getting the job, and perplexed by the attitude Professor Wilbur had expressed as the basis of his choice. He returned to his own apartment to tell Kitty the good news and to ask her if she did not think the attitude of Professor Wilbur rather strange, since he had merely praised Nathaniel Burke for his professional ability, which was unquestionable. Kitty was not at home, however, and Monroe never found out what she thought on that subject, for she had left him, placing a brief note on his pillow, in which she said he was too good for marriage, he was really devoted to the things of the mind, so she was going back to live with her parents for a time. Monroe was quite perplexed and distressed. He tried to call Kitty, only to learn that she had not, in fact, returned to her parents. Hence Monroe concealed the fact of her departure from the parents, so that Kitty would not be embarrassed and her parents would not be alarmed. Doubtless this was a passing mood. When a week had passed and Kitty had not returned, Monroe was astonished and gratified to find that he did not mind her absence at all. During the summer he prepared for the courses he was to teach the following fall, and he resumed his practice of betting on the horses in a purely theoretical way, accumulating a large theoretical fortune in a very short time.

Ellsworth encountered Monroe in Pennsylvania Station one day three years after, when he was hurrying to take a train to Chicago, and as he explained his haste he asked Monroe whether he enjoyed his job. Monroe said that he enjoyed it very much, and began to tell Ellsworth that he had returned to the system and that he had made over three million dollars.

"I wish I had the time to hear about it," Ellsworth said, "but I just have to make that train." And he waved his hand and ran, toward the gates which were beginning to close.

"If you see Sidney," Monroe called after him, "don't forget to tell him: the system really works, I've made over three million dollars although I only put it to use on paper, during the summer time—"

Sidney encountered Kitty by accident not long after Ellsworth had walked into Monroe in Pennsylvania Station. He had come into a big drugstore on Times Square to get a pack of cigarettes, and as he turned to go he saw Kitty at the soda fountain counter, seated on one of the backless stools, munching a club sandwich and sipping a malted milk. She looked as pretty as ever, and she looked voracious, munching and sipping as if, unless she hurried, her sandwich and her malted would be taken away from her.

"How are you? It's wonderful to see you again," Sidney said, seating himself next to her, and only then perceiving that Kitty was not alone, but the husky young man next to her, crouched over a bowl of chili con carne, was with her. Kitty took the straw from her mouth, set down her sandwich, looked sideways at her young man, and said, "Oh!" She was clearly so embarrassed that she was speechless, and Sidney was immediately certain that she was ashamed of the young man with her, who somehow seemed to Sidney to look like a truckdriver at the ballet, or a pacifist at a bullfight.

"How are you?" Kitty managed, finally, to say, "and how is Monroe? I have not heard from him since we were divorced. Did any of you boys ever tie down that colossal fortune you were after?" And then Kitty looked horrified by the rudeness of her question, which was entirely unlike her, and Sidney, seeing the ways of things, told her that he had just stopped for a moment and had to hurry, and that he was making out fairly well and Monroe was too, he was a very popular teacher and would soon have a permanent appointment and a full professorship.

As he departed with rapidity and awkwardness, Sidney recognized how fortunate Monroe, whom he had not seen nor heard from for years, really was. He had no need of anyone or anything; he had no need of a drugstore, a soda fountain, a wife or a colossal fortune: he was his own colossal fortune. He was very lucky, Sidney said to himself, and now understood for the first time that he himself had no desire, really, to be very lucky or to have a colossal fortune.

The Hartford Innocents

I

Red Bananas

When, very early one very cold and gold morning in December, an infant was left under the front stoop—to be exact—on the doorstep of the barred downstairs entryway of the handsome brownstone mansion in which the Manning family lived, the fearful, fugitive and luckless mother would hardly have known with what immense joy the infant would immediately be welcomed, by all six of the Manning children, and soon after by Dr. Manning and Mrs. Manning. The mother had certainly chosen the Manning family, among many possible choices, because they were sure to be kind to an abandoned child. Dr. Manning was a minister famous for his unconventional and liberal social views, and the Mannings were clearly quite rich and very fond of children, since they had six, three or four more than most families of the same social and economic status.

There was every reason for choosing the Manning family rather than any other in the large mid-western city, yet had the mother known what was to occur as a result of her choice —beginning with the profound delight and unmixed enthusiasm of the Manning children and concluding (insofar as one can speak of a conclusion) in railroad trips, plane flights, long distance phone calls, national scandal, nationwide publicity, a severe crisis on the directorate of a famous philanthropic foundation, and the intervention of a congressional investigating committee—had she·known of any of these or other of the consequences of her comparatively simple act, consequences which bordered on the indescribable and were immediately characterized as unprecedented—it is quite probable that she would have preferred to bestow the child upon another family: she might even have chosen to keep the child, if no other alternative than the Mannings had been available.

Among· those who became involved in the disposition of the child, only Candy Manning would have wished the Manning family to be chosen once again; although she might have hoped that others would have acted and responded to the finding of the child differently than in fact they did, it is clear that she would have acted and responded again and again just as she did. Candy—or Candida, her given name, but used only by her mother—was the oldest of the Manning children: she was seventeen years of age on that cold December morning just after Christmas and she had come to the door of the entryway to take in the family's daily four bottles of pasteurized milk when she saw the infant in his bassinet, carefully bundled, quietly sleeping, as innocent as each of the four bottles of milk, covered by linens as white as the milk and whiter than the snow piled up, like anchored rowboats, against the curbstone.

"A baby!" Candy exclaimed, "How cute!" She gasped with joy. And her pure delight became incoherent as she picked up the child, forgot the milk and raced up the stairs, crying: "A baby! A baby! Someone left a baby on our doorstep!" It was thus that the astonishing event and advent was announced to Candy's younger brothers and sisters. Soon all six of them— even William Wordsworth Manning, the genius of the family, were stamping up and down the carpeted stairs and shouting,

shouting and stamping up and down, so much that the chande-
liers in the drawing room tinkled and the goldfish in the goldfish bowls trembled as the waters shook. The uproar was a
violation of the ironclad discipline of the household imposed
or dictated by Mrs. Manning and it soon brought her forth from
her bedroom in her new peignoir: she was the absolute monarch
of her family and ruled it from dawn until midnight with a
relentless set of rules and laws and tasks.

She came downstairs, her face made expressionless by cold
fury, but when she saw the child, she too was immediately
enchanted, and in her enchantment, she went straight to the
sofa on which the child in his bassinet had been placed, thrust
aside two of her children and inspected the infant herself with
unconcealed delight, forgetting her anger with a quickness
which was wholly uncharacteristic of her.

Each of the Manning children had suffered the same acute
disappointment for the past eighteen months: William Wordsworth Manning had stopped being the infant and the baby of
the family with an abrupt suddenness. He had been unsatis-
factory from the very start and he had not been the youngest
child of the family for an adequate length of time and he had
disappointed Candy most of all for she had long delighted in
the role of little mother of the family—the phrase her father
had used time and again—and there had always been a baby
of the family for her to mind until William Wordsworth stopped
being the baby of the family. Then there was no one for Candy
to mind.

Soon after William proved to be a severe disappointment,
Candy had entertained the thought of becoming a nurse until
she was a wife and a mother herself and had her own darling
little baby. William had been very trying from the time he
was born and finally it was decided that his misbehavior and
his antics were such as to suggest that there was something
seriously wrong with him and he had been taken to the university psychological clinic after a particularly inexplicable,

unprovoked and extremely violent tantrum. At the clinic it was discovered that there was only one thing wrong with William: he was a genius, a truly extraordinary genius, so much of a genius that the doctors who gave him the psychological and intelligence tests had to admit that they were astonished and had to confer with each other on the possibility that the tests as such were inadequate or wrong. William had broken all the I.Q. records, amazing and dazzling everyone, including the teachers and doctors at the clinic, and including also, Mrs. Manning herself, the most difficult of human beings to impress, for seldom or never did she seem to be impressed or surprised by anyone or anything. The only one who remained unmoved by the record-breaking performance was William himself. He had returned with Mother wearing the same look of indifference and boredom as he had presented when he departed: it was the look which the other children usually reserved for boring homework.

When William and Mother returned, Mother summoned all the older children and announced with appropriate pomp and circumstance that William was a certified genius and that as a result he was to be released from the obligation to obey the rules of the household and the round-the-clock family discipline which made every waking hour of the day a matter of order and discipline. Since he was a genius, Mother said it would be wrong to expect him to do anything except what he wanted to do: he did not have to make his bed unless he felt like it, he did not have to go to school unless he felt like it, and anything which he did do was to be regarded in a new light, the light of someone who had been certified as a genius. In addition, William was released from any obligation to obey Candy, and Candy was no longer to regard him as a child in her care.

So, for almost two years now, the family had been deprived of the joy of having a baby in the family or a youngest child; the other children had felt the deprivation almost as acutely as Candy herself: and it was when her dissatisfaction became

most acute that Candy announced at dinnertime that she intended to become a nurse, only to have dear Mother say to her
in front of the entire family: "Candida, your desire to be a
nurse is immature and premature."

A week after, at dinnertime once again, Mrs. Manning had
announced to one and all that "although Candida is probably
not college material, she will be sent to Hartford for at least
one year." Then it was that dear, gentle Father had protested
gently, as if he were joking. He had called Mother the well-
known dean emeritus of the Ivy League, but Candy knew very
well that he was not joking because she happened to see the
shocked, angered look which appeared and disappeared on
Mother's face. It was just like the time Father had said to
Mother: "My dear, Reality is merely your ingenious and skillful
secretary and research assistant." "Yes, I have often thought
of Reality in that light," Mother had answered serenely, a
majestic smile upon her face. And then she added, "Reality is
merely my silent partner: silent! my dear, and present only
at the proper time, and briefly, like the male in procreation.
And just as the male is absent during the travail of child-birth,
so it is appropriate that the male should be absent or silent
during periods of profound crisis and indescribable pain, as in
giving birth to a child."

If Mother and Father spoke like that in front of the entire
family, what must they say to each other when they were alone!

Coming home from Hartford more than a thousand miles
distant was almost unbearably exciting. It was so wonderful to
see everyone so pleased when Candy rang the doorbell, even
William had smiled with a look of faint pleasure when he saw
her, and Mother had lifted her eyebrows as if to conceal the
joy she felt that Candy was home again after all the months
that she had been at Hartford and when Mother squeezed her
hand very tightly, Candy thought that she would burst into

tears of pure joy. Christmas was more wonderful and charming than it had ever been in the years gone by, but it was all over so soon, even though the Christmas tree still glittered and everyone was giving parties to which Candy went where everyone said: "O Candy, what a big girl you are, it seems but yesterday that you were a child in the cradle, a kindergarten tot." By the middle of the week between Christmas and New Year's, everything and everyone were just as they had always been, all along, before she went to Hartford: William was unbearable, Mother was stern and severe and very critical and always correcting her, whatever she did, and adding, "I assure you, Candida, I am only calling your attention to this for your own good; surely you wouldn't want me to remain silent and to keep from you the painful insights which are among the few rewards and certitudes of experience," and Candy had begun to think of going back to Hartford when she went downstairs to get the milk in the morning and saw the infant on the doorstep and cried, "A baby!" at the top of her morning voice.

The Manning house had six bedroroms and each bedroom had a bathroom and the cellar was also equipped with a tiny toilet and there was a bathroom in each guest room and thus there were nine bathrooms in all: Candy had been very much perplexed when, at Hartford, this fact about the family house had become known, for another girl, a junior girl who came from the same city but, being a junior, saw little of Candy, had told several other Hartford girls about the nine bathrooms. The topic had become the cause of discussion, and disbelief until finally one girl asked Candy if she would mind answering a personal question. Candy answered that she loved personal questions, but when the question was asked, she was disappointed: what was personal about living in a house with nine bathrooms? Candy thought it quite peculiar that it should seem strange to anyone that a house should be equipped with nine bathrooms. Instead of being strange, it was sensible, convenient, and part of the living equipment a house with so many children ought to have.

Candy thought about the bedrooms and bathrooms as she rested after lunch in one of the guest bedrooms, waiting and resting impatiently because she was eager to see the adorable baby again, when he was fed at two o'clock. She wondered if her parents would want to keep the baby and was sure that they would and then she wondered if the baby, when adopted, would have an official birthday and whether his birthday would be the day when he was found on the doorstep or the day when he was officially adopted, or the day of his baptism.

On each birthday, each and all of the children were summoned by Mother to her bedroom, and when the children were convened about her canopied bed, having come in stately and solemn procession, the bells rang all over the house. Father although supposed to be so helpless with his hands had installed a complicated system of bells, demonstrating an electrical cleverness which had impressed some guests and embarrassed others by the sudden need to suppress a smile. Mother held her levee like a great queen: indeed the bells were the first part of the ceremonial and the enormous canopied bed was too and the way in which Mother reclined in it, propped up by three fat pillows, looking exalted and yet a little bored too, or at least Candy suspected that she was bored. When all the children stood in his or her proper place, Mother then would command her favorite of the moment to crouch down and get under the bed and draw forth the tree of red bananas which, until she was thirteen, Candy had supposed Mother kept under her bed all year long. Then each child would receive a red banana from Mother with the gesture and official dignity which was just like a high school graduation when the principal gives each of the graduating students a diploma: the only real difference was that Mother remained stately, solemn, and silent throughout and did not attempt to pretend like high school principals that they were unbending and acting towards each student as to a new or an old friend.

Impressive as each red banana day truly was, it was surpassed as an event by the days when Mother and Father—after long seclusion and never a sound, behind the closed, locked door of Father's study (where he wrote and read his sermons aloud to himself)—emerged, rang the bells to summon all the children and to announce, with suitable solemnity—that their number would be augmented by one in the near future. "How soon?" Lewis Carroll Manning once asked, and Mother answered coldly, "Comparatively soon," an answer which all the children strove for weeks to understand and interpret. The cold look on Mother's face was so severe that thereafter no one dared to ask questions on the occasion of the ceremonial announcement of a new child. Nevertheless there would be an outburst of uncontrollable glee: the news was the cause of a feeling of wild excitement and was so exciting and thrilling that there would be another red banana day and it meant that there would be another human being to think about, to mind, and to watch. The announcement of the coming of the baby who turned out to be William Wordsworth Manning caused so much excitement that Lewis Carroll and Candy ran outdoors and turned in several fire alarms until a policeman saw them and made them go home: and after that, for several weeks, the neighbors and the neighbors' children made supposedly witty remarks about the parson's arsonists.

When there were six birthdays and thus six red banana days, Candy, Lewis and Emily Bronte Manning discussed the meaning of the house being equipped with nine bathrooms, and Lewis said then that it must mean that there would be nine children in all, since there were nine bathrooms, a calculation reinforced when one of Emily's school friends remarked at a party, long before Candy was questioned at Hartford, that there was something strange about having nine bathrooms, no one else had so many, not even people who were newly rich. "No one else has six children," Candy said, answering for her younger sister, astonishing herself and dumbfounding the other girls who heard her so completely by the pure, impeccable logic of her answer that when Candy told Lewis they both agreed that nine children in all was an absolute certainty.

From noon until nightfall, joy over the coming of the child rose higher and higher by the hour: by dusk all the children felt triumphant, and expressed their sense of delight by more and more expressions of pleasure and excitement. Even William Wordsworth Manning had interrupted his private studies which he conducted in arrogant secrecy, to join his brothers and sisters whenever they watched the baby being given his bottle. As Candy collected the baby clothes which, until that morning, she had been sadly convinced would never be used again—save perhaps in her own home and for her own darling first baby —she remarked upon William Wordsworth's sober and studious presence to Lewis Carroll, the brother who was truly her next of kin since he had been born one year after her birth.

"Maybe William wants to find out," she said to Lewis, whispering and giggling, "if the new baby is a genius too?"

"O no," said Lewis, *sotto voce*, "William is here because the baby does not yet know that he is the genius of the family, the boy who broke the scales at the psych clink when they weighed his intelligence. He wants the baby to know that he is a big genius as soon as possible and without any further delay."

At dinner, after grace had been said by Father, Father then looked at Mother with a faint smile, and added a sentence to the usual grace, thanking the Lord for the unexpected gift of the baby. Hearing this, all the children broke into cheers, but suppressed them because it was the sort of thing which would be impolite and disrespectful just after grace had been said. When dessert had been served, all the children rushed through eating up the plum pudding, eager to get dinner over with so that they could go upstairs for the baby's next bottle

and see how the baby looked now, after sleeping some more
and after being in the Manning family for a whole day, his
first day. But Father held up his hand and told his children
that he must detain them for a moment—Mother had surely
insisted, unnecessarily, to Father, that an official statement must
be made about the baby by the official head, or figurehead, of
the family—Father was always required to pronounce and
formulate the family's official attitude and he sometimes described himself as Mrs. Manning's Secretary of State, since
Mother always told him what to say and he always said what
she had commanded him to say but added a few sentences of
his own which made the announcement very different from
what Mother intended, to judge by the look of suppressed fury
upon her face. Mother would tell Father—Candy had overheard
her telling him once—to make a lucid statement of what she
called "the proper sentiments, the Christian and civilized attitudes, the guidance most likely to be profitable to the family
as a whole, as a living unity."

"My dear, dear children, six in all," Father began, speaking
in his comic serious tone with a faint and sly smile upon his
face, "now that you are seven in number—"

The children broke into jubilant uproar, the sort of uproar
Candy could hear in the autumn when at the football stadium
the University was playing a big game, hailing a halfback who
had broken loose and was running to a touchdown unexpectedly:
this addition of the child to the family was what the children,
one and all, had immediately desired when they saw the baby
in the morning and hoped for intensely all day long, fearing
only that something would go wrong—the mother might come
back and ask for her darling baby or the orphan asylum people
might demand the child—and now what had been almost certain
was a certainty: this confirmation of their devout hope, of the
acceptance of the baby, was the reason they were yelling,
despite Mother's clear disapproval of what she called "excessive
and unsound emotionalism" and "vulgar demonstrativeness."

"Yes," said Father, smiling and continuing as the yelling died down and the handclapping stopped, "this child must become as one of us. And I must, as your mother rightly insists, attempt to say something of a delicate and important matter concerning the new member of the family. This infant is a natural child, a child of love: such an infant is known also, in vulgar parlance, which, in this instance, expresses a profound darkness of heart, as a bastard. And in the chill spiritless jargon to which vulgarity and self-hatred or fear of love often forces those who are too sensitive to speak freely, the quasi-legal phrase, an illegitimate child, is often used as a shuddering euphemism. The cruelty which society inflicts upon children of love has diminished somewhat during the past generation and particularly since the labors of the compassionate Professor Kinsey of Indiana University: but the stigma of the bar sinister, another ancient and proverbial phrase—that is to say, of having no recognized parents, no family and no family kinship, in which to take pride and seek sanctuary—remains unaltered for the natural child of love. Hence we must never permit, insofar as we possess the power to govern our minds and the humility to understand our hearts, we must never, I must say again, permit the cruelty of polite society, or the hypocrisy of the conventional standards—to affect our own sentiments about this little child, or our attitude toward him. This unexpected gift should forever make us remember, whenever we forget, that we are all members one of the other, as St. Paul so truly said. This unforeseen, small and beautiful stranger who has come among us is no longer a stranger, he is now one of us. We must begin to think of him thus, in this way, now, long before he is capable of conscious observation and sensitive to the slightest differences of attitude, tone and affection. The only difference between the little child and each of you is the inescapable difference in age, and all of us participate in this difference in one or another way. Thus, as the poet says, 'if you are worth my hope,' and worthy of my prayers, when the child is old enough to go to school and go among strangers and encounter the inevitable malicious remarks about his origins by strangers who through accident or resentment are likely to be evil in tongue and in heart, at times (often because they are loveless and unloved, often because the world is loveless and loved too much), this child will be protected by the armor of our love: his sense of being loved by us and his sense of being one of us will give him strength to disdain the mockery of tongues and the self-hatred of the insecure. I must add that if you are not worthy of my hope, you will be worthless and hopeless.

"We must remember, it is true, that the pursuit of tolerance, as an end in itself, is often the confession of spiritual bankruptcy, the sign and pain of that profound sickness, the loss of belief in the meaning of life. It is all too easy to be tolerant of belief when one believes in nothing, and this is the state of mind of many human beings today. Indeed, it is difficult not to be tolerant, since if one believes in nothing whatever, one is forced into tolerance of one's fellow's childlike superstitions. Most human beings tend, now, to speak of the virtue of having 'an open mind,' but a good many of them cannot distinguish between having an open mind and a hole in one's head—or an empty heart. True tolerance is difficult—it is very difficult—to those who are possessed by belief intensely and cannot understand why others are stubborn enough to resist the beliefs which they find so irresistible.

"These two very different forms of tolerance often have been and often will be confused with one another.

"Nevertheless this confusion, however regrettable or hateful in itself, is infinitely more desirable than any form of intolerance. It is better to be tolerant because one believes in nothing than to be a bigot, or a snob. It is far, far better to be a crackpot than a tyrant; a fool is to be preferred to a fascist; a pig is less odious than a prig; and it is far better to be a publican and a sinner than to indulge in the self-righteousness of the Pharisee and the Philistine: May God in His infinite mercy grant us the love which is the source and beginning and end of human existence and of all those inclinations of the mind and the heart which make us human beings. May He give us the strength and the self-understanding which will make it possible for us to be neither empty nor narrow, neither bigoted nor insensitive, neither foolish nor cruel. Let us remember what the greatest of all poets made his beautiful heroine, Isabel, a noblewoman of Vienna say in *Measure for Measure*:

> Alas! Alas!
> Why all the souls that were were forfeit once;
> And He that might have best took the vantage
> Found out the remedy. How would you be
> If He, which is the top of judgment, should
> But judge you as you are? O think on that;
> And mercy then will breathe within your lips,
> Like man new made.

This is birth and rebirth and life everlasting; all else is a long and living death."

"Father, you are just wonderful," Candy cried, clapping her hands and trying not to let the tears well out of her widened eyes: so moved was she, so overcome, by the Christian charity, beauty and compassion Father had described so clearly in a low and gentle voice.

"Yes, Father, you are really and truly wonderful," Lewis exclaimed, passionately, with the most passionate admiration in his voice and eyes.

"Father, you ought to be President of the United States of America!" William declared with an unprecedented enthusiasm, an exultation and exaltation entirely unlike him or unperceived before this evening. William's remark was not only sensational in itself but all the more unique because it had been uttered by William himself, for the genius of the family was subject to such high standards that he had never been capable of genuine admiration of his own powers and gifts.

"Well said, William," said Mother warmly. She was clearly very pleased. Although very critical and at times scornful of her husband, she naturally and spontaneously approved of all expressions of admiration directed toward authority and parenthood.

"Thank you, William," Father said, a serene look upon his face, a look which meant that he was really very much amused. "The pleasure your esteem gives me is not at all lessened but rather increased by the certainty that there is no likelihood whatever of my occupying the White House."

"How many bathrooms do they have in the White House?" asked Tina. She was the youngest of the girls and her full name was Christina Rossetti Manning.

"Tina!" said Mother severely. "You are being either ignorant or satirical."

"What's satirical?" Tina asked Father and William at the same time. But everyone had begun to fold his or her napkin of the week and attach its clasp. Everyone was impatient to go upstairs and see the new baby again when he woke up for his next bottle. Tina hurried to follow her brothers and sisters. She was not at all troubled by her mother's comment and judgment and she was entirely untroubled by her ignorance of the nature of the satirical and the meaning of satire.

II

The Flight of the Innocents

When the train finally departed— after what seemed to Candy an unbearable delay of a few minutes according to her wristwatch—a few minutes are sometimes longer than forever, some

Hartford senior girl had said last autumn—Candy felt relaxed enough to sit back on the green plush seat of the compartment. She felt sufficiently safe to look at the baby in his bassinet next to her and rehearse to herself, as the long night of train travel began, all that had happened which had forced her—she felt sure that she was forced and compelled, although only by her own conscience to take the baby and to take the train, disappearing in the middle of the night after writing a note which her parents would find in the morning. There were all the wonderful things that Father had said two days before and these sentences of Father's were still continually ringing through her mind as the train began slowly to pick up speed and the successions of rhythm became customary enough to be unnoticed by the entire body as well as by the delicate ear.

He had spoken these wonderful sentences during a family council, as Mother had called it, to discuss what name to give to the little baby.

"To give life to a human being has a close kinship to giving that new human being a unique name," Father had said to his children assembled in the study where they seldom were allowed to be. "A given name is necessary to signify the uniqueness of each immortal soul as it issues from the hand of God: combined with the family name, it affirms not only the bonds which unite it immediately to a few other human beings living in the same house, but it is a vivid and concise symbol of the coexistence of uniqueness and kinship, identity and resemblance.

"Your mother and I have agreed that in this instance a different procedure would be appropriate. This beautiful child —the most beautiful child I have ever seen (and I do not forget how enchanting each of you were at the same age, long before you left the bassinet each and all of you have occupied in turn, and at a time of life when to an outsider an infant is most likely to resemble dried apricots heaped in a laundry bag)—is not your mother's child and mine alone but your child as well as ours: we are all in a profound sense, in a profoundly spiritual sense, the parents of this dear newcomer. He will be, I assure you, a trial and a burden, a trying responsibility, a distressing burden at times. He will not be at all times the delightful creature who now interests all of you so much—and interests me just as much, I freely confess. This is a fact which you must not forget: and the privilege of naming the child since it is a profound spiritual privilege too, should be for each of and all of you a symbol, a vivid symbol, an oath of honor as binding as a promise and a pledge of one's heart."

"But Father," William had inquired solemnly, "our having a voice and a vote in the naming of the child seems to me inconsistent with your noble instruction to us that there should be no distinction between the new member of the family and the rest of us. Perhaps I am wrong," he added: it was the first time he had ever been known to entertain this possibility, but he spoke of his possible wrongness in a way which transformed the meaning of what he said and declared his conviction that he was not wrong, but attempting to be polite.

"On the contrary," William was told by his father, "the naming in which we are now engaged will be but a distant memory to all of us and something unexperienced by the child himself by the time he knows what his unique name is. He will assume that he acquired his name just as you acquired yours. But your attitude toward him beginning now and for years to come will be influenced by your participation in his naming now."

The train was moving very quickly now, going south, toward Chicago: it was just good luck that Candy had been able to get a compartment on a train which did not stop at Chicago, except for a few minutes, at two o'clock in the morning: otherwise she probably would have had to change trains at Chicago and even if it were not necessary to change at Union Station for an express train, it would still be nervous-making to know that when the train did stop for a few minutes in Chicago, detectives, summoned by her parents, might board the train and arrest her for kidnaping the dear, darling creature or take the child from her. It was still possible that this might happen anyway, but it seemed less likely by far to Candy at two o'clock in the morning and once the train left Chicago, she would be able to sleep in peace and be free of being stopped or arrested or deprived of the dear creature until the train arrived in Albany early in the morning.

Candy looked from the train windows at the sordor and slum, dark and white, of the winter night and sighed to think how evil the most noble of human beings sometimes were. Father was surely one of the most noble of human beings, but all his fine words and all his fine sentiments and all his exalted ideals and attitudes collapsed like a house of cards the moment they were tried by a crisis in his own family. It was Mother's fault, Candy knew that it was Mother's fault, for Mother had cowed and crushed Father since the first year of marriage. Father was a noble human being, but he was weak; Mother was strong, but she was a tyrant and her tyranny would not have been harmful, if only she had not been so strong and had so cruel a hold on Father.

How close she had come to being caught before she left the house with the child: and how quickly she had had to act, after observing the look upon Mother's face and soon after upon Father's that morning at the breakfast table! Her female intuition had told her immediately that something was very wrong, and she had been sure she was right when Mother and Father retired to Father's study after breakfast was over. Father's face was shaken and Mother's was stony. Mother had casually opened her mail while sipping her breakfast coffee and then she had read the awful letter—the letter which said that one or the other of the child's parents was a Negro. It was probably true that the mother was partly a Negro: it was very difficult to be sure whether it was the paternal or maternal parent of the child, but it was much more likely that it was the mother and perhaps the mother had told the father only after she became pregnant.

How delightful everything had been on Saturday and Sunday. It was on Saturday that the discussion of the naming of the child had occurred and the voting, or the choice, as Father called it. It was perfect irony and too delicious to be true that William had voted that the child be named Abraham Lincoln Manning and Father had gently used his power of veto, declaring that although Abe Lincoln was perhaps the greatest of all American Presidents, nevertheless it would be grandiose, pretentious and hence vulgar to name the child Abraham. Mother had murmured something deprecatory which Candy did not hear clearly except for the words "Irish Rose."

And then again on Sunday Father's sermon had been so inspiring, so noble! *Misère!* there was an enormous gulf between what human beings professed to believe and the actions which they performed whenever a real crisis occurred, or threatened to occur: that was just what Father had said in his sermon on Sunday, and he had provided on Monday pure and perfect proof of how cowardly a noble human being, who believed in courage and was often very courageous, could behave when he was really on the spot.

On Monday at lunch time Candy had recognized how sad-faced Father looked and how stony-faced Mother was and Candy's woman's intuition told her that the baby was not going to be adopted the moment she looked at them. When lunch was over, Father said that he had a painful announcement to make, the announcement that for various reasons the adoption of the baby would have to be postponed for several weeks at least. Candy looked quickly at Mother, saw the displeasure flicker in her eyes and knew then that Mother had expected Father to announce that the child would not be adopted at all and Father's announcement had been a false compromise, a compromise between the dictates of his conscience and the dictatorship of his wife which would result in only one conclusion: the sending of the baby to an orphan asylum. Candy did her best to conceal her own feelings, confided in no one, and took a taxi immediately after lunch to the bank where all her savings were. She withdrew all her money from the bank, took a taxi to the depot, reserved a compartment on the night train, despite the supercilious and doubtful expression on the face of the man behind the ticket window who Candy feared might call her parents. Then, after dinner she composed a careful, polite and tactful note which her parents would find upon her bed when they discovered that she had kidnaped the poor creature.

At eight-thirty Candy told Lewis to get her a taxi and meet her two blocks away and when he wanted an explanation, she told him that if he did not do exactly what she said he had to do right now, she would never speak to him again. This made Candy feel guilty but she felt justified and innocent as soon as she took the baby down the stairs and out the front door while Mother was reading in her boudoir and Father was suffering remorse in his study.

Lewis was where Candy had told him to be and a taxi was waiting and she kissed Lewis goodbye and told him to say nothing of what he had done and she was doing and soon the taxi was on its way to the depot. At the gate where the train was waiting she told the conductor who asked silently for an explanation that she was taking her sister's child to Boston. He said nothing and Candy was afraid again but nothing happened and at ten o'clock, just before the train finally left, she gave the dear creature his ten o'clock bottle.

During the trip, sometime after midnight, Candy read the current *New Yorker* which she had taken along with her and came upon Edmund Wilson's review of *The Collected Works of Abraham Lincoln*: "In great contests each party claims to act in accordance with the will of God. Both may be, and one must be wrong. God cannot be for and against the same thing at the same time . . . it is quite possible that God's purpose is something different from the purpose of either party; and yet the human instrumentalities, working just as they do, are of the best adaptation to effect his purpose. I am almost ready to say that this is probably true; that God wills this contest, and wills that it shall not end yet. . . .' " . . .

> The baby is in his bassinet,
> After day's fitful fever he sleeps well.
> Bias has done its worst. Nor *Mère*, nor *Père*,
> Malice domestic, race prejudice, nothing
> Can harm the child once Hartford is his hearth.

Candy had fallen asleep while reading the *New Yorker*.

III

A Confidential Report

Dear Quincy,

Before the meeting of the trustees occurs—I am assuming, perhaps wrongly, that there will be a meeting and not an eruption of indignation which will lead immediately to resignations *en masse*—I think it might be best for me to write out this account of "the facts" which I have carefully and indeed painfully unearthed after conferring with everyone concerned, except the infant himself. I doubt that anyone who has not yet taken all the pains that I have to find out "the truth —the whole truth—and whatever other kind is there, after all?—will have any genuine knowledge of what actually occurred. The unwillingness of most human beings to face the truth and their unawareness of it when they are forced to confront it—is something I need not expound to you. And I need hardly tell you that most human beings possess im-

mense resources of ingenuity, disingenuity, and imagination
which enable them to transform whatever happens to them
into the most amazing fabrications. The repugnant actuality
was far from being a candid and open thing at the very start;
and the mixed-up status of the entire affair has been increased
by the confusions of the press, further confounded by the
students and the faculty of Hartford and the nearby men's
schools—who were so excited that they issued statements, mani-
festoes and threatening ultimatums each more drastic than the
preceding one, in an unprecedented fashion—and the entire
affair has finally been blown up into a hideous pandemonium
by the sudden descent of Cobb's Congressional committee.

Nothing can be done about demagogues like Cobb directly.
But I assume that the trustees, like most human beings, are not
self-seeking opportunists who have a vested interest in denying
the truth, but like most human beings, are sincere and honest
in their evasion of the truth. They will act as I imagine a con-
gregation of Christian Scientists acts at the funeral of a devout
Scientist, denying the truth of evil, disease and death, yet nevertheless attending the ceremony and permitting the undertaker
to place the body of the dear departed one in a coffin, to transfer
the coffin to a hearse, and finally to bury the coffin in a newly
dug grave.

I must say more about the difficulty of communicating the
truth in this instance, but perhaps I had better summarize "the
facts" before proceeding to the sophisticated and complicated
matters which are beyond most of the trustees' minds or consciousness, at least insofar as they are merely trustees.

During the Christmas recess, an infant was placed upon the
doorstep of the Manning house where it was found by Candida
Manning. When I questioned Candida, it was difficult to get
her to commit herself as to whether there were reasons to think
the poor mother had chosen the Manning family rather than
another one, but I persisted and despite Candida's indignation
and excitement, I verified what I had suspected immediately

—that the Mannings had been chosen, it is almost certain, because the mother knew of Dr. Manning as a minister of unconventional views—he had preached a sermon only the week before on Christianity as a scandal to the world of propriety, respectability, and middle-class morality—and it is entirely probable also that the Manning family was chosen as quite well-to-do, full of children, extremely liberal, extremely well-meaning, and, most important of all, eccentric and Bohemian in certain ways which would be remarkable anywhere and are all the more remarkable in the Middle West, and in that particular city of two hundred and fifty thousand human beings. Had any other family been chosen by the hapless mother, the result, surely, would not have been a national uproar. And since it is incontestable that the Mannings were selected rather than so many others because of the kind of a family they are and others are not, I think that this is the first "fact" to be emphasized: for it is enough in itself to show that what has occurred has virtually nothing to do with Hartford's intrinsic nature as an educational institution and just as little to do with the grants for sociological studies provided by a philanthropic foundation, unless we assume that such grants are to be given only after all the families of the recipients have been carefully investigated, as if they were destitute human beings who want to be placed on the relief rolls.

Soon after Candy, as everyone calls her, took in the infant, there was boundless excitement among all the Manning children and the parents too were delighted, so that by nightfall Mrs. Manning consented to the adoption of the child. It was only after several days of rejoicing and rapt interest in the new child that trouble began: and I think that this is the second point to be emphasized, the fact that at the outset and for almost a week the entire affair was confined wholly to the Manning family and had nothing whatever to do with Hartford or with the sociological studies of some of the Hartford students. The trouble began when Dr. Manning and Mrs. Manning each received a letter—the same letter, but two copies, as if to be certain both husband and wife possessed the information, and as if the writer knew they did not always consult each other—a letter which asserted that the infant was a negro; and added, with devious directions, an offer to provide the incontestable evidence that this statement about the infant's paternity was true, if the would-be foster parents wished to be convinced that the anonymous informant was telling the truth!

Knowing that all their offspring would be not only acutely disappointed but shocked that the infant was not, after all, going to be adopted into the family, Dr. and Mrs. Manning conferred for a long time in Dr. Manning's study: the problem was not at all simple, for the sudden change of mind would have to be justified to the children and Dr. Manning's passionate social avowals would have sufficed to make it very difficult to tell the Manning children the truth about their reversal: in addition to Dr. Manning's pulpit denunciations of segregation in the South, Mrs. Manning had often told her offspring with much pride of her New England forebears and had dwelt fondly on those among them who had been ardent Abolitionists before the Civil War. Dr. Manning thought it would be best to attempt a detailed explanation to the children, telling them with care and candor that the ideal state of society which all human beings of good will desired and wished to further had not yet come about and would not be near realization for years to come so that until then it would cause the infant more harm by far than good to be part of a white family. Mrs. Manning insisted—rightly, I suppose, in view of how young most of the Manning children are—that this was too complicated an explanation. She said that the children had shown no evidence of a capacity to understand the meaning and necessity of piecemeal progress, limited objectives, and "gradualism," the word Dr. Manning had used in speaking to her. She wanted to explain matters to the children on the basis of "family," on the basis, that is to say, of a distinction between the ideals to which one is devoted as a part of the community and the very different criterion one had to adopt within the heart of the family.

During the past two and a half years, Mrs. Manning had been very much alarmed when, in rapid succession, the three daughters of her best friend had contracted entirely undesirable marriages, one to a Czech refugee, one to a Jew, and one to a young man who was of an Italian immigrant family. Hence it seemed both sensible and important to use this comparatively minor crisis to suggest to her daughters that however devoted one might be to the ideal of a truly democratic social order, nevertheless the community was not the same thing as one's family and the nature of the family was such as to make intermarriage unwise, at least in most instances: this was a good opportunity precisely because it was an extreme and unlikely situation—none of the girls would want to marry Negroes, of course—to instruct the children in how dangerous intermarriage was, how the offspring of such intermarriages very often suffered from a loss of identity and worse, from a shame about part of their family background which led to cowardice, guilt, evasion, or an over-assertion which made them reject with cruelty and unfairness that part of the family background which posessed social superiority in a conventional sense.

Dr. Manning was very much distressed, for he had never before perceived with complete clarity what his wife's underlying attitude was, how the liberal and unconventional views she seemed to accept were based upon an intense belief that she was far superior to most other human beings, who were equal to his wife solely because they were so inferior to her and to her Bostonian forebears. Troubled as he was, Dr. Manning made little protest: his wife's explanation seemed just as complicated as his own and less justifiable because it was in part a denial of the truth and in part an exploitation of a half-truth governed by ulterior motives. Dr. Manning did say that he was unable to see how Mrs. Manning's justification would seem to justify anything to the children, but he knew it was useless to contend with his wife whenever she felt strongly about anything.

They had not decided exactly how to formulate an explanation to the children when the servant girl knocked on the door of Dr. Manning's study and told them, in a panicky voice, that the infant had disappeared Mrs. Manning knew immediately that Candy had eavesdropped upon her parents—this had occurred before—and had taken the child. Questioning the other children, the Mannings learned that Candy had been outraged at her parents' "snobbery, bigotry, cowardice and hypocrisy"—the very words she had used to her sister Emily, and had departed with the child to save it, Candy told Emily, in tears of indignation, from a fate far worse than death—an orphanage, segregation, social injustice, and racial prejudice. By the next morning, Candy had returned to her dormitory at Hartford with the child and was soon so preoccupied in preparing the baby's formulas that she apparently was hardly aware of how, so far, she encountered no opposition or criticism, or that her arrival at school with a newly born infant had not been the cause of extreme astonishment solely because most of the students had not yet returned from the winter recess.

Soon after Candy's return, her parents had called her long distance. Speaking first with her mother and then with her father, she had answered their carefully restrained and measured pleas to return with the infant. With an expression of stubborn anger, at the start—speaking to her mother and telling her that she had not been surprised by her "reactionary" attitude— and then, speaking to her father, whom she loves with just as much integrity as she dislikes her mother—she had controlled herself for a time by restricting her refusal to a statement of how disappointed she was to find out how he really felt. When he continued to plead with her, she had let herself go and accused him of being disloyal to his principles, a hideous snob, a ghastly hypocrite, a whited sepulchre, and worse, a coward who feared his wife. Naturally the parents were thunderstruck as well as very much wounded, for Candy had never before made explicit the intense resentment she felt towards her mother and how critical she had been for some time of the way in which Mrs. Manning dominated her husband and her entire family.

Here again it is important to underscore what will be overlooked or disregarded—as it has already been—Candy as a unique individual of a remarkable family in the midst of which she had lived most of her life. Her attitude toward her mother had been one of half-concealed, half-revealed resistance and rebellion for several years, at least: Mrs. Manning had declared that Candy was not "college material," two years before the question need have been raised: Candy retaliated by announcing that she was going to become a nurse, which sufficed to place her mother on the defensive and enable Candy to get to Hartford. Soon after arriving, she shocked the other students by volunteering to pose in the nude as an art class model before a mixed audience, an offer accepted in silence and soon abandoned when Candy discovered that her nakedness attracted no amorous attention whatever, but presented merely a problem in drawing. Thus it is clearly true—and clearly it is just as difficult to be explicit about this truth—that Candy's seizure of the infant was inspired first of all and above all by her family role and the feeling and motives she acquired in the midst of the family realm, while being crushed by a matriarchal dictatorship: Candy was moved by extreme resentment, by sexual curiosity, eagerness and precocity, and by a conscious determination to enjoy in her own right her mother's dominion and eminence.

I know how impossible it would be to make these preceding occurrences a matter of direct presentation in explanation—an almost total explanation—of Candy's refusal to return the infant. Yet it is this point of Candy's responsibility, and equally, her parents' which has vanished entirely from everyone's mind, if indeed it was ever taken into account. If either or both parents had immediately appeared at Hartford, during the winter recess

—which still was more than a week long—then the intolerable aftermath would have been avoided, and no one would have known anything whatever about the entire affair outside of the Manning family.

This cannot be presented as indisputable evidence, since it did not occur, although it is as likely as any course which could have and did not occur that the Mannings could have regained the child by invoking their rights as parents who had taken out adoption papers; but surely it is possible, however extreme, to compare Candy's appearance with a newly born infant to the appearance upon the Hartford campus of a homicidal maniac. The exaggeration is justified, surely, since it is the best way of pointing out that there is nothing intrinsic or essential to Hartford and those related to Hartford in one or another way which involves the sudden appearance of students with infants of dubious origin. No one would suppose that the administration at Hartford fostered and encouraged an un-American state of mind and un-American ideals among its students when extraordinary and regrettable behavior of another kind occurs. It is probably useless to insist on the point, but I have looked up statistics of the same sort regarding the incidence of drug addiction, sexual promiscuity, sexual deviation, and the like at the leading schools in the East, most of them far more conservative than Hartford. Every year, consistently, a certain number of students are attracted to these vices, some of them become seriously addicted or suffer serious emotional disruption: yet no one has been foolish enough to suppose that because these vices occur at an educational institution, it is the institution which has encouraged them, aided, abetted, incited them, by the policy of the administration and the intrinsic nature of the curriculum, the subjects which are taught.

After questioning both parents, I was forced to conclude that both parents failed to act quickly for fear that their action would be publicized and their championship of various liberal and advanced causes compromised. The fact is clear that this would not have occurred, even if, as Mrs. Manning insists and Dr. Manning denies, Candy hinted or clearly threatened to publicize any effort of her parents to take away the child from her. For Candy would have done nothing of the sort as long as it was solely a family question: her instinctive loyalty to her family is far too strong, however much she resents her mother and thinks of herself as a very advanced young lady.

The Mannings, by hesitating, by permitting themselves to be intimidated by Candy's unexampled fury of accusation, allowed a situation which was a family responsibility only and could only have come into existence in so remarkable a family—to become a Hartford question, and then the cause of national furor. The coals of fire were suddenly placed in Goodknight's hands. It must be admitted that he did not act very well, but it is hard to see precisely what, at that point, he could have done. This was his first year as president, he was still a comparative stranger, he was naturally determined to move slowly and avoid trouble when it was avoidable until he had become familiar with all the problems involved in directing a progressive school for young and wealthy girls. Now, suddenly, he was confronted not only with a *fait accompli*, but one which had no precedent whatever, since nothing of the sort had ever occurred before, either at Hartford or elsewhere. This intensified his natural inclination to be circumspect, to move slowly, to be non-committal. At first Goodknight maintained that the infant would not be given the proper care at Hartford, an argument which was manifestly untrue, at this point, since no detailed plans had been made for the disposition of the child and only an orphanage had been proposed, while the child obviously flourished very well in the care of Candy and the friends who lived in the same dormitory. But again it is foolish to condemn Goodknight, or to be critical of him, since he had not been informed—how could he have been?—that among the duties of his office was that of judging whether an infant is getting the proper care—he and his wife are childless—while an even more important duty of which he had not been informed was that of securing an adequate home for children who were abandoned, illegitimate, and colored.

He finally proposed—when it was far too late, so excited, determined and dedicated were Candy and her friends—to secure a Negro couple and have them adopt the infant, subject to the approval by the students, of the Negro couple. Had Goodknight unearthed this couple at the very beginning of the new term, he would not have prevented some of the most excited of the girls from condemning this arrangement as a clear betrayal of the principles of a democratic society, principles continually being taught at Hartford, but at least this would have stopped the affair from getting beyond the limits of the academic community. But the girls involved had been antagonized by Goodknight's first statement of policy during the fall term, when he proposed that the Hartford curriculum be given a new and what he called scientific orientation as opposed to the preoccupation with literature, the arts, the drama and ballet which had prevailed until his installation that September.

Goodknight's explicit justification for an altered curriculum was extremely foolish. This must be admitted without qualification. He declared that the beginning of the atomic era signified the conclusion of that concentration upon the master works of high culture which had hitherto marked the Hartford girls and which had been overestimated by being called "creative." Young women who wished to be truly creative must now be concerned first of all with the responsbility which would be theirs when they were citizens endowed with suffrage, and as wives and mothers burdened with all the tasks and all the anxiety of womanhood. This would have hardly apealed to any of the young ladies under any circumstances and no matter what the reasons of the President. The extreme and somewhat self-righteous formulation made matters worse: not only were a good many Hartford girls immediately disaffected, but the faculty also

was outraged, particularly since the statement included a re-
duction of the budget expenditures for the drama, ballet, and
art, to make possible increased expenditures for the study
ot atomic physics, adequately equipped laboratories, and
the like. Several instructors resigned immediately and were
persuaded to wait until the end of the year: an inclination to
rebellion and to self-assertion existed at one or another degree
of intensity upon the campus. Thus when Candy appeared with
her infant bombshell, the entire school was prepared: the girls
and their teachers had been in a volcanic state, latent with
indignation and protestation and detestation of authority. The
teachers behaved very well when the winter recess ended
and everyone had returned to Hartford: they refused to be
critical of Goodknight yet it is also true that they did not express
any strong dissent or disagreement with Candy's attitudes which
had by that time become those of a number of girls who were
united enough to be called a kind of party.

Clearly it can be said that no one was in the wrong and at
the same time everyone was in the wrong, for all were involved in
an original experience, an experience so original that nothing
in the past experience of anyone was a preparation enabling
one to recognize the new experience: forgive them, it might be
said, they not only did not know what they were doing, but
they had never before done anything of the sort, in ignorance or
with conscious intention, and once the school was in session,
the situation possessed a momentum which was unsuspected
and uncontrollable: as Yeats speaks of the Magi encountering,
in bewilderment, "the uncontrollable mystery upon the bes-
tial floor," this is an instance of an uncontrollable hysteria at
the scholastic door, upon the campus and in the dormitory
where nothing of the sort—nothing more serious than a panty
raid—had occurred before.

Indeed the entire episode draws one irresistibly to a long
excursion—which I will suppress—on the American character,
on the innocence of America, and of American womanhood,

such as Henry James dramatized so well in another young
American girl, Daisy Miller: Candy resembles Daisy very much,
and the differences such as they are are without meaning, for the
behavior of Candy and her friends and their "child's party" is
rooted in the dominant patterns of American life. The majority
of the girls who go to Hartford come of good families, either
families of wealth or of good social standing in Boston, New
York and Philadelphia. They come to Hartford, instead of the
older and more conventional girls' colleges in the East, because
they are already much involved in a repudiation of their family,
the career of the debutante, and the customary studies of undergraduates. Hence Hartford is not the product of a theory of
education, as it seems to outsiders, but the result of something
which the students and their parents both refuse to recognize,
the girls' profound dissatisfaction with their social class, social
status, the natural or, if you like, customary expectations of
their families. The girls of Hartford have committed themselves
to a profound rejection of the entire way of life of the upper
middle class in our society. This is the root truth of the incident,
useless as it may be, and difficult as it certainly is to explain
to anyone not already acquainted with the root truth, to whom
no explanation would therefore be necessary.

When school was again in session, Candy's party immediately attracted new and passionate supporters. Pressure was
brought to bear upon the acting chairman of the social science
department to allot part of the fund for projects in which
students attempt "to determine the compass of the problems
with which social sciences must deal when it is rooted in reality."
The result of these projects in every instance is just as an un-
equivocal one as it is, for the most part, unrecognized: reality is
the silent partner of the imagination. Reality in this instance
seemed to Candy and her friends to be rooted with overwhelming
clarity in the problem of the care of an abandoned colored infant.
The acting chairman of the department refused to make any

such allotment. Hearing of his refusal from the girls, one could hardly avoid the impression that the girls—in some part of their hearts, some region of their minds—desired eagerly to be refused. The reason for refusal was again viewed as a mere pretext and hypocrisy: the acting chairman said only that since the actual chairman was in Europe on a Fulbright, he lacked the authority to make the allotment.

The refusal caused a new clamor: the girls claimed that if the true chairman had been present, he would have given his blessing, support and financial aid to the adoption of the infant by Candy and her friends. And then one clever girl suggested that the true chairman be questioned by phone or cable as to his view, and this led immediately to the office of the president. Goodknight rejected the bold proposal, saying that it was an undue imposition on the absent teacher and that he was, in any case, not likely to be willing to intervene and judge when he was so far removed from the campus and the local scene: as, in all truth, he was, for the abyss of the Atlantic was not the only obstacle to an understanding of the growing crisis.

It was then that Goodknight began to move forward with unquestionable gentleness but clear resolution to the point at which he told the girls that the infant must be surrendered to the proper authorities.

"Who are the proper authorities?" Candy asked quickly. "Are there any?" one of her friends added. And a third spoke with the same heat and speed: "Either we have not been taught the truth, or the truth which we have been taught is being deliberately ignored."

"You are just like my father, Mr. Goodknight," Candy exclaimed with passionate indignation and a barely suppressed sob in her voice.

This immediately placed Goodknight upon the defensive: and though the interview was short and did not long continue, to be an accusation of the President, Goodknight perceived very soon, with characteristic and absolutely incredulous amazement, that Candy was literally and entirely sincere when she said that she was not afraid of expulsion. And the other girls echoed her, and if they were not all as determined to follow the dictates of conscience as Candy, nevertheless Goodknight was unable to deceive himself: this was not a teapot tempest, but a genuine emotional tornado, whatever its causes might be and Goodknight suspected that its causes at heart were not purely social and political, he knew that as a unique emotional tornado, it might very well lend to calamitous and unpredictable consequence.

Since expulsion did not trouble the girls in the least, Goodknight felt paralyzed: his paralysis took the form of expressionless silence and since he was a fluent man, on all occasions, the girls interpreted his silence, naturally enough, as the intransingent unwillingness to yield on the part of an authoritarian and a despot.

As the girls made a sullen departure, Goodknight could think of only one resolution of the crisis: the passage of time: summer would save him: but it was mid-winter at Hartford. Goodknight feared precisely what Candy's parents had feared. He felt certain that if he expelled Candy as the ringleader and some of her more assertive friends, they would not be troubled, they would be delighted. Delighted in principle to make the entire affair public: the girls had been taught that this was an essential part of the democratic process. In the last resort, as in a serious strike, American public opinion would decide who was right and who was wrong. Indeed one of the less voluble girls had murmured during the interview: *"Vox populi, vox dei*—you can't fool all the students all the time."

The publicity which Goodknight feared descended upon Hartford soon after, bringing pandemonium, chaos, metropolitan reporters and flashbulb photographers. However, neither Candy nor her friends were directly responsible, although perhaps they might have made such a move after a time. A student at one of the men's colleges fifty miles distant from Hartford—who had been paid for the previous two years to supply tips of information—called up several nationwide press bureaus and several gossip columnists in New York, Philadelphia and Boston.

As it happened, before nationwide publicity descended upon Hartford, the Hartford girls, reacting with the savagery of youth to Goodknight's misunderstood silence, had set in motion a campus campaign to demonstrate the stalwart reality of their principles and convictions. Some of the girls appeared to believe that they were employing the method of trade union leaders in an industrial strike and there was some talk of a sitdown strike in the classrooms. But before any further action and before the arrival of the press, the blackboards bore, on the morning after the interview with the president, these sentences and others of equal brutality:

GOODKNIGHT IS A CRAVEN KNAVE AND A PRETENTIOUS HYPO-CRITE.

LINCOLN HAS BEEN ASSASSINATED A SECOND TIME.

GOODKNIGHT IS GOOD FOR NOTHING.

HARTFORD IS HEARTLESS.

DON'T BE A FOOL AND BELIEVE WHAT YOU ARE TAUGHT IN SCHOOL.

THE PRINCIPLES OF DEMOCRACY AND EQUALITY EXIST ONLY FOR THE WHITE RACE.

HITLER, YOU WERE AHEAD OF YOUR TIME.

THE CIVIL WAR WAS FOUGHT IN VAIN.

SUFFER A LITTLE CHILD TO COME TO US AND TO SUFFER.

The teachers, coming into their classrooms, and finding these sentences chalked upon the blackboard, tried to be neutral, neither erasing the sentences nor acting as if they were aware of their presence.

The arrival of reporters broke the back of the conflict during the next two days. For as soon as nationwide publicity became an actual fact and ceased to be a threat and a dreaded possibility, the little champions of the child discovered that they no longer had any power whatever to exercise: for the administration felt, for the time being at least, that the worst that could occur had already occurred. No educator, however aware and prudent he was, could have foreseen that a congressional committee, starved for publicity and for new grist, would seize upon the excitement at Hartford. The truth is that if the most hostile students had envisaged the possibility of Senator Cobb's intervention—they all detested Cobb and it was Cobb above all and what he represents that they supposed themselves to be attacking—then a compromise and silence might have been accomplished, or, at the very least, the stalemate and impasse would have continued and have been confined to the campus of Hartford.

Hartford is in the depths of the most rural countryside: the nearby village is not even a whistle stop, it is merely a country store and post office: the nearest township is twenty miles by car and it is important to bear these facts in mind first because they indicate that the girls were innocent of the uses which Senator Cobb might make of their protest and rebellion and second because the welfare agencies for the destitute and for orphans, who might have been summoned to the scene if Hartford had been near a fairly big city, were too distant to be called in promptly. Goodknight should have attempted to make this move in any case, despite the distance, as a possible means of shifting the burden of judgment and responsibility to agencies which exist solely for the purpose of social welfare problems. But he would have had to act more quickly than he— and most educators in such a situation—are disposed by temperament, training, tradition and precedent to act. It is not true, however, that Goodknight is, as some of the columnists loudly implied, a member of the light brigade; to be exact and just, he is simply genteel, slow-moving, and dislikes scenes and crises so much that he behaves more or less as one's maiden aunt is expected to behave. After all, the poor man, when he became President, had no way of knowing—no one did—that he would have to cope with situations which began with the slave trade, reached a climax in the Civil War, and have been made more difficult than ever before by the Supreme Court, the Soviet Union, and the Cold War.

The Hartford girls were, to their own immense astonishment, very much disturbed by the experience of nationwide publicity. It gave them a sense for the first time that what they were doing did not appear to the outside world as being a pure and dedicated action—clearly and obviously. The girls had supposed that only reactionaries would fail to recognize or to admit that their motives were principled and purely democratic. Moreover, the gossip columnists had suggested sexual immorality among the Hartford girls; and the sexual frustration of late adolescence had been the explanation of a metropolitan sob sister of all the tumult intensity. Since most of the girls are—in a good as well as in a bad sense—children of good families, they have an instinctive distaste of newspaper publicity as vulgar, unbecoming, and unfair. It was this instinct which immediately asserted itself among a good many of the girls after the first onslaught of publicity. There was a lull upon the campus, suddenly: a shock of real disturbance—some of the girls' parents had called long distance —and there was, during the lull, a feeling of relief and relaxation. The students and the faculty both believed that a hurricane had whirled through the little school, caused damage, produced unnatural insinuations, endangered important and valuable things, particularly since the columnists' insinuations had made the girls' sexual behavior a matter about which the public and people and their own parents might wonder. So, for a short time, the school as a whole thought that the sunlight of normality was shining again, albeit few would have admitted that it was a progressive school for girls' normality.

This intermission and delusion would not have occurred if anyone had kept in mind Candy's role: but just as no one foresaw the later complication of the legislative pack, so at this point no one reckoned with Candy's resourcefulness and determination. Candy moved quickly, once she felt a wavering and uncertainty among her hitherto passionate supporters. She moved just as quickly and in precisely the same manner as she had in taking away the infant from the Manning household to the Hartford campus: she took the child to the country house of Julia Sorel, an alumna of Hartford's first graduating class— she had almost been expelled several times for a variety of sexual escapades during her years at Hartford. In the fifteen years since being a Hartford student herself, Mrs. Sorel had become a well-known surrealist painter married to a Belgian modernist composer: and she had permitted her painting and drinking to be interrupted only by the report that a Hartford girl was being subjected to injustice in the very way that she had fancied and still fancied herself to have been mistreated—for reasons of prudery, bigotry and the self-righteous puritanism of the blue-noses on the Hartford faculty.

Mrs. Sorel was deceived about the injustice she had herself suffered (she enjoyed what occurred: it was a form of intense attention), but even more deceived, as the years passed, for the little basis in truth which her sense of injustice had had when she was a student was entirely a matter of the past during and after the second World War, when so many rules and regulations had to be suspended: but that's another matter except insofar as Mrs. Sorel mistook whatever happened in the present as being identical with her own experience many years before; and as a result—so she thought, at least—she felt obliged to provide a kind of Bohemian sanctuary, or asylum—asylum is more exact—for Hartford girls who were in a condition of desperation, resentment, jilted love, escapade, or, to be completely concrete, in need of an abortion.

Mrs. Sorel had taken an immense liking to Candy the year before, and Candy liked Mrs. Sorel very much too. When Candy turned to her, finding new support and much stronger support at a distance of forty miles and across the state line to boot, the feelings of Goodknight and his assistants on the faculty can well be imagined. This was the last straw, the very last straw, the final crisis. For Mrs. Sorel is not only an adult, a fairly well-known artist, and an alumna; she is also very rich, so rich that she has never known, nor had to know, immediately, just how rich she was at any particular moment. She gave Candy every kind of support—financial, emotional, unconventional, and legal, and made possible actions which had been beyond Candy's scope until then. Candy's position became impregnable when Mrs. Sorel summoned her lawyers who rushed to her country place with a speed that suggested transit by helicopter. The lawyers took charge with a decisiveness based upon knowing Mrs. Sorel for years and being well rewarded for their pains. It was at this point, then, that Goodknight's inertia and passivity, hitherto so damaging or disastrous, became wisdom itself: he said nothing: and if this hesitation until then may be regarded dubiously, it was the perfect attitude to adopt once a change of locale had occurred, and new circumstances existed. Mrs. Sorel was a whole set of new circumstances by herself and in herself: she would have welcomed the attention of the newspapers with a joyousness only her husband could have surpassed, for he loved public attention even more than his wife and was as ardent a Bohemian.

Nevertheless, some sort of truce might have been reached now that the child was no longer under the immediate jurisdiction of Hartford, and this truce would surely have become a kind of *status quo* until the end of the school year—and Hartford itself would have escaped the worst consequences of the entire affair—which was still no more than a Quixotic escapade of schoolgirls—had not there been a renewed rumor that Candy was in actuality the mother of the child and the father of the child a Negro. This rumor persisted until it attracted the attention of the Congress of the United States, in the form of Cobb's investigating committee, which descended upon Hartford and began an inquiry into Hartford's educational principles and methods, the sexual chastity and national patriotism of the Hartford girls, and the extent to which the girls and Hartford itself were being supported in activities which were un-American at the very least, by a philanthropic foundation. Had not Candy taken the law into her own hands again, announcing as soon as she and the infant were at Mrs. Sorel's house, that she was engaged to be married, matters might have been terminated prior to Cobb's descent. She still feared that the child would be taken away from her long before Mrs. Sorel could become its legal guardian.

*   *

*

The intervention of Cobb's investigating committee was the introduction of an entirely new dimension. The imputation of sexual irregularity—that is to say, of promiscuity or of a lack of chastity had merely been a side-issue until then, the subject of gossip and nothing more. Cobb, however, appeared to feel that an attack upon the educational methods of Hartford as an indoctrination into un-American and socialist ideals was insufficient. He wanted, and his assistants had no difficulty in helping him, to link disloyalty with immorality, illegitimacy with miscegnation, and complete sexual licentiousness with Communism. His assistants seized upon the suggestion which had been made at the very start that the now celebrated infant was in actuality Candy's own child, and it immediately became a question of proving not that this was true, but that the accusation was untrue, for in Cobb's mind, as ever, everyone was guilty until proven to be of an innocence incompatible with anything but sleeping sickness or a catatonic attack: and it was admitted, was it not? that Candy favored social equality for people of every creed and color: otherwise what was all the shooting about? In addition, the rumor that the child might in fact be Candy's had been first expressed and bruited about (but only on the campus) by other Hartford girls, those girls who had for some time been antagonized by the snobbery—the literary and intellectual snobbery: it was not social snobbery, of course —in Candy's circle. It was then that it occurred to Goodknight to indulge in the most interesting speculation of all—which he did not hesitate, for once, to express to others on the teaching staff.

"It is fascinating to ask," Goodknight said softly and in a pained voice, at a faculty meeting, "which occurrence would cause a greater degree of shock, a more serious disturbance— the fact that Candy wished to adopt a Negro child, or the fact that she had given birth to a child who had been fathered upon her by a Negro."

The teachers who listened to Goodknight were dumbfounded and few of them understood that he had been forced to this kind of facetious morbidity of speculation because he had felt so much humiliated by the written and chalked insults of the Hartford girls.

It was agreed at this meeting that no action whatever should be taken, except the most superficial, with regard to the Cobb committee's investigation: the files were not to be denied to Cobb's assistants, but no further aid and no discussion, sympathy or cooperation was to be manifest on the part of the faculty: Goodknight gained unanimous support for the attitude that Hartford did not recognize the need or the right of the congressional investigating committee at Hartford.

At the same time, Cobb's assistants began making inquiries among the Hartford girls, and the results were what one would expect: a complete confusion, comprehending the most scandalous suppositions on the one hand, and on the other an affirmation of moral purity which would have done credit to a nunnery. Cobb himself questioned the very much preoccupied Candy, who had been visiting the infant she had chosen to defend so valiantly every other day at Mrs. Sorel's, and it was this questioning of Candy which brought into the open a new state of mind, a new attitude, on Candy's part and that of her friends: a reversal of attitude such that it has to be called an unsuspected curve and bend in the dark labyrinth of the entire Hartford affair.

"My father has often said to me," Candy replied to Cobb, ignoring the question he had asked her, "that a husband and a wife are not really married unless they have a child: they are just having a prolonged affair! A house without a child is not a home and a childless family is not truly a family. I am sure my father is right!"

Cobb was left gasping: he had not inquired about Dr. Manning's view of marriage, but whether Candy thought that it was necessary for two human beings to secure the permission of the clergy or of the state in order to be truly married. Candy had seized upon the concept of true marriage, quoted her father with approval, and come forth with an answer so completely respectable, conventional and irrelevant that Cobb was left, for the first time in a long time, speechless.

After he had recovered and emerged from bewildered silence, he asked a direct question of Candy which was intolerable in itself and also intended as a trick. Hs asked her if she was, in fact, the mother of the child and hoped—knowing very well that she was not, despite the administration's deliberate failure to deny the accusation—that she would say she wished she was the mother of such a delightful child, thus admitting an inclination to miscegnation. Candy, knowingly or not, sidestepped the trap again with a beautiful directness and concision:

"How can you be so silly as to ask such a question, Senator?" Candy said with a chaste demureness. "If I were the mother of the child, this entire unpleasant and trying dispute would not have occurred at all and you would not be here and I don't think you should be here, anyway."

Again Cobb was left gasping and speechless.

And again, he decided to break down the stalwart Candy in the most vicious manner.

"It is fairly well established, Miss Manning," Cobb said, with the slight trace of a leer upon his fat face, "that at least half of the girls at Hartford are not and would not wish to be virgins after their first or second year at Hartford. It will not appear unseemly, I trust, to ask you then if you are still, in a physical sense, a virgin, Miss Manning."

Those who were present had begun spontaneously to groan in protest at Cobb's obvious and unnecessary bad taste when Candy answered in so spectacular a way that the listeners forgot their indignation immediately in uproarious laughter.

"You are not a gentleman, Senator Cobb! Would you ask your daughter or your sister a question like that?" Candy spoke with the same demureness and absence of malice as before. "You ought to be ashamed of yourself!"

Cobb was annihilated, perhaps most of all because the reporters, aware—as others, including myself, were not, that this was the sort of question which a waitress or a barmaid might have asked *circa* 1900—were enchanted and intoxicated by the cleverness of Candy's innocence and the deftness with which she had made the accuser the accused one.

"Suppose that someone wanted to know if your mother was a virgin until she was married to your father: what would you say then, Senator Cobb?" Candy said then, following her advantage: she had knocked the Senator down by making it clear that she did not think him a gentleman: now she was determined to keep him on the floor of the ring by questioning him as to his mother's chastity. In all his sensational adventures as an investigator, Cobb had never been faced by an opponent so quick, agile, guileless and capable of blows to the solar plexus.

"My dear Miss Manning," Cobb replied, stammering, because he was as sentimental as he was brutal, "you are hitting below the belt. You ought not to bring my mother into this questioning."

The uproar which greeted this weak protest stopped in mid-air so that Candy's comment could be heard.

"Now you see: one must draw a halt somewhere, Senator

Cobb," Candy said as if she were a young schoolmarm and Cobb a neighborhood hoodlum and ruffian, "Rules cannot be disregarded with impunity: fair play ought to be observed. It is about time you realized the significance of standards of decency and honor which you have so often disregarded in favor of libel and slander, in the name of patriotism and hiding behind the cloak of congressional immunity!"

When the uproar of delight which arose at Candy's answer had been silenced by Senator Cobb's severe and forbidding stare, he then turned and glared at Candy, in a rhetorical silence.

"I can see, Miss Manning," he said, moistening his lips and speaking as if he were sucking in his underlip and biting it, "I can see that you do not like me as a person. But that is beside the point: and you have not yet reached the age where you have a right to the vote, so that we can dispense with your views of the investigation here or any other congressional effort on my—"

Candy broke in Cobb indignantly and spoke with passion.

"Senator Cobb," she exclaimed in a voice nervous with excitement, "I may be presumptuous, but since you have come here to Hartford to question us *qua* Senator, the fact that I can not vote makes your right to question me dubious, at best! and what I have to say must have some meaning: otherwise you would not be here, as a demagogue. You should liten to me and try to understand what I say. I believe I have a far greater understanding of life than you do. I know about girls: you do not: I think it extremely probable that you have never been in love and that you have never been a child. Moreover, some of the questions you have asked are not only pointless, but they are not in good taste. 'The heart of another is a dark forest,' said Turgenev, 'but none more so than the heart of a young girl.' I suppose that I had better tell you that Turgenev waks not and is not an ardent advocate of Soviet Communism, but a very great novelist."

Candy's speech left everyone in dumbfounded delight, and a silence of astonishment which included Senator Cobb and Candy herself: she hardly knew what she was going to say before she spoke, but her intense sense of the wisdom of the heart gave her complete and serene assurance, devastating and spontaneous insight.

"Young lady," said Cobb after a paralyzed and shocked silence, clearly surrendering all effort to conceal the fact that he was enraged and insulted in the extreme. "Just what is it that you are trying to say? And just what is it that you want?"

Candy faced the audience, her look unaltered, speaking with the superb presence and the unwavering courage of conviction.

"Do you really wish to know what I want, Senator Cobb? Do you really want to know?" Candy asked a question but spoke as if she were stating an accusation. And then, continuing with marvelous poise and dignity, she said, "I dare not ask for what I hope: if what I hope were probable, I would not fill my throat with a single incoherent syllable!"

"Is that a quotation? Who told you to say that?"Cobb stammered, bewildered and irritated. "Has someone been coaching you? One of your teachers?"

"Senator Cobb, I have a mind of my own. I have been trained very well at Hartford. No one has coached me: only the experience of living in the United States and moving among people of every kind and station."

"Young lady," Cobb said in the utmost fury (making all present freeze in shocked protest), "Do you believe in birth control? Do you believe in marriage between white girls and Negro men?"

"Senator Cobb," said Candy, undisturbed, in calm hauteur, and with the resonance of victory and duty fulfilled in her voice, "You have a black tongue and a dirty mind. No question of birth control nor of inter-marriage brought you and your committee to Hartford. Hence, I need not answer your irrelevant and vicious questions. There is a saying that 'the heart cannot be commanded.' I follow the dictates of my heart, Senator Cobb!"

An overwhelming ovation of virtually hysterical applause saluted Candy's declaration. Cobb threw up his hands, as if admitting defeat, and walked away, murmuring to one of his assistants that he should have known very well that he would merely make a fool of himself if he questioned a sophisticated child who was, in addition, a Hartford student and the daughter of an eloquent minister.

The extreme delight—indeed rejoicing—which had greeted Cobb's discomfiture was so intense that not until the next day did anyone recognize the reversal which had occurred: Candy had not only made Cobb look dishonorable and ungentlemanly and foolish, but she had defended her father and Hartford, after all the days and weeks of sustained and overwhelming attack upon her family, upon the authorities and the administration at Hartford, and upon the great betrayal of democratic principles directly involved in the official and parental attitude toward the infant.

Those who saw that a shift had occurred were too delighted to see Cobb made to look like a vulgar fool and crude bounder by a little girl, to be troubled by the fact that at this point, chaos and confusion had been confounded and compounded beyond any ordinary possibility of clarification. Candy, suddenly, was the heroine of Hartford to the administration, to all the students, to Mrs. Sorel and to the reporters who had been present very often on other occasions when Cobb attacked confused and helpless human beings, and they had never seen any witness penetrate Cobb's malicious composure—to say nothing of the fact that she had accomplished far more and for the first time: Cobb was badly shaken. No accusation had troubled him until a little girl had slapped his wrist and told him that he was not a gentleman, a status far more important to Cobb, in his present state of mind and heart, than that of being a United States Senator. Hardly a newspaper and few cartoonists failed to make the most of Candy's beautiful coup.

Ralph Williams, enchanted like everyone else by the way in which Candy had made a United States Senator and the most feared man in the United States look like a crude and cruel buffoon, supposed like everyone else that Cobb would forget or pretend to forget Hartford and return to opponents whom he could intimidate more successfully. The Hartford girls possessed an innocence which adult human beings seldom sustained save through some identification of innocence and naiveté: most adult human beings existed in a state of guilt about one or another relationship, past or present, and although what they felt guilty about was hardly ever what Cobb attempted to establish, nevertheless they looked guilty, when they encountered the accusation of guilt, however inaccurate.

After the passage of a week, it became clear that Cobb was not going to forget about Hartford, but to attack the grants for projects in sociology which had been made by one of the most famous of the foundations; and it was then on a Sunday afternoon, seated in his study after going through the huge Sunday edition of The New York Times, that Ralph Williams reviewed his own impression of Hartford and the Hartford Affair.

He had come to teach at Hartford at the beginning of the fall term, he had never been in America before, and his experiences from the start had been different from anything he had known in England where he had been educated, or in India where he had been the child of Anglo-Indian civil servants which, as you know, is as distant as anyone can be from the New World, if only in that Williams had grown up in England's class society and in a caste system made all the more other than America by Albion's aloofness, shyness, or disdain of the Brahmin and the Maharajah. His impressions had been so different and their rapid succession so delightful and delightfully novel that he had scarcely attempted to come to any conclusions or pass any judgments about life in America and at Hartford.

It was certainly true that in America the rich and their off-spring regarded the possession of money as a grant of freedom, and this was perhaps most clear of all in what he knew of the attitude of the Hartford girls—of some of the Hartford girls—when it was a question of sexual freedom, sexual experiment, and sexual involvements which excluded marriage or disre-garded the fact that they had become involved with a married man. It was far from true, as the tabloid newspaper had sug-gested insistently day after day, and as Cobb had assumed entirely true, that all Hratford girls had affairs during their years at the school. It was a half-truth and like most half-truths amounted to a total falsehood, for the positive instances were what one called to mind and the negative instances were over-looked or unknown. The actuality was as different from the assumed reality as the daily newspaper's representations of what occurred on the previous day: in reading the daily news, coming upon accident, catastrophe, debauchery, murder and suicide, one hardly, or at least habitually, kept in mind the fact that on that very day hundreds of millions of human beings had lived through another uneventful day and night—a day marked, perhaps—for some of them at least—by happiness.

So it was with the supposed sexual promiscuity of the Hart-ford girls. None of them were, in fact, promiscuous in the sense of having more than one affair at a time, and indeed this was exactly what the most advanced girls regarded as truly immoral: to be involved with more than one man during the same period of time, to fail to break off one affair when one became interested in another man, or to be guilty in any way of a lack of candor and honesty about one's feelings.

Williams felt sure his impression was accurate that at least half the girls and perhaps more than half did not in ac-tuality go—to use their phrase—the limit with any man. Per-haps the restraint was merely a physical one and self-deception for a good many who remained chaste, but it meant a good deal to these girls, nevertheless, partly because they were afraid, rightly or wrongly, that an affair before marriage might make it more difficult for them to get husbands. Certainly there was an immense amount of freedom of speech and reference among some Hartford girl's circles, including Cardy's circle. And it was a freedom of language such as the most Bohemian young women in London would have thought shocking, despite the fact that their behavior comprehended a good many actions which, probably, most of the Hartford girls knew little or nothing about. Nevertheless it was merely the racy speech of upper middle class and literary girls: only the old-fashioned and the foolish would assume that the brouhaha of the girls' conversations was the verbal equivalent and direct evidence of wanton sexual activity. The statement of one columnist—that a Hartford virgin was a contradiction in terms—was quite untrue. During the descent of the Cobb committee, few girls questioned the likelihood that Candy had had an affair, but none of them knew that she really had except for the tendency among the girls to become more and more reticent about sexuality once they had begun their first affair: the avid discussions—which the girls called "bull sessions" since that was what the boys at the men's colleges called their own dormitory exchange of impressions—was prior, almost all of the time, to the real thing. There was a great deal of talk, a good deal of necking *in extremis*, an occasional venture across the borderline unknowingly or in the midst of infatuation, but almost never the deliberately cold-blooded and calculated promiscuity weekend after weekend which the press had described and which the press had, in fact, invented.

The truth is astonishing, probably the truth always is astonishing: the truth is that a strong sense of guilt about making love still existed, and was as intense as it had been in the past, among the girls and their young men, and this was all the more marked in those who took the most pride in their modernity of attitude, their freedom from puritanism and prudery: these attitudes merely masked the powerful feeling of fear which torment the girls and their young men too, whether or not they are chaste.

Candy's announcement that she was engaged to be married to Mrs. Sorel's younger brother renewed and augmented the problems which the Hartford faculty thought had been set to one side, at least, by the departure of the infant from the Hartford campus. It once again became necessary to be explicit and maintain an official attitude toward the infant and toward Candy's relationship to the infant. And now it was all the more difficult to decide on the most prudent attitude, since if the child was, in fact, Candy's child, her desire to keep the child presented itself in a very different moral and legal context; however regrettable her maternity prior to marriage might be, it could hardly be condemned as equal to abandonment, nor for that matter, an effort to secure an abortion.

Moreover, if the child was Candy's own child, marriage was in itself desirable; the actual father might be a Negro or of mixed blood, but Candy was going to marry a white man now and could not be accused of miscegnation continued and made permanent. Nevertheless there was no doubt then that the child was a Negro, however lightskinned, and thus that one parent was Negro to some degree. Thus the question of race prejudice and bigotry remained directly before the Hartford administration in a somewhat outlandish way, but—like the Great Wall of China—for whether Candy was the actual mother or the adopted mother, she had adopted a child of black skin: if the official Hartford attitude was silence, then silence was consent, as in the pursuit of love. On the other hand, any expression of disapproval would bring on another verbal riot among the Hartford girls, for it would be taken as renewed or new evidence that Hartford was based upon systematic hypocrisy.

Before continuing, I had better say that there is nothing whatever in the suggestion that Candy was the actual mother of the child—this would be clear as a matter of date of birth and the like, if there were any doubt. And it is equally and categorically true that Candy's sexual innocence has survived until the present moment, although she has been the object of much attention and pursuit on the part of the young men from nearby colleges and it may be that her chastity is a purely physical and quite trivial matter when set in contrast with the ardor and inclusiveness with which she and her friends engage in what in our youth was called necking. For all her deviousness and rebelliousness of character, Candy has a strong sense of propriety also, and whether this explains her innocence—which is not characteristic of her own circle of friends, I should add—is somewhat beside the point now: the point is that she has been slandered and libeled in a legal sense.

Mrs. Sorel first came to know Candy on one of the occasions when she was helping a girl of Candy's circle who had been trapped into unpremeditated pregnancy during a casual sexual adventure, and Mrs. Sorel did tend to support and encourage what she still calls "free love" among Hartford girls: she does not know how old-fashioned the phrase is! It is a long long time since Edna St. Vincent Millay sold free love to the women's clubs of America and burned her scandals at both ends, but Mrs. Sorel truly acts and believes that the present time is the same period of time; she is still in her first youth and it still is necessary to fight against the hypocritical constriction of the prigs, the prudes, the philistines and the puritans: for all I know—and to judge by the way she drinks—Mrs. Sorel may not have been informed that Prohibition has been repealed and she has not secured her liquor from a bootlegger or made gin in a bathtub!

Candy's circle has consisted of girls who have "a working understanding" with a fraternity at the nearest of the men's colleges—the young man who called the Associated Press belonged to this fraternity—and although there are no sororities at Hartford, and the fraternity system is frowned upon, as one would expect, by Candy's circle as entirely undemocratic, nevertheless Candy's circle functioned in relationship to this fraternity in just as conventional a fashion as that which exists between a fraternity and a sorority at any of the conservative, traditional and Ivy League schools. The behavior and the customs are just as adolescent, barbaric—and, I confess, just as charming, at times: secret societies delight, as you know, in codes, passwords, and secret or private nicknames: Candy's code name was Cold Cream, and her roommate Martha was known as Cream Cheese, while the fraternity in question were known, quite aptly, it appears, as the Martinis, a word chosen to unite the idea of a clan of Indians, the idea of braves, and the Dutch bravado of a cocktail party. The purpose of the working understanding, pact and compact between the boys and the girls is clear enough, although I doubt that they are conscious of the purpose: young men and women who have arrived at the exalted age and state of post-adolescence (which is to say, they no longer live at home with their families or under the rule of a headmaster) are protected from the infamy of adult society and can move about freely without fearing the scrutiny and criticism of their elders. The *entente* appeared at one point to be on the verge of making a decisive difference in the uproar about the infant, for some of the young men of the fraternity raised a fairly large sum of money to help Candy and secured pledges of further sums, a move which, before Mrs. Sorel entered like a *dea ex machina*, enabled Candy and her friends to issue a devastating answer to Goodknight's proposal that he secure a Negro couple as adopted parents for the infant: the sum of money raised and pledged was fairly big, in itself, and Candy's natural inclination to dramatize her feelings by exaggeration made her suggest that more than triple the amount was available, so that it was quite ridiculous and it was, in a like way, quite disingenuous for Goodknight to argue that the infant would fare far better in a Negro family than if Candy remained the infant's ward and guardian.

Before I continue, I must confess that as I go over the notes I have made—and again and again as I examined the situation and engaged in the questioning upon which the notes are based —I am, and I was, overcome by a sense of guilt such as I have not felt for many a day—not since the time when, during the Second World War, I had to make unfavorable comments about a close friend to the F.B.I. and another government agency: it is the kind of guilt, I mean, which one encounters when one is compelled to pass judgments which are of a different order from the sentiments and touchstones governing purely personal relationships. The realm is one in which intellectual analysis and logic are foremost, and exclude any entertainment of sympathy, compassion, pity or charity, any influence—so far as that is possible—of forgiveness, forebearance, and acceptance of another human being upon which all personal relationships, all intimate friendships and above all, the family itself, depend.

You will soon see how direct a bearing these feelings and this sense of guilt has upon the Hartford affair. It should make clear the degree to which what occurred at Hartford is the sort of thing which—as we live through it—draws from us a spontaneous affection and allegiance—just as, before we live through it, it represents to all of us as natives of the New World—the ultimate aspiration of innocence and goodness and nobility. Once we have lived through it, and taken serious account of such an affair, we must face the fact of the ultimate innocence of most forms of aspiration, an innocence unaware, deliberately or not, of the nature of reality and the nature of the reality of a human community, to such an extent that the only possible conclusion is the recognition of the infamy of innocence, an infamy all the more destructive because its basis is precisely this: the ignorance of innocence, the deliberately cultivated disregard of all consequences and of all possible injury to actual human beings in the name of one or another exalted principle: *let there be justice, although the heavens fall.* The Hartford girls disregarded the extent to which they might be the cause of injury to the school, to family, and their parents: they brushed aside as sophistical the possibility that their behavior might be harmful to Negroes. They became monomaniacs: the fixed idea of *loyalty* to a principle was more important, it seemed, than the specific principle as such. The principle was, to be sure, drawn from the democratic ethos to which America is committed: but the girls became more excited about loyalty, than about democracy, about being principled than about the problem of integrating the Negro as an oppressed, underprivileged minority.

The infamy of innocence begins by concerting a valid legal postulate—that all human beings are *born* equal—into an ideal and an absolute which must be realized immediately; if it is not, we are all unconscionable scoundrels and hypocrites. The desire for the immediate realization of principle (which other schools will face soon, I fear, when fraternities try to prove their democratic faith by admitting Negroes) is ruthless and possessed by all the overbearing cruelty of youth: this is the reason that the Hartford girls were so stubborn, tenacious, immovable, satirical and denunciatory throughout what I cannot help but think must be called the crisis of their innocence. Idealism rideth to a fall, like pride itself—it is a form of immense and self-righteous pride—and innocence goeth before cynicism, disappointment being the midwife of the bitter change; worst of all, innocence soweth the grapes of Quixotism and drinketh the wine of chaos; and radicalism, triumphantly established, becometh nihilism. The sons and daughters who were such passionate embodiments in Hartford's self-righteous innocence may be expected to go through these and like transformation and gyrations in later life—when it is too late.

This is hardly the conclusion to which I expected to come when you sent me to Hartford so that you might have an independent report on the so-called Hartford scandal. I expected, as, knowing me, you must know, to conclude that what occurred at Hartford, no matter how destructive and childish it was in some ways, was one instance of the kind of the calculated risk necessary and indeed inevitable in an open, free, democratic society; and I expected to be able to express this conclusion in a form which would appeal to the trustees as parents and seem persuasive to them as responsible and realistic adults. When you send your child to school, permit him to go on an excursion in the mountains or on the high seas, boating or riding, or, equally, when you buy him a sports car, you risk an accident which would not be likely to occur if he remained at home and were denied a high-powered vehicle. There is the same choice between inevitable alternatives at every turn: as devoted parents, one chooses between a calculated risk and the more dismal prospect of keeping one's son or daughter in a state of permanent childhood, immaturity, or sheltered adolescence—in short of making one's progeny domestic pets, safe in the asylum and sanctuary of the home. This outcome, I intended to point out to the trustees, is far more repugnant—and in any case, it may not be foolproof or lasting—than the risk of the other and, for the most part inescapable alternative—inescapable in the sense that civilized society could not exist for very long if most human beings were kept in a state of safety and security excluding all possible risk, hurt and harm. This is to say almost nothing of the fact that these young men and women would be spoon-fed, or continually hiding under the bed so much of the time that they would become human beings who would be regarded with contempt and disliked; human beings, moreover, who either dislike their parents or liked them with the craven affection and fondness of spaniels and lapdogs. Finally, as if the calculated risk were taken too late—and this, in actuality—happens most often—the son or daughter is plunged from complete security to an insecurity which is unsuspected and hence overwhelming which makes their adult lives a state of drunken resentment: they are like football heroes, child stars, infant prodigies and lyric poets: they cannot forget the privileges, indulgences, security, attention or limelight which they once enjoyed and which nothing, prior to the loss of the privileged phase, prepared them to expect or helped them to accept as inevitable.

I knew very well that this kind of appeal would not persuade every one of the trustees, and there are a few of them to whom the statement that in human existence there are always threatening situations suggests only a memory of the occasion in which they had done the threatening: but it seemed certain that a sufficient number would be won over merely by their own sense that one can never guard against all dangers and one can always be so careful that one is too careful and this in itself attracts perils of all sorts. Midway in my investigation, as I began to be aware of how inadequate my own attitude was —I was defending the right of a son or a daughter to drive a car when it was a question of flying a plane across the Atlantic, swimming the English Channel, or climbing Mount Everest— the risks were far greater, were too great: it was true that there were always threatening situations, but they might become situations so threatening that experience was an uninterrupted nightmare of terror—and nothing is as terrifying as innocence and that boundless idealism which is innocence's chief aspiration. Innocence was sowing the seeds of extreme disillusion and nihilism. The attitudes and principles meant as theoretical limits of the structure of a democratic society had become not the boundary lines they were meant to be but the center of attention, consciousness and action. The Hartford girls, in their disregard of all but principle, acted as if human beings existed for the sake of having a democratic state, rather than the democratic state for the sake of the human beings inhabiting it.

This is far from being an isolated or abstract question as the trustees, perhaps, can be persuaded by citing the attitude of the Hartford girls during the past generation towards divorce, and thus towards marriage: the two have become inseparable in their minds with the passing of the years, and it is now wholly forgotten that it is one thing to make divorce justifiable as a last resort when a marriage has failed and its continuance will merely be continual harm, and to liberate the act of divorce from the stigma which was until recently attached to it. It is another thing to make the possibility of divorce an integral part of the rapidity and rashness with which so many of the Hartford girls rush into early and heedless marriages. Whatever misgivings they may envisage are banished by the simple and sure safeguard of divorce as a cancellation and purgation, without aftermath, of an unfortunate error, passing infatuation, or, to be blunt, the desire to copulate under comparatively stabilized conditions, rather than in hotels, motels, and the back seats of automobiles. The actual result is that there is an extreme heightening of the very instability, impermanence and insecurity which makes existence difficult enough for most human beings in America. When the social mobility which is so fundamental to American society becomes an integral part of love, marriage and the family, at the very beginning, at the time when young men and women decide to get married and become involved in the most intimate of relationships, what can be expected but a continual collapse into chaos? Mobility is desirable only where there is an underlying stability. This must be true even of those families who live in trailers: they stop at night, to gain refreshment from that fountainhead of life, sleep. The tendency and direction which the Hartford girls illustrate can conclude, if it continues unchecked, in some insane version of existence as a perpetual marathon dance, an unending six day bicycle race, a senior prom in which the couples keep cutting in on each other in dances which continue, with brief halts, throughout adult life.

As I write and look back at what I have written, I see I have taken a long time to come to a conclusion which is not an answer—not an answer in the least—but a question, a whole set of questions: and the questioner looks like an inquisitor to a directorate who have come to hear answers, and not to begin to ask questions. The conclusion to which I come is merely a starting-point: we must begin to question all the assumptions of human beings who live their lives in American society. On other occasions, at other schools, it has been clear and obvious that an institution of education is an epitome of America itself, a microcosm of the great, sprawling, rich, and somewhat disunited states. The microcosm of the school, precisely because it is small, and because it is unified enough for inspection, is a combustible version, a fermenting bottle, a small volcano in which the major and half-hidden conflicts which run through American life come to the surface and erupt. This is all the more true because the young men and women are free—they possess more freedom because they are not yet adults and hence have no serious responsibilities—and their freedom is intensified by the vitality one enjoys at that age and by the sense of an open future awaiting them. Finally they are free in the most irresponsible sense—since they are no longer children but still for the most part adolescent—they are free to be the carriers —the *kamikaze*, I am almost tempted to say—of every impulse which can be destructive and annihilating and catastrophic (I do not exaggerate at all) when disconnected from the unity of human community and all its needs, concerns and interdependencies: but these impulses, on the other hand, cannot be condemned and prohibited without banning—if it is, indeed, possible —the very *élan* of America, the sense of existence which is native to a nation which began as an escape *into* freedom. Again, the automobile provides an apt metaphor: one cannot ban the use of cars by the young because some of them become hot-rod fanatics.

The girls at Hartford are the daughters—or perhaps, by now, some of them, the granddaughters, of Edna St. Vincent Millay; Gertrude Ederle, the girl who swam the English Channel; Ruth Elder, the girl who tried to fly the Atlantic; and Amelia Earhart, the girl who was lost in the Pacific: they are the great-great-granddaughters of Margaret Fuller, the very intellectual young lady who was Emerson's friend and terrified Hawthorne at the Utopian colony of Brook Farm. Before she drowned, on her honeymoon, crossing the Atlantic with her Italian bridegroom, she announced to Emerson: "I accept the universe!" You remember that when Emerson told Carlyle of this extraordinary remark, Carlyle said with stupid irony: "She'd better!" But Carlyle missed the point, naturally enough, since he knew nothing about American girls. The girls at Hartford regard the question of accepting or rejecting the universe as a very important and serious one: and they usually conclude that they wish to transform the universe, or at least to make some alterations. The universe and American life (the two are identical in their minds) is a place which they are determined to improve so that first of all they can feel creative and second so that they can be certain that the world is a nice place in which to live. The world at which they look is a late Victorian mansion, full of outmoded horrors, gingerbread, skeletons in the attic, mansard roof and dormer windows: nothing short of a transformation of this anachronism into the sane, efficient, bare and inhuman iceboxes of Frank Lloyd Wright or the Bauhaus will satisfy them—at least for the time being.

So too, the girls at Hartford are often the darlings of economic freedom, and it is clear here, as elsewhere, that money is freedom, clear that the Hartford girls possess a very real degree of freedom which is precisely what they had begun to use as capital when they were faced with the question of taking care of the kidnaped child, using the freedom of money with the utmost drama and efficiency in those disputations about the baby's fate in which they were told that their attitude was one which disregarded the child's future as an adolescent and an adult. They immediately collected and pooled funds and replied in triumph that no infant would flourish better in an underprivileged family!

The Hartford girls have tasted of the apple of freedom and found it enchanting. They want to continue to munch freedom's apples indefinitely and endlessly—which is to say, what they want is freedom for freedom's sake, freedom as an end, and not a means to comprehensive choices and commitments such as are inevitable in adult life. Thus what they want is nothing less than infinite freedom, like a machine for perpetual motion, or like spending the whole of one's life in an amusement park, rising and falling on carousel horses, dangling on Ferris wheels or screeching as the roller coaster dives and soars. Freedom is an automobile, a car that will take one anywhere, except to the kind of place where one can stop for good. They do not know that this is merely the dream of freedom and that if it were a reality, they would suffer boredom, nausea and vertigo. And some of the girls who have been at Hartford in past years are now living and will always live in this foolish paradise of endless experiment, endless freedom, playing their roles in a fantastic and unparalleled masquerade: it is a masquerade in which they suffer from the hallucination that it is possible to be a purely free being. At the most abandoned of masked balls, there was never any pretence that the dancers would be able to conceal their identity or change partners not only all through the night but all through life. Doubtless the girls would seek to abolish the law of gravitation—as a restriction upon their freedom—if this abolition could be accomplished through legislative action.

I could give specific examples if the mere accumulation of instances would make the point any more lucid. To be as concise as possible, the only conclusion I can reach is inconclusible: the inconclusible conclusion is a desperate dilemma which I cannot resolve nor avoid. As the assistant director of a shaken foundation I must confess that there are only two choices—two more, indeed—than most of us have after the age of thirty in most of the problems and choices which confront us. I must choose between Candy Manning and Senator Cobb both of whom are characterized by absolute self-assertion which is one of the reasons that they cannot ever arrive at a truce. It is almost needless to say that my heart belongs to Candy but that as a responsible and adult human being the prospect of the American girl regarding Candy Manning as the model *par excellence* of the American heroine is terrifying. It is entirely needless to say that Senator Cobb has terrified millions of human beings by his tactics as a senator. Faced with this choice one can only attempt to refuse to support either the young lady or the infamous senator. To support Senator Cobb is to support fascism: to support Candida Manning is to support boundless and uncontrollable freedom. The child is, to paraphrase the great poet, "the uncontrollable mystery on the scholastic campus." Candida Manning must be defended from herself: her unwillingness to be compromised or to realize principle through patience will lead her, unless she is protected from herself, to the martyrdom of an American Jeanne d'Arc!

If I seem melodramatic or grandiose, it is because I am tormented by a sense of unsuspected ignorance and undreamed of depths of self-hatred, bewildered and perplexed more than at any time prior that I can remember, I can think of only one possible counsel: it is to be found in Kierkegaard: "Reality is something which must be experienced; it is not a problem to be analyzed, discussed, and explained before the future has become the past."

If this were explained to Candy Manning prior to experiences which she has not yet had, that precocious little girl might very well quote Kierkegaard in reply: "To will one thing is purity of heart." And needless to say Senator Cobb could quote Holy Scripture as well as Satan himself. Just think of what he might make of the Old Testament episode in which Abraham is commanded to sacrifice his son Isaac; and if he happened upon Kierkegaard's commentary on the episode in *Fear and Trembling*, demagoguery would become a filibuster during which Cobb would convince millions of Americans that all foundlings and orphans are Danish agents of the Russian secret police, wearing blackface or foisting themselves on us as Aryans, despite their dark Slavic and African forbears. This is grotesque and extreme, but an expression of genuine emotion. What else can one say, confronted with a cynical opportunist who may declare that spaghetti is un-American and chop suey the insidious propaganda of Communist China?

I hope you will see that I have done the best I can—and the best is far from enough. Please don't hesitate to ask me any further questions before the meeting of the Board.

(May the inconceivable future have mercy upon us)

Yours ever,

(Signed) DeWitt Howe

The Statues

To Meyer Schapiro

The snowfall began at five on the afternoon of the 8th of December. Faber Gottschalk, a dentist of thirty, walking to his office to meet one of his patients, was hardly aware of the first few feathers of snow. He had had a whiskey and soda but a moment before, and the pleasant bonfire liquor created in his whole being permitted him to think of the next hour without his customary distaste. Intimacy was what he resented most about his profession, the necessary acquaintance with the interior of the human mouth. To seek out decay, and pus, to do this day after day, to have this in the forefront of one's consciousness—these central aspects of his profession he disliked, did not get used to, and would never regard with anything but aversion. Consequently, as a habit of mind, he constantly evaded what immediately presented itself to him, the dinner he ate, the street on which he walked, or as on this afternoon, the first signs of the white whole and visual absolute of winter, the snow.

It was night before the sidewalks were covered over, and midnight before the remarkable character of the snow was evident. Hence, only the nightfolk, the police, the watchmen, the sleepless, and the drunken knew before morning that an extraordinary, inexplicable, and even terrifying event had occurred. Not only had the snowfall formed curious and unquestionable designs, some of which were very human; but also the snow had the hardness of rocks and could not be removed from the pavement.

The morning newspapers devoted three columns on the first page to this strange event. They commented especially on the difficulty of removing the snow, and printed photographs of the statues, as the snow objects were soon named. The photographs had been made before morning with the aid of flashes, and this heightened their uncanny and startling appearance.

Soon after, the newspapers of the late morning editions described the entire event as something quaint and full of human interest: there were stories of how different kinds of persons had responded to the whimsical and comical aspects of the snow, stories about the amazement of the housewife, the joy of the school children, and the inevitable fabulous lying of the old timers, who asserted that they had seen this sort of thing before, and in better style. Soon, however, this point of view was surrendered, because the entire populace was affected very differently by the statues. The stillness which comes with any great snow, the muffling and muting of sound, the slowing of pace and movement, the luxurious drag and trek of car and truck—these changes seemed to have entered into the very being of the citizens, so that they spoke slowly and softly, they moved serenely and as if soundlessly, they looked about with long stares, they looked about as if they were dreamstruck or abstracted or profoundly in love. The effect was much like that of a street-organ's operatic outburst, in which the music seems to take all the motions of the pedestrians into its flowing order.

Hence it was that the whole day after the snowfall became an unofficial holiday or fete. All private concerns were ignored, all tasks absentmindedly attended to, all other things put aside while everyone discussed, analyzed and sought an explanation of the remarkable statues of snow. The day was warm, sunny, and glittering, as often happens after a snowfall's catharsis, and the air was of a delightful purity and sweetness.

At noon the Mayor issued a statement to the press in which he promised that the snow would be removed as quickly as possible. This brought about the first example of the unanimity and intensity of feeling of the city, towards the statues. Everyone acted at once and in the same way precisely. The Mayor was overwhelmed by phone calls and even telegrams protesting against the removal of the snow. Even the Mayor's secretaries and assistants joined in exhorting him to do nothing about the snow, although some were anxious and unable to understand their emotions in this matter.

Faber Gottschalk, however, went even further. He attempted to visit City Hall, astonished at himself, unable to understand his passionate concern about the statues, but determined to do naught all day but walk about and look at them. Promised by the secretary of the Mayor that nothing would be done at present about removing the statues, he was left suspicious and unassured. No sooner had he left than he was disturbed by the ambiguous character of the phrase, "at present," saying to himself that that present was already past.

Faber Gottschalk cancelled all his appointments until further notice.

A mathematician at Columbia University, upon being interviewed, stated that the strange occurrence was proved by the laws of probability to be one which would probably have occurred, sooner or later.

Ministers of the various organized religions rewrote their sermons for the following Sunday, most of them adopting the view that the curious snowfall might be regarded as a literary allegory, so to speak. None of them ventured to suppose that any supernatural agency, divine or evil, was involved.

The children during the first day delighted in the comic strip surface of some of the statues, but soon some of them became annoyed that snowballs could not be fashioned out of the snow. In their frustration, they threw other available objects at each other, and one boy went so far as to open his brother's skull with a hockey stick.

Faber Gottschalk walked from the apartment which was both his home and his office to the Battery. Since this apartment was on Washington Heights, his walk was one of approximately ten miles, from one extreme to the other of Manhattan's long and narrow spine. Then he walked back again, surprised to find that the statues which studded his route disclosed new and even more interesting aspects when they were regarded for the second time. In fact, he attempted the experiment of circling a city block immediately after a second view of one statue, to see what new impression would occur. And there were new impressions, and they were very interesting, and it seemed to Faber Gottschalk that the statues had an inexhaustible nature.

By evening, he had returned to his apartment. Seated by his radio in the living room, he sought to understand the emotion which had overwhelmed him at the sight of the statues. As he reviewed the day in his mind, he smoked one cigar after another, gratified by the tobacco and yet able to distinguish clearly between the pleasure of smoking and the great happiness which had come upon him when he had awakened to see the strange snow things below his apartment window.

In seeking an explanation for his emotion, Faber Gottschalk thought of his past life, of the pattern, fate, or host of accidents which had brought him to this day. He had been persuaded to study dentistry by the uncle with whom he lived after his mother's death. His first ambition had been to be an athlete, and, failing in this, to be a sportswriter. Actually, he was not sure which of the two activities he desired more strongly. At any rate, the small complete world of the professional athlete interested him above all things, and since he had not the equipment to be very good at any sport, he had soon resigned himself without difficulty to being merely a spectator.

To be truly a spectator, however, is a great deal, for it involves the most intense partisanship, a life of the emotions which is at the mercy of success and defeat every day. In major league baseball, Faber's favorite sport, a fan follows the odyssey of his team for six months and more in every year, beginning with the spring training camps and culminating in the extraordinary excitement of the World Series. And this is a matter of a journey to eight cities, again and again, a trip which the fan endures in mind with no little anguish because it is more difficult for a team to win on a road trip than when playing before its own applauding audience.

Faber's uncle had pointed out to him that as a dentist he would have a modest income, and he would be able to arrange his hours of work in such a way as to permit him to follow the sports which absorbed his free attention through the year. Faber had no reason to regret the fact that he had acted on his uncle's counsel. He had arrived at the age of thirty, moved by the profound disgust with his profession which has alreay been noted, but he had been free to develop and satisfy the habits and appetites of a spectator. Although he felt that his life was a might-as-well matter, he had no reason to suppose it might have been better, if he had striven more.

During the long evening, seated in the darkness of the living room and going to the window from time to time to look down at the city street where the figures lay, blue-white and ghastly like shrouded corpses, Faber Gottschalk was unable to explain to himself by his examination of his past life the reason for his emotion about the statues.

II

The huge event was succeeded by a week of perfect weather. The snow did not melt, nor did the statues alter. They remained firmly attached to the pavement as if they were a natural outgrowth of the asphalt, and automobiles found it necessary to move circumspectly and circuitously about them.

When the newspapers had exhausted all the approaches to the subject of which they were capable, when thousands had come from suburb and distant city to see the new sights, and then remained, unable to depart, fascinated and obsessed, then a broad and sharp change took place in the consciousness of the populace, among the rich and the poor, the middle-class and the working-class. During the day, many would go to the window to look down at the statues, and many during the lunch hour would eat hurriedly or would not eat at all or would munch sandwiches in the street that they might be able to look longer at the creations of the fall. The strikes which occurred at this time continued without abatement, but the pickets were often absorbed in the figures outstretched upon the white ground; and in this contemplation, in this absorption, they were often joined by the police, who, despite this unity of interests, did not cease to check them. Even a boss at times would pass, pause to look at the statues, then look up again at the pickets with undisguised hatred. In general, everyone did what he was expected to do, but in a new way, with more concentration, with more devotion, and more efficiently. At certain moments, everything stopped and was motionless, as at a red light on a great avenue; and in this motionless period, complete attention was given to the statues, as when a noble man's death is regarded.

From each borough of the city of New York came news of the variety of the statues, and reports of the absorption of the citizens in the statues, an absorption which seemed to rise above the habits and acts of daily existence, but not to destroy them. Faber Gottschalk alone surrendered the being of his past life utterly, ceased to practise his profession, and went through the conscious day throughout New York in an effort to see all the statues.

Many of these statues were grotesque. Some were monstrous. Some resembled human figures, and although they were of a perfect verisimilitude in all else, the faces were at times blank as a plate, distorted like gargoyles, or obscene, as when, in certain suburbs, figures clung to each other in an embrace which was hardly ambiguous. Elsewhere, however, the statues had the rotundity and the plumpness of the cumulus clouds of a summer's day, the solidity and the stillness of fine buildings, or the pure and easy design of some flowers. Everywhere were forms which delighted the eye either as fresh complexes of previously known designs, or compositions which seemed to exhaust the possibility of arrangement. The populace's fondness for the statues continually increased, and soon many of them were given nicknames: one was called "Versailles," because of its glitter in the sunlight, like light shining upon many mirrors; one, a great gross one, was named, "Caliban"; then there were such names as "Sky Folly," "Sestina," "Chios," "Hallucination," "Plum Elected," "Old Nick" and "Shelley."

In certain quarters, and indeed everywhere at times, there occurred much speculation as to the source, sources, cause or causes of the phenomenal snow. Soon it was decided that the entire system of the snow had been a wonderful chance like perfect weather or a rockface. Some for a time spoke of the fecundity of nature; some—these were the ones who were often alone—thought that this was indeed the way that the haunted and hunted lives of human beings took shape by an unpredictable and continuous fall to which little or no designing agency could be attributed.

Slowly, after much thought, waking from troubled sleep, or pausing on a stair, Faber Gottschalk recognized that for him, at least for him, these wonderful objects were of such grave interest because they resembled the white teeth which were, so to speak, the subject-matter of his profession. But, recognizing this, he was merely confronted with a greater degree of perplexity. Why should he take such delight in the statues, since teeth were an abomination to him?

At art galleries and theatres attendances became meager. The chief attraction at the moving picture houses was the newsreel in which it was possible to see figures which were in other distant parts of the city. The audiences at these newsreels regarded the statues with an interest which was equalled by their interest in the attitudes and emotions of citizens photographed in the act of looking at the statues. (Here we must presume that it is possible to draw a valid distinction between the interest in the statues and the interest in the spectators, for they were always part of one scene.)

No one laughed at the rapt expressions on the faces of some spectators (they were, the audience, too enraptured themselves), nor at the old men who seemed to become statues too, as they stood in stillness staring at the statues. But one audience did become very angry when a boy of thirteen was shown in the act of drawing a mustache on one of the figures' faces. Apart from this resentment of any act of change, the audience were of a pure seriousness as they gazed in the darkness at the screen. And one woman broke into tears when she saw a crowd of men standing before a statue and looking at it as if they regarded Niagara Falls.

Bars, restaurants, theatres, and museums lost a great deal of patronage. And yet those most directly concerned, the owners and the managers, did not seem at all troubled. Perhaps this was because of the general and indeed unanimous feeling that all was well, at least for the time being.

Yet, if many of the figures were of a matchless beauty, there was one which, as a literal thing, was so shocking, so appalling, and outrageous, that certain citizens petitioned the mayor to the effect that it be removed at once, by dynamite. This was the cause of one harsh conflict of this period of good feeling, for overflowing crowds, hearing of the petition, protested immediately, demanding that nothing be done. The sentiment thus became explicit and conscious that every object of the wondrous fall was somehow of a perfect preciousness and importance, and must be guarded with the utmost care, preserved at all costs, and never destroyed. Faber Gottschalk hearing of the petition a little late, came hurrying to the scene, the most avid advocate of the preservation of the statue.

III

On a street corner, near a lamp-post, standing on the rumbleseat of a motor car, he harangued a crowd which was decidedly in agreement with him. As he neared the end of his speech and sought a certain conclusiveness or resolution, he was troubled by the sense that he himself did not truly understand what he was saying.

"So I say to you," he said, "there is every reason to believe we have no right to modify any of these new things. Those who have been in favor of getting rid of this statue, which they avow to be obscene, tell us that the children will be corrupted by it. I will not say in reply that we cannot permit our lives to be determined by what the children will or will not see. Such an answer would be too easy, although true enough. I will not advance the argument that those of us who really know children and have lived with them know very well that it is the children, not the adults, nor the statues, who are corrupt, whence it is that our adult lives are a long suffering and chiefly unsuccessful attempt to free ourselves from the utter corruption of childhood, infancy, and the egotism contracted in the womb. I myself remember very well, how at the age of eight, on a visit at my aunt's, my two female cousins, twins, took me into the closet and taught me certain things of which I must already have been somewhat aware, because I was scarcely surprised by what they did to me.

"But apart from these considerations, and apart from the children, who can be trusted, I assure you, to take care of themselves, I want to impress upon or rather recall to you something on which we are certainly in some sense agreed—"

(Here the speaker showed his hesitancy most of all.)

"To anything which is beautiful, to anything which is true, to anything which is good we are committed, though the commitment jeopardizes our lives. Furthermore—"

(This last word bore in tone the lack of conviction felt by the speaker.)

"—since we really do not understand these extraordinary objects, must we not, from motives of humility, prudence, and practicality, regard them as sacred mysteries, at least for the time being? Who knows what relationship they may not have to our lives? What natural or supernatural powers may not, through them, be signing to us? Do any of you have the presumption and insensitivity to maintain that you do not know more and honor more in the nature of things than you did at the age of fifteen?—"

Few understood the latter remark, but the crowd cheered Faber vehemently as he dismounted from the car. They liked his tone and they were in favor of his emotion. When one listener, an intellectual, sought Faber out in the bar of a nearby restaurant, he was at first merely interested in repeating what he had just said, and emphasizing again and again the close relationship he felt between teeth, sports, and statues. Some peculiar and necessary importance seemed to be involved in their connection.

When Faber's questioner kindly suggested to him that he ought not to permit this passion to disrupt his life, since there were, after all, other important and necessary things, Faber replied: "If one becomes sufficiently interested, wholly absorbed, and absolutely involved in any one thing, or any passion, then that thing or that passion becomes the whole world for one, the whole world appears once more in it, and with more intensity and clarity. The same difficulties, the same duties and necessities reappear, translated into the terms of this purely important thing. For if one becomes completely interested in any thing, it ceases to be a thing among other things, it ceases to be a thing in essence, it becomes the whole world."

Seldom have the mouths of dentists uttered sentiments so serious and metaphysical.

Gottschalk's speech and the solidarity of other like-minded persons won out, and the obscene statue was left intact. The enchantment which had made New York a sleep-walking city of contemplatives continued with no diminution of attention. At the conclusion of the tenth day of the presence of the statues, a period of unblemished weather, it was felt by many that these marble white beauties were permanent parts of the city. The gross figure resembling a giant pharoah which had descended upon an Elevated station was washed clean by a troop of painstaking Elevated passengers, after the soot of the city had darkened it. Like acts of pious ablution were performed all over, which seemed to show through this unanimity of feeling a new kind of *Burggeist*.

And then, without warning, a tireless and foul rain descended and to everyone's surprise utterly destroyed the fine statues. Their disappearance was noted on the first page of the next morning's newspapers, but not in the headlines, as with their arrival. Everyone resumed the customary problems, old enmities were revived as if they had not been interrupted, as if their continuance had not been lifted to a new level for a time; and immediately the motion-picture theatres, theatres, libraries, and galleries enjoyed a sudden flood of patrons.

A particularly brutal murder was committed in Brooklyn, the sport pages carried much news about ice sports at winter resorts, a boy of seventeen, scion of a very rich family, disappeared from his home and was found only after two weeks in Iceland, Faber Gottschalk jumped or fell in front of an onrushing subway train, and only a few were sufficiently disturbed to keep in mind, with the help of photographs, the holy time when statues had presented their marvellous forms everywhere in the city of New York.